A SEAL AT *Heart*

ANNE ELIZABETH

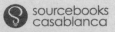

sourcebooks
casablanca

Published by Sourcebooks Casablanca, an imprint of Sourcebooks, Inc.
P.O. Box 4410, Naperville, Illinois 60567-4410
(630) 961-3900
FAX: (630) 961-2168
www.sourcebooks.com

Printed and bound in Canada
WC 10 9 8 7 6 5 4 3 2 1

*This book is dedicated to our outstanding Navy SEALs
and our men and women in uniform and their families.*

*Thank you for your tremendous dedication,
your sacrifice, and your service.*

Chapter 1

If you're not gonna pull the trigger, don't point the gun.

—James Baker

Operation Sundial, at an undisclosed location deep in the jungle

BLOOD DRIPPED DOWN HIS FOREHEAD AND BLURRED HIS vision. Wiping it away, Jack forced his eyes to focus. He squinted, but it was useless.

The helicopter downwash whirled mud and dirt into the air faster than he could blink, and the clouds of grit stuck to his face. Nothing shielded him from the suffocating pelting of the brownout, making him blind as hell without his protective glasses.

Gathering the five-foot-ten-inch form of his swim buddy Don into his arms, he duckwalked as low as he could, heading toward the belly of the helicopter. Luckily the rain had stopped momentarily as the rotor blades cut the air, but it made the moment more surreal.

Whup, whup, whup…

He blew air out of his mouth. His nostrils were caked with grime, but he could still smell the blood seeping from the bandages he'd fastened around Don's chest. He squeezed his swim buddy tightly, trying to keep pressure on the wound.

A stray bullet ricocheted, displacing the air near his face. Where the hell did that shot come from? The helicopter was *so* goddamned loud.

The door of the copter jerked open; the blessed haven was dead ahead. The two door gunners laid down suppressor fire, but it was short-lived aid as enemy bullets took them down. They fell back just within the side door of the helo.

"God help us," Jack muttered under his breath as he finally reached the opening. The men in front of him were practically cut in two by the rounds. There wasn't time to think about them or their families now. With a mighty heave, he lifted his buddy onto the helicopter floor and scrambled in after him.

Coughing the crap out of his lungs, he dragged Don over to the far wall, away from the doorway, and stood up to scan the interior. It took him a minute to take in the carnage. He tried to wipe the image from his eyes as his mind put the gory pieces together. The pilots were shredded. *Damn*.

Making his way to the cockpit, he could see that the glass dome had been compromised and the entire enclosure looked pretty chewed up. "Please let this thing fly." The blades were still turning, so that was a good sign, and neither the cyclic nor collective were hit. But would it be enough to get them out of this hellhole?

He touched his throat to activate the comm mike. It didn't respond. He spoke softly, trying again, "Whiskey. Tango. Foxtrot." *What the fuck!*

Where the hell is everyone?

The rain was starting again, angling into the copter and hitting his face.

Another series of blinding flashes—hard to tell if it

was lightning or shots—from outside, but it forced him to move Don, to stash him deeper in the belly of the copter, and momentarily duck for cover.

Pwing! The bullet bounced off metal.

He was pretty sure it was only a small number of insurgents and one sniper firing wildly. Random shots in the dark. Problem was, even a broken clock was right twice a day, and the dead airmen were horrific evidence of the sniper's success.

A volley of shots. A few rebels cross-fired at one another, sending shouts of anger into the air. *Go to it. Maybe you'll hit each other.*

The only good news was that if he couldn't see them, they couldn't target him directly either.

There was no point in sitting tight. He needed to find his Team. After securing Don and rigging a piece of equipment to hold pressure on his swim buddy's wound, Jack went back to the open door. A glimpse of rag-covered muddy boots to the right let him know that an enemy was approaching. Moving quickly into the disrupted cloud of crud, he positioned himself so his vantage point was optimal.

Two Tangos dressed in frayed pants held Russian 9mms at the ready. Instinctually, Jack withdrew his Sig Sauer, took a breath, and squeezed off several rounds. They dropped instantly.

He checked their pulses. Dead. Now, where were the others? *Here, birdie, birdie, birdie…*

Working his way quickly out of the cloud of dust, he knew he would be vulnerable, but this was his best option. He had to know what was going on. This mission had gone sideways long ago.

Coming up behind a rebel who was caught up in dislodging a jammed gun, Jack holstered his own weapon and, using bare hands, silently broke the enemy's neck. Slowly, he worked his way around the perimeter of the helo. For now, it was clear.

Lightning split the sky, bathing the area better than a floodlight. It was the vantage point he sought.

A noise caught his attention as a door from the factory flew open, banging against the siding. That was them—his Teammates—sprinting from the interior as flames engulfed the structure. They were coughing and several of them appeared to have minor injuries. Jack held his ground, preparing to lay down cover fire, if required. His eyes were desperately searching for a subversive threat, when an explosion lifted him from his feet and threw him to the ground.

Bam!

Thrown backward from the blast, the back of his head smacked something hard. Black spots danced in front of his eyes and bile scored the back of his throat. Swallowing the harsh rush of acid, he lifted his hand—gun gripped tightly in his fingers—trying to focus on the enemy that should have been coming over the large boulders a few feet in front of him.

Nothing. No one.

The smell of C-4, with its acrid ether odor, filled his nostrils even as thunder shook the sky and rain barreled down.

A sharp burning sensation seared the back of his skull, going from ten on the pain scale to numb within seconds. Another wave of nausea made his stomach roll and quake as he deliberately forced his way to his knees and then his feet.

The clock is ticking. Fighting the dark spots, he stood wavering for a few seconds before his sight returned to normal and he could search for them... The enemy. His buddies. Or any signs of life.

His eyes widened.

Giant pieces of seared, cloth-covered flesh were scattered over the ground. It didn't compute at first. Those were his buddies, Teammates from SEAL Team ONE, Platoon 1-Alfa, and only a few of them were moving.

Jack was instantly in motion. Grabbing the body closest to him, he felt for a pulse. The steady thump sent a surge of adrenaline through his system. He gathered the man to his chest, trying to keep his hands on his buddy as he dragged him toward the helicopter. The path was wet with blood and mud, and repeating the task several times, he slipped in the sludge as he loaded the bodies closest to him on board.

Only one Teammate, Gerry Knotts, was left and remained exposed. Jack would be a moving target—a perfect bull's-eye—for the enemy's shoot-'em-up game if he attempted it.

Eyes sought his. His Teammate was alive and signaling him. Jack understood and moved to a rock as far from Knotts as possible. Lifting his 9mm, Jack fired several shots. Bullets peppered around the rock as he quickly belly-crawled back to his original position.

Knotts fired several shots, nailing the Tangos.

Moving up into a dead run, Jack reached Gerry's side and then helped him stand. Together they rushed into the cloud of dirt and grunge, going for the helo.

They left long streaks of mud along the deck as they rolled inside.

Jack checked…seven men loaded, and he was lucky number eight. His life meant nothing without them.

Finally able to close and secure the door, Jack shoved debris aside until it was easier to move around the cockpit. Quickly moving the pilot's body to properly reach the controls, he straddled the chair and checked the instrument panel.

He held his breath, watching the RPM gauges of the turbine and rotor. The helo hovered. The controls required constant small changes to keep the bird in the air. Sweat dripped off his face. "Come on, baby. That's it! Into the storm.

"Now, let's get the hell out of here." As the helo responded, he sighed with relief. He'd only piloted helicopters a couple of times—all his experience was in fixed-wing aircraft—and he was hoping his brief lessons would be enough to get them back to the rendezvous point.

He had to hand it to her—this bird flew, even all shot up. Just as he was beginning to feel okay about the flight, he noticed black spots at the edge of his vision. With the back of his thumb, he rubbed one eye. Nothing prepared him for his sight going, leaving only one eye functioning.

He squinted at the instruments. The radio was blown and there was no luxury of an autopilot. Keeping a helo in the air was a constant struggle against the torque, the wind, and the pilot's ability. "Come on, Jack. Concentrate!"

Wind buffeted his face courtesy of the bullet-shattered windshield. The smell of ozone was heavy and ripe. He hoped the lightning was over.

Wetness dripped down the back of his neck. He

wiped a hand against the warmth, and it came away with fresh blood. His.

Fuck, fuck, fuck!

Looking over his shoulder, he saw the bodies of his Teammates. He didn't know if they were alive or dead. But he could never let them down. He'd get them all to safety—make them secure—even if it was the last thing he ever did.

———ᴡᴡ———

Coronado, California

No other place on the planet was like McP's Pub in October—the seagulls circling and crying overhead, and the women just as raucous. He took a long pull on his beer.

"Welcome home, Jack," said Betsy. The friendly blond waitress with a wide, pearly white smile and a set of 44Ds grinned knowingly at him as she walked by. Hers was the kind of walk that had her hips swinging, and her tight apron full of change played a musical medley to the movement of her sexy saunter.

Some women can move like their hips are on springs.

For those around him—the suntan worshippers—almost any hot spot on the planet would probably suffice. But for Jack, this tiny island town between Glorietta Bay and the Pacific Ocean was uniquely qualified to be his home. Having been assigned to SEAL Team ONE and with an apartment only ten blocks away from the Amphib base, Jack thought this was a snapshot of perfection.

He scratched at the gooey tape mark behind his

ear. The bandage around his head was gone and he was no longer hooked to IVs or being pumped full of fluids and painkillers, but he wished there were an antibiotic or balm for the one place he hurt the most, his soul.

At Balboa Naval Hospital, the medical staff had told him his number one job was to relax until he was fully healed and had his memory back. There were too many holes, too many memories missing from the last Op. The worst part was... his best friend was dead.

Jack couldn't reconcile it and didn't know how to fix the situation.

The rub was... if he didn't take care of himself, fix the recollection issue, he'd be stuck with the label "acute psychological suppression"—forever. That didn't bode well for him.

Do the familiar. Take it easy. Those were the orders from the medical staff.

With those directions rattling around his brain, it meant finding a place to unwind where he could feel the sun's raw heat on his skin, taste the tang of salt on his lips, and have a cold brew sweating in his hand as he savored each sip. Well, maybe not the alcohol part, but everyone had a vice and his was simple: fresh air, exercise, and a bit of the barley.

Ah, beer! The first sip was always sweetest.

At first, being back in Coronado had been difficult. The layers of emotion had punched him in the gut practically every few minutes. Drink in hand, his mind had started to go numb, turn off, and he went whole hog for the break. McP's was the perfect place to just... be. Where men and women interacted, doing a dance as primal and ancient as time itself to attract each other. As the action unfolded in front of him, he saw a few younger brethren had scored, snapping up the curvy and very willing quarry to set off for more serious play somewhere else. Nature's fundamental dance never ceased to intrigue him, though he wasn't looking.

Listening to the slap of the waitresses' tennis shoes against the slate wasn't quite as sexy as the click of a stiletto, but he couldn't complain. Most of them were paragons, Madonnas—look but don't touch—because they were SEAL wives or friends.

A loaded hamburger with a crisp green salad was placed in front of him. Steam rose from the burger and his nostrils flared. Of course, *this* tasty morsel he would be willing to sink his teeth into anytime.

"Just the way you like it, and on the house," said Jules with a wink, another one of McP's waitressing angels. "'In Xanadu did Kubla Khan, a stately pleasure-dome decree…'"

"'Where Alph, the sacred river, ran through caverns measureless to man down to a sunless sea…'" The reference from "Kubla Khan; or, A Vision in a Dream," by Samuel Taylor Coleridge, was a favorite of his and McP's was a home of sorts, his own pleasure-dome. A framed copy of the eighteenth-century poem sat on his nightstand, a birthday gift from Jules and all of the waitstaff at McP's. Even now he could recite each and every line verbatim. His own life was like that poem, a journey, and very much unfinished. He wanted that chance… to explore.

"Thanks, Jules." Jack grinned, unusually grateful for

the human connection. He shifted uncomfortably on the chair. Maybe the incident overseas had shaken him more than he realized. "Hey, how did you know exactly what I wanted?"

Her smile was sweet. "The same way I've known for years that you'd rather drink your calories than eat them. Enjoy lunch, Jack. You're looking skinny." She leaned down and kissed him gently on the cheek.

"Thanks." Part of him wanted to add a sentimental comment about her being a sweetheart or maybe ask about her husband, who was in Team FIVE and probably deployed, but being sappy wasn't his thing. Life was easier with the walls up.

"Don't forget to eat your vegetables." She gave him a big smile before she went back to attending her other customers. Did she know how her aura of bubbling beauty affected men? Probably not.

Releasing the grip on his beer bottle, he placed it on the table and then attacked the salad. It was significantly better than hospital food and MREs. Hooking his fork into the meat, he pulled it out from between the buns. As a SEAL, he was always in training, and he would rather carbo-load with a brew and burn it off running. He wrapped the burger in lettuce and took a bite. The meat was savory and juicy, filling him with welcome satisfaction.

News droned in the background until someone had the good sense to flip on a ball game. There was something peaceful about that... as if it were Saturday and he was a kid again.

Methodically, he ate until the burger and salad were gone. The french fries sat untouched next to the bun halves and a very sad-looking pickle. He lifted his brew, and his lips drew tight, pulling the cold liquid down his throat.

He'd been in the Teams for eight years, and being a SEAL was the basic foundation of his soul. Another enlisted man might state that the military was important, but to Jack it was everything. If he couldn't deploy anymore… well, the concept was too harsh to even contemplate.

His eyes searched, looking for a distraction from his musings. For several seconds his gaze stopped on a large, agile man until his inner gauge dismissed him as a nonthreat. Ever vigilant, there was always a part of him searching for trouble and ready to respond.

At the next table, a dog happily lapped water from his complimentary "pup" bowl. A man in his fifties, probably the owner or an overindulgent dog walker, dropped parts of a hamburger into the water and the dog went crazy—busily fishing pieces out and then chomping, chewing, and swallowing the tasty morsels down as if no one had ever fed him.

Life must be so much easier as a dog. Someone is there to make the meals, walk side-by-side, play, and run. Was that what he wanted? Did he want someone feminine, curvy, and sweet to be there, too?

He'd be better off with a dog. With his schedule he didn't know if either was a realistic wish. His ideal state was being deployed, which didn't leave much time for a home life.

Gripping the cold bottle of beer like a lifeline, he lifted it to his mouth and drank deeply. *God, that tastes good! And it's predictable. Every swallow is the same.*

Off to the side, he could hear the faint buzz of cars

and trucks as they sped down Orange Avenue, confirming that everything was in sync here, normal. That was reassuring to a degree, witnessing the commonplace; this is what "everyday" was supposed to resemble. Calm. Steady. Regular.

Why isn't that me? His mind and body couldn't slow down. Closing his eyes, he forced himself to let this familiar place and a beer soothe him. At least he hoped it would. McP's was a special home for his kind. Owned by one of his brethren, there was Navy SEAL memorabilia on the walls, a trident on the T-shirts, and oftentimes the bar would fill with sightseers and froghogs—women who hopped from frog to frog. In the Underwater Demolition Team, or UDT—the precursor to the SEAL Team—these Navy sailors were called frogmen. Later on, the name was changed to better show their areas of operation: SEAL—SEa Air Land—but the age-old name for the women who pursued them never got updated.

Half his Teammates were in committed relationships, and the rest dicked around almost constantly. Lately, his celibacy walk had turned into a preference. It had begun as a way to concentrate on work, and now…

Maybe he just didn't have what it took—a crap tolerance—to be in a relationship.

The back of his head exploded with a sudden and sharp pain. His hand lifted automatically, rubbing over the healing wound and stubbly blond hair.

"Red Jack!" His eyes whipped open, and for a second, he could have sworn that he'd heard Don. That was impossible. His swim buddy was dead, and there was nothing that could bring him back.

Pain squeezed his neck. His vision blurred and for a moment an image of his friend flashed before his eyes.

The rush of emotions for his swim buddy was the kind of tidal wave that could take out a city, and equally as devastating as it crashed over him again and again. He'd have done anything to have Petty Officer Second Class Donald Dennis Kanoa Donnelly alive and well. Sorrow punched his heart, but he'd never show it, especially not in public.

His phone vibrated. Jack had the cell in his hand before he remembered he was supposed to be on vacation—no one would be calling him for sudden deployment.

Punching a button, he accessed the email. Appointments had been scheduled for him: group therapy and individual sessions. *Can't this Frankenstein wannabe leave me alone? I don't need a doctor.*

He just needed to keep it together long enough to go operational again. Being on medical leave was like swallowing two-inch nails whole: it hurt the entire way down and out. He had way too much time on his hands to think. He needed action.

"Petty Officer First Class John Matthew Roaker."

His name was a command that had Jack sitting up straight in his chair. Any other service would have a guy standing at attention before the rank and name had been completely spoken. Spec Ops was different, more laid-back.

"Taking a trip down memory lane?" commented a gruff man with salt-and-pepper hair and a long bushy mustache. His sideburns were like hairy caterpillars perched on the side of his face. The man took a step closer to Jack and grinned. A fat cigar was clamped between his lips and his voice had lost the hard edge and was warming progressively. "Shit, you look like a newbie jarhead, Jack! We're going to have to mess you up a bit! So you look like a fucking SEAL."

"Good to see you, Commander," replied Jack, already proffering his hand to greet his former BUD/S Instructor, now mentor. With a grin on his lips that spoke volumes of the man's capacity for jocularity, Commander Gich didn't appear to be the kind of guy who could teach you fifty different ways to kill with a knife.

His gaze connected with the Commander's. Jack took comfort in the stare. Emotion hung like a bad painting just behind his own eyeballs, but he pushed past the weight of it. "Sir, it's great to see you."

Jack stood and the men embraced, slapping hands on each other's backs in heavy smacks and then briskly separating. There was a tremendous sense of the familial. Jack needed that right now.

"You too!" said the Commander. "How's the brain? Is it still swelling? I can think of better things to make swell."

"Christ! They're not sure. You know docs. Though, I'm pretty sure the fracture's better." Jack reseated himself, eager to change the subject. "I was thinking about my first drink here, and then there was the Hell Week celebration, when you and I drank until the kitchen opened for the early birds' lunch the next morning." He could practically taste the stale alcohol. Bile threatened to rise, but he shoved it down. Yep, that memory was definitely intact! Why couldn't he have lost that day, instead of the events from the last Op? He needed those memories.

"No shit! You were so hungover from those shots that you puked your guts out in the back of my car." Gich signaled the waitress for a beer. "Still doesn't smell right. But it's easy to find Blue Betty in the dark." His grin could have lit up the darkest depths. "So, how's it going, Jack? What's with the shrink-wrap therapy? I may be retired, but I'm still in the loop."

Shaking his head, Jack said, "I don't know. It's been…" He searched his mind for the word, but he couldn't even find that. Who really wanted to know the inner workings of a SEAL? They might not like what they find in there, and then what? SEALs had more layers than an artichoke.

"Hard, complicated, and disillusioning to come back from a mission that's seriously goat-fucked. You're not the first, Roaker, and unfortunately, you won't be the last. Just don't become a poster boy, it's not your gig."

"Yeah, me a poster boy! Could you see me in Ronald McDonald hair?" cracked Jack without missing a beat. It felt good to have someone giving him shit. Everyone had been so "nice" to him lately that it creeped him out. "Sure I can pull off the look, but all those hands to shake, personal appearances, and then there goes your private life."

"Wiseass!" A shapely blond waitress who could easily be a modern-day Marilyn Monroe placed an icy beer in front of Gich. "Thanks, Betsy. I knew you'd remember how I liked it."

"Anything for you, Gich." She winked at him and headed back inside. The bar was pretty empty for a Tuesday afternoon, but it'd pick up tonight and be packed with military personnel on the hunt for hook-ups and single ladies on the quest for the golden ring. That was old hat for him, and he'd rather work out, clean his guns, anything…

"I can make a few recommendations. There are a couple of medical professionals who use unconventional methods. Alternative healing… it might help." Gich looked at him over the top of his beer as he drank. "The person I'm thinking of does acupressure. Did wonders for my knees and lower back."

"Doctors aren't my preference." Jack contemplated getting a pain pill out of his pocket, but he knew it'd be a dicey mix with the alcohol. He preferred to drink, so he left it in his pocket and took another sip.

"Roaker, you can talk to me," said Gich, drawing on his cigar and puffing out a long thin stream of smoke.

Jack sat silently, briefly weighing his thoughts before he shared them. "Six weeks ago when I left here, I was ready for the mission. Even though there were a couple strikes against it. First, Tucker kept getting changing Intel on the location and how it was laid out. Second, the resources seemed underkill for a plan of this magnitude, and whenever I brought it up, they told me to add as much as we needed. So I did, but it never felt like enough. Third, when we got there, nothing was as discussed; the place was a ghost town outside with only a few people inside. Either the information was terrible, or—"

"You were being set up. Seems unlikely, in the Teams," said Gich, softly leaning forward. "What happened next?"

Jack shook his head. "I don't know. I don't remember.

I can see my feet hitting the dirt and watching everyone take position, and then... nothing."

Gich took the cigar from his mouth. "Did you see Don die?"

"I must have..." Pain ripped through his heart as he pushed hard to make it go away. "But I don't remember any of it. What the hell am I supposed to do? I'm beached like a whale until I can remember, and it's ripping me apart to be this still. I need help."

"You need to get out, have some fun. Don't think. Just react and let go of everything." Gich surveyed him with a critical eye before turning his gaze back to watch the shapely blond go through her routine of serving drinks and taking orders. "The watched pot never boils, or in our case, the undrunk beer only gets warm and flat."

Jack gave a half smile. "I'm not really in the mood for socializing."

"Come on, you'd have to be dead not to appreciate that," Gich said, motioning toward the waitress.

He had to admit the bending and reaching of the busty waitress was rather compelling, but he had more important stuff on his mind and couldn't even consider flirting right now. Shifting in his chair, he found a more comfortable position and said, "What I want to know is how do I... get my warrior mentality back?"

Those words captured Gich's attention as his eyes locked on Jack's. The lesson of finding his equilibrium and balance had been the hardest trick for Jack to learn. Gich had worked doubly hard with him on that one. They'd developed all sorts of techniques to help him out, but right now, Jack felt like his skin was crawling off his body and he had to nail himself to a chair to keep still. Did other SEALs feel like an alien in a human body?

With a deliberate and slow movement, Gich brought his hand up and rested it gently on Jack's arm. But no matter how slowly he'd moved, Jack still flinched and had an urge to pull away. Forcing himself to be still took some concentration.

"Give it time. PTSD happens. Ride it out." Gich leaned forward and whispered, "And while you're waiting, go get your whiskers wet and your dick licked. You're a fucking hero; you should take advantage of it." He pulled back his hand, grabbed the neck of his beer, and chugged it down. When it was empty, he waved it in the air. "Tonight, Dick's Last Resort. There are all sorts of SEAL fans there. I'm sure the Naval Special Warfare fund-raiser crowd would benefit from laying eyeballs on you, too. Why not go get your pick of the, uh, ladies? Tour some sweet spots and give your brain some time off."

The idea of being surrounded by that many people made Jack's stomach clench, but he knew Gich was right. He had to get back out there. Going from the Op to the hospital, and now home, had not afforded him the opportunity to decompress, let alone figure out how to socialize with anyone of the fairer sex.

Maybe getting hot and heavy would help. He could love 'em and leave 'em as easily as the rest of them, though it seriously had been a while. Love just wasn't a priority the majority of the time, though sex was almost always welcome.

When Don had been alive—God, those words stuck

in his throat—it had been easier to go out for a night on the town. His buddy, though married, was a perfect wingman. He would wrangle the ladies in Jack's direction and it was a sure thing that his pocket would have a few phone numbers. Sometimes, he'd even take someone for a spin on the town.

Shit! When the fuck would he feel like himself again?

"Promise me you'll go tonight." Gich was studying him again. A man's word was a bond that was never broken in the SEAL community. Might as well have said, "Put your balls on the table, and if you don't do as I say, I'll slice 'em off and pocket 'em."

Gich would badger him until he agreed, and the Commander ten times out of ten knew best. He'd give it a try. What could it hurt? It couldn't be any worse than spending weeks in a hospital bed.

"Yeah," said Jack. "I'll go." Though he knew he'd probably not enjoy it.

The back of Jack's head squeezed tight again, reminding him that the head injury was still an issue. But as the Commander was fond of saying, "Where the body goes, the mind follows." Maybe a little interaction—some puss and hoots—would go a long way toward finding some kind of relief or momentary happiness.

The beat-up yellow Jeep slid into an empty parking spot only a few blocks from the Naval Special Warfare fundraiser. Jack didn't bother securing the torn soft top. There was nothing of value inside, not even a radio. Though he did shove the Bluetooth speaker under the seat.

The last vestiges of light were slipping from the sky

as the ripe smell of seasoned meat filled the air. He was tempted to ditch the NSW event and go to the Strip Club for a steak.

A memory flashed through his mind of grilling T-bones to perfection with Don, his wife, and their five-year-old daughter. God, it was barely two months ago! They'd feasted and Sheila had announced she was pregnant at the meal. A game ensued of toasting her all evening long until she drove the lot of them home.

"Shit!" Jack swallowed hard and forced the vivid moment from his mind. Dwelling on the past, especially the loss of his swim buddy, was not helping. He knew he needed to deal with his friend's death, but until he knew what had happened on that mission, he didn't know how. Maybe once he remembered, he'd finally be able to look Sheila in the eye.

Rubbing his hand over his head, he lingered on the scar. If his buddy's death was his fault, he'd own it. If someone else were responsible for Don's death, he would bring justice.

Without that missing bit of knowledge though, he was in limbo.

Let it go. For at least one night, Jack, you need to be someone else. Take a break from yourself. He nodded his head, deciding his gut was providing good advice.

Pointing his feet in the direction of Dick's Last Resort, he set off. The slap of his feet against the pavement felt good. Anything physical seemed to be healing. This morning he'd run six miles and swum for an hour. His body had felt somewhat spent, but his mind was still spinning on the hamster wheel.

"Hey, Jack, good to see ya!" Hank Franks, a Master

Chief in SEAL Team THREE, slapped his back and then enthusiastically shook his hand. His arm felt like a pump trying to pull up water from a rusted pipe. "Are you on your way to Dick's? Have you met Dan McCullum, our new weapons specialist?"

Jack nodded and shook Dan's proffered palm. "Good to see you again, Dan. Been a while."

"Yeah," said Dan warmly. Pointing to his head, he asked, "How's the noggin? I heard there was some action."

"Healing." Jack withdrew his palm and looked forward. He didn't want to say anything about the Op.

Franks wrapped an arm possessively around the woman walking next to him. Her heels clicked a swift staccato on the sidewalk, keeping time with their pace. "Hey, have you met my wife?"

The lady beside the Master Chief smiled shyly. "I'm Rita. Happy to meet you, Jack." The emerald dress hugged her body as if she were a pinup girl, but it was the humor and happiness in her eyes when she looked at her husband and then switched that intense gaze to Jack that held him captive for a few seconds. He caught the residual affects of her joy and the strength was Grade A.

"Nice to meet you, too," he replied, relieved that he hadn't blurted out some silly comment about Hank's wife having a nice rack or the fact they looked good together. His guess was that Hank had already measured those assets for himself. Giving them all a smile and a nod, he slowed his pace and let them surge ahead.

Social graces weren't his thing. He hadn't been to Dick's Last Resort in years, but his recollection was that the food was tasty and the beer was ample. That had to be enough to work for him tonight.

After making a show of eyeballing his phone, he pocketed it. Then he looked in the windows of several nearby stores. *Stop stalling!*

He forced himself to walk the extra twenty feet, flashed his military ID, and went inside. The din of voices and music was momentarily deafening. A passing waitress pushed a beer into his empty hand. He gripped it gratefully.

His instincts took charge, taking him to an optimal vantage point, one that afforded him an overview of the comings and goings of the bar. Nothing could halt either that habit or the training, except a conscious decision to set his back to the door. When that happened, he'd have to trust the expressions of the people around him to alert him to danger. It was a hard-earned skill to be able to utilize ordinary passersby as mirrors.

As he drank, he watched a couple argue. The wife was seriously pissed. Jack was glad he wasn't in that guy's shoes. At another table, a group of ladies were making plans for later. Then there was the small group of retired military men lined up on bar stools, chatting about the good ole days, wearing jackets that read Old Frogs and SEALs. Across the room near the bar, several wives gathered together, laughing and pointing as they discussed the auction items and sipped delightedly on mixed drinks. Jack smiled as their conversation turned a bit more racy. He was glad he could read lips.

An alarm beeped on his wristwatch. Time to take an antianxiety pill. Anger lanced through him. What was he, some hundred-year-old man who had to take his medication? He would not die without that little pill, and there was no way he'd let himself get in a situation where he was addicted to something… anything or anyone. Unwilling to spend even another minute contemplating it, he stepped toward the closest trash can and dropped the bottle inside. Relief swept through him. He knew he could do better than those "hunt and peck" doctors who were actually using the process of elimination to guess at courses of action. Besides that, he didn't want to pollute his body with crap.

Beer was his only vice. Basically, it was his carbohydrates—liquid bread.

Ah! He swallowed down the rest of the cold brew.

Another body pushed into his, and suddenly the crowd, the noise, and the smell—everything—was too much. It was overwhelming. And that was his cue to go.

He placed the empty bottle on a passing waitress's tray and headed for the door. He'd done his duty. He came, he drank, and now he was leaving.

The door he had selected as his escape hatch opened before him and a gorgeous brunette stepped through, wearing spikes and a black dress with a very short skirt. Her skin glowed as if she'd just come in from the sun, and she was slightly out of breath. A large basket filled with goodies that she balanced on one hand wavered and then tipped.

In one motion, he was by her side, catching the basket before it reached the floor.

"My hero," she said. "Is this a side job or do you do it professionally?"

A grin split across his face; he knew it must look pretty goofy, but he couldn't stop it. "Which one do I win brownie points for?"

"Depends…" She smiled, and her eyes sparkled like

diamonds in a darkened cave. "I'm Laurie Smith." She held out a now-empty hand.

He shifted the basket to one side and reached forward to take it.

An abrupt woman wearing a badge that read "Salia Sedgwick, I am the Queen! Don't make me fetch my 9mm!" interrupted him before their hands could connect. This rude lady was actually standing between them. "Laurie Smith! You're late. Give me that basket. This was supposed to be here two hours ago. How am I supposed to do my job when other people aren't doing theirs?"

Jack inserted himself into the conversation. "Ah, Ms. Sedgwick, I'm sure she has a good excuse, or does Ms. Smith need a note from her mother?"

The woman frowned at him. "Well, I never!"

"Never what?" he asked innocently.

Laurie did a lousy job hiding her smile behind pursed lips.

As the organizer snatched the basket and hurried away, Laurie's laughter burst out. "Thank goodness, she left. I almost laughed in her face." She touched his arm. "Thank you. Salia Sedgwick is a handful…"

"A handful of what? Pudding? Meanness? Squishy resentment?"

"All of the above," she said, presenting her hand again. There was something light about her, and as he leaned forward, he could smell a hint of lilacs, as if she'd been rubbing the silky petals on her skin and hair.

This time, his hand connected with hers. As his palm engulfed her tiny fingers, a small bolt of electricity raced up his arm. Perhaps he could stay at this event for a little while longer.

"Hooyah! Hooyah! Hooyah!" The sound of the crowd grew louder, chanting as glasses were raised. The noise grew until his ears rang, yet it didn't stop him from trying to speak over it.

"My name is Jack."

Chapter 2

It is better to live one day as a lion than a hundred years as a sheep.

—Italian proverb

"WHAT DID YOU SAY?" YELLING IN HIS DIRECTION, SHE wished the crowd would lose some of its cheery enthusiasm so she could hear what the heck this man was saying.

He squeezed her hand. Now she was glad she had made it to the salon—had her hair and nails done, eyebrows waxed, and all of that important girly stuff. Meeting someone like him might make the pain worthwhile.

She smiled up at him. Twice he had scored points in his favor: making her laugh and coming to her rescue. Those were excellent qualities. It didn't hurt that he was built like a quarterback.

The decibel level dropped slightly and she heard his voice. Delight laced through her.

"I'm Jack Roaker." Like velvety warm hot fudge, the timbre of his words made her smile. Could a man's voice heat her insides and stir her interest this quickly? Perhaps, if it's the right voice, it could. She could imagine him whispering in her ear, and the fantasy of his lips being so close to her made heat rush into her cheeks.

A man bumped hard into her, sending a plate full of chips and guacamole onto her dress, and pushing her into Jack's arms. He caught her, steadied her, and as her eyes met his, she murmured, "Hi, Jack. Nice to meet you."

Taking a step away, she tried to regain her composure. "Is it hot in here?"

"Very," he replied. "You okay?"

"Sure, I live for attending events where I get yelled at by a hormonally hopped-up menopausal woman and get to wear guacamole on my new dress." She sighed as she tried to wipe the green mess off with nothing but her hand. *Yuck!* "See you around."

"Wait, I'd like to talk to you."

"Really? I mean, great." A blush threatened to engulf her already-flushed face, so she broke the gaze and looked around the room. The fund-raiser was wall-to-wall with patrons. Not the best place to get to know Jack better.

"Beer, anyone?" A waitress, who amply filled her Dick's Last Resort T-shirt and very short black skirt, eased her way through the crowd, balancing a tray. Her long fluffy blond ponytail swished in her wake as she arrived in front of them.

Here and there, people grabbed a cup and dropped money on her tray. Having large plastic cups was a wise move for this crowd and had been arranged by the NSW fund-raiser coordinator. Glass could become dangerous. But the way this waitress looked at Jack had Laurie understanding a new kind of threat.

"We'll take two." Laurie snagged a couple of napkins from the girl's tray, cleaned her hand off, and began fishing in her purse for some singles, until she spied a five-dollar bill. Searching for the proper change was helping to steady her nerves and she owed this guy for rescuing her. Perhaps the use of *we* would make this waitress take the hint.

The waitress looked at Laurie for a long moment, caught the hint, and moved off. "Enjoy yourselves," she added with a big smile.

"I believe we will," Laurie said as she presented a cup to Jack and lifted one to her own lips. She drank deeply. In truth, she was more of a "vodka and grapefruit juice" girl, but this would do in a pinch. A Girl Scout like her knew how to make the best of any situation.

He drained his cup and then said, "So, Laurie, tell me about yourself. Do you live in San Diego?"

"Point Loma." It was dorky, but she liked the way he said her name, as if it had tons of syllables. "What about you?"

"Coronado," he said. She noticed he watched her as she finished the beer and then placed both of their cups on a side table. She liked the way his eyes stayed on her—as if he didn't want to miss one movement she made.

"Nice place, Coronado," she confirmed. It had been a long time since she dated anyone, and she'd lying if she didn't admit she was intrigued by this man's singular attentions. She couldn't stand the men who flirted as they scanned the room for someone to upgrade to, or worse yet, make an overt swap or substitution call for their original date.

"I'd like to get to know you better," he said flatly.

No way! Did he just say that? Isn't that the lamest line in the world, right up there with "What's your sign?" At least he's honest about it.

"Me, too." The words popped out.

A grin lit his face. "Come with me." Taking her hand, he led her closer to the wall and the wished for possibility of silence. The music cranked up louder, canceling any chance of a stolen moment or a few audible words.

He said something.

She shook her head.

This silent-movie version of events was getting old, fast.

His body language spoke volumes as he leaned closer. The scent of aftershave tickled her nose. Not bad. Definitely spicy! Those wide shoulders and huge biceps practically had her panting, too.

"Isn't there any other place we could talk?" she yelled. He sure was cute, with his buzzed blond hair, gorgeous eyes, and chiseled features, but she didn't really get physical on a first date. Not that this was a real date.

The music stopped pulsing and for a few seconds there was an abrupt silence. As voices started to fill in the break, she took her chance.

"Jack, do you, ah?" She licked her lips again and watched his eyes follow the movement of her tongue. *Heavens, I'm sweating! The man is making me perspire. I hope my deodorant holds up.* "Do you work in the area?"

"Yeah, Laurie." His voice sounded like clover honey. "What about you?"

"I have my own practice." Her words were cut off by music blasting through the speakers.

He took her hand. Every nerve ending fired again as he held it.

Damn, I need to get a grip! Going all gooey while

surrounded by half her childhood friends would undoubtedly make her die of embarrassment.

On the other hand, her secretary would say, "Way to
go! It's only been… how long?"

"So, you're donating a gift to the auction." The corners of his lips turned up at the edge. What gorgeous
full lips.

"Yes." She swallowed hard. She thought to ask him
how he was associated with the Naval Special Warfare
Foundation, but the muscles of his biceps flexed, stretching the fabric of his shirt, and the thought drifted away.

Heaven help her! Her hormones were out of control.
She never thought she could get such nerve-racking
lightning sensations from a handshake. Her body was
screaming that this was a man worth experiencing.

She had never been the type for one-nighters, but Jack
was making her reconsider. She was a grown woman.
Wasn't it time for her to take a risk?

The list of dos and don'ts was rapidly playing in her
head. But she wasn't interested in listening to the "chat-
back"—that moral-based sound track that so often took
the fun and spontaneity out of everything.

*You don't know him! You shouldn't hook up with him.
Think "stranger"!*

However, her libido was in charge, and it didn't
give even a second's notice to the words screaming in
her head. The happy-joy-juice feelings were too great.
Instead, she leaned forward, giving him her sexiest smile
with her best come-hither gaze.

Within seconds of that look, his hand was on the small
of her back, guiding her toward the bathroom labeled
Handicapped. There was so much action happening

around them—plates of food, waitresses with trays of beer, music, someone making announcements, and more—that no one paid any attention to them. She was relieved by that. Was she really going to have a quickie?

The bathroom wasn't much to look at. It wouldn't be making the cover of *Architectural Digest*, though it wasn't bad enough for a makeover show. The odor of disinfectant permeated the air—*that* was reassuring—but there were only a few extra feet of space.

As the lock clicked into place, she had a moment to breathe and decide. She could still turn back. Her feet were backing her up, putting distance between them. When her back hit the wall, she had to stop. She took a deep breath to calm her pounding heart. She was going to do it.

She shoved her small black clutch handbag between the handicap rail and the wall in one smooth motion. Her eyes captured his and then dropped down to devour him. They continued all the way to his well-polished shoes and then raced upward to his piercing gaze, which promised complete and unadulterated satisfaction.

Oh, yes! She wanted him—his hands on her skin and his mouth driving her heart rate through the roof. Excitement raced through her veins, and her heart pounded hard as if she were running a marathon. She was drawing air in so fast it was hard to catch her breath. Short of passing out, nothing was going to stop her from enjoying this illicit moment.

"You smell good, like lilacs." Jack leaned down, close to her, their mouths only inches apart. "My mother used to grow them. So lovely." He kissed her and she was lost in myriad sensations.

His hands slid under her elbows, lifting her against him. She wrapped her arms tightly around his neck, losing herself in the strength of those burly, safe arms.

Lips rubbed gently against hers—asking, questioning, needing—and the tenderness swayed her. Opening her mouth to his want, their tongues touched and a teasing duel had her smiling into the kiss.

Moving his lips against hers, he said, "You're not a wilting flower, are you?"

"Why wilt, when I can give as easily as I take?" She felt his lips smile against hers. "What do you think of them apples?"

"I love apples, but I'm hungry for something else." His lips laid siege, and her hands dug into his back, steadying her before they wandered up to play with the fuzz on the back of his neck. *I haven't had this much fun since high school…*

His hands slid down her back and then back up again to cup her head. He kissed with a focus that was transporting. She drifted further and further in his world of sensation, seduction, and teasing satisfaction.

Thud! Thud! A pounding at the bathroom door interrupted them, dragging her abruptly back to reality.

"Just a minute!" she yelled. Slowly, he lowered her feet to the floor. His shirt was askew and there was lipstick all over his mouth. Her clothes were wrinkled and the back of her dress was partially unzipped.

Pushing the strap of her dress back up her shoulder, she did about a hundred moves to pull the zipper up all the way.

"Um, I think you might want to wash your face." She gestured with her hand.

"Thanks." He smiled as he turned on the sink and did as she suggested.

Fetching her purse from where she'd stashed it, she fixed her lipstick and was semiready to exit the bathroom.

———~~~———

On the other side of the bathroom door, they quickly skirted the line. These people actually wanted to use the facilities. Heat rushed to her cheeks. She was mortified—necking in the toilet like a teenager. What on earth had gotten into her?

Jack touched her elbow, guiding her to a semiquiet niche. Squeezing into it, they stared at each other.

Ugh! She hated that awkward moment when the physical attraction was cooling and reality was setting in. Not that she had a ton of experience, but she had some.

"So, Jack, what would you like to do next?" She began chattering to fill the silence. Though perhaps she shouldn't have led with that question. Now that the crazy, lust-fueled moment had passed, she was starting to feel back in control. "I mean, what do you do for a living? What's your job?"

"I'm a Navy SEAL. I thought you knew." His head tilted to the side as if he was studying her anew.

Crap! Crap! Crap! "No, I didn't. I, uh, don't normally date military guys." She spoke the words a little vehemently. *I shouldn't have kissed him.* Seriously, it wasn't this guy's fault that he was Spec Ops. Whom did she expect to meet here? "Sorry, I just—"

"Does that mean you date military women?" he asked with a smirk on his face.

"No!" She laughed. "The military—in all its forms—isn't my normal preference. I like nine-to-five guys. A man who comes home every night and is there on the weekend. Someone stable."

"You ever date a SEAL?" he asked. The question sounded curious, not judgmental, so she answered it.

"No."

He looked at her intently. "How can you know you don't want something if you've never tried it?"

"Inside knowledge," she stated. He hadn't earned the right to her history yet.

A grimace passed over his features. He grabbed his calf and massaged the back of it.

"Cramp?" she asked.

"Yeah, I get them when my potassium is low," he confessed.

"I have just the trick." She pulled his hand away from the ailing muscle and pushed on various spots on and around the muscle. "I do acupressure. This should loosen things up."

"Yeah, that helps. Thanks." Lowering his leg, he stared at her, and then he straightened his collar, flipping it out to land on top of his jacket.

She searched in her purse for her business card, plucked one out, and handed it to him. "Laurie Smith, physical therapist." His eyebrows furrowed. The smile melted away, to be replaced with a very deep frown. "What the hell? Is this some kind of setup? Did Gich put you up to this? He mentioned something about acupressure. I fucking knew you'd done this before."

"Done what? How do you know Commander Gich?" Laurie was confused. Could he insult her any more deeply than thinking her a prostitute? What was with this guy?

"Hold up! You need to explain yourself, Jack." Anger built in her gut. Had Gich set *her* up with *him*? Was all of this a game to get her back into the groove of dating and living? Gich wouldn't do this! She was a paragon, basically a nun, in his eyes, almost as pure as the Virgin Mary. None of this made any sense! Feeling a hard edge creep into her thoughts, she said, "You need to be up-front with me. What's going on?"

Stepping closer than was necessary, he looked down at her with a frown on his handsome face. "You can tell Gich for me that I don't need any charity. Anything I have to face, I'll do it on my own." He turned away from her and then stopped. Looking over his shoulder, he said, "For what it was worth, you're not half bad."

The comment hit home. She couldn't speak past the knot in her throat.

Just then the music started up. "Fuck you, Jack!" She yelled, but he was gone. The man slipped through the crowd as if he was butter on a hot pan.

No one paid him any heed as he made his way to the door and left.

She watched him go. Tears welled in her eyes, blurring her vision. *I won't do it. I won't cry. Jerk!*

Honestly, what had she done wrong? Besides make out with a total a-hole!

I told you so, said the voice from inside her head. *You should have gotten to know him better. Then you would have realized he was a loon, or just another egocentric, self-involved guy like the last few dead-end souls you dated.*

As she wiped the wetness off her cheeks, she said, "I promise. No more leaping before I look, and no more spontaneous moments." Part of her couldn't deny, as awful as the parting had been, that it had been one of the most memorable kisses of her life. For a few minutes, Jack Roaker had made the whole world melt away.

Laurie quickly shut down her little pity party. She was there to support her business and the SEAL community—she always did her duty. The party was in full swing and she should circulate.

Plastering a professional look on her face, she smiled bravely as she walked around. It was pure torture. All she wanted to do was go home and pout. She'd had a string of horrifically bad luck in the romance department lately. There was Patrick, who'd slept with her ex–best friend, and the last loser was Kenny, who'd thrown her against a wall in a fit of anger. She'd never told Gich about him. Her adoptive dad would have killed him!

Those guys had the moral fiber of dock rats, and that was insulting the rodent population. Add in the military element— soldiers and sailors who wanted to get drunk every time they had access to alcohol and get laid every night—and you had the definition of bad-relationship material. Not that she was opposed to sex or that everyone in the military was like that, it was just hard to find the good ones. Honestly, she loved sex! But talking was necessary to her and usually underrated in their minds. What she needed was a regular guy, maybe a lawyer or an architect. But not a doctor; her childhood friend married one and he was rarely home.

Scanning the room, she didn't think she'd find any-one like that at a Navy fund-raiser.

Sure enough, other guys hit on her. She walked away from a few propositions midsentence and went back to holding up the walls. That's where Hank G., Bruiser, and Jimmy—cronies of her dad's from UDT (Underwater Demolition Team) 11—found her and hov-ered close. They amused her with stories she'd heard a hundred times.

"Your dad ran naked onto the beach, having snagged his UDT swim trunks on some barbed wire. Didn't stop him from slitting two throats before he stormed…" Jimmy's voice was so familiar and the Southern twang was melodic, making her mind wander. If her dad were alive, maybe things would be different.

"Yeah, Dad was a hero." She was a military brat who had basically been raised by the West Coast SEAL community. Her mother had died when she was a baby, and her dad had drunk the pain away. Gich had stepped into the gap, and though the Commander was a bach-elor, he was a pretty good father figure. She remem-bered her dad going out for milk when she was little and coming back two days later. An hour after he left the house, she'd called Gich and he had stayed there the whole time, playing Barbie. Gich might have had a proclivity for the same things her father did—alcohol and women—but Gich had rules and never let anything bad affect his life or hers. She wished her biological dad had been smarter about his choices. Was she follow-ing in his footsteps—making dumb mistakes or risking herself on the wrong things?

"You're not laughing, Laurie. Bruiser, do your thing.

Make little Laurie laugh." Jimmy poked his friend in the ribs.

"A cow and a goat walk into a bar…" started Bruiser. His breath was laced with the smell of rum and his beer sloshed over the rim of his cup as he spoke. Within the hour, his daughter would be swinging by to pick up the lot of them and drive them home. They had two hours of socializing time, which was their SOP.

"Thanks, guys, but I'm really tired. Do you mind if I call it a night?" Drawing in a deep breath, she let it out slowly. She wasn't in the mood for being "cheered up," and the only lure right now was the silence of her bedroom.

"Sure, good night, Laurie," said Jimmy. "Drive safely."

Each of them hugged her, patting her back gently. Somehow the sympathetic twist was the hardest part to take. As she walked away from them, she was glad there were people in her life who cared, but somehow her dad's neglect had really damaged her. It made her more cynical about life, the male sex, and the military in particular. Hard to escape what you're born into as well as shake events and impressions that had imprinted on the psyche.

As the crowd thinned, a few insular clumps waited for the raffle to conclude. After that, they would most likely scatter like church mice, all except for those die-hards who couldn't pass up a one-dollar cup of beer. Those folks were definitely going to be praying to Ugh, the porcelain god, later tonight.

A hand caught her arm as she neared the door and wrangled her into an embrace.

"Hi, sweetie. How's the lovely and successful Laurie

Smith tonight?" It was Gich. The man in question had actually showed up at the NSW fund-raiser. Hell *must* be freezing over!

"Hi, Papa Gich." Laurie hugged him close. The smell of beer and cigars wafted off of him with an undertone of musk that was all Gich. She could close her eyes and find him in a crowd. There had been so many times he tucked her into bed, held her while she shivered with a fever, or wiped her tears. Tonight, she was definitely grateful to be in his arms. Her arms squeezed tight.

"Hey, are you okay, little one?" His voice held concern. He always said he hated to see her cry. When she was a child, she'd scored a lot of candy with a sudden outbreak of tears. Though he was no one's fool and could always tell the real deal from the faked.

Bowing her head, she murmured, "Yes." But she didn't mean it. Suddenly the urge to bawl was so intense, she bit the inside of her lip to squelch it. A single tear slid down her cheek. The solitary cry for help was wiped away by the tip of his thick index finger.

She waved her hand, and said, "I'm okay, Papa Gich. I'm just tired."

He didn't seem to buy the excuse, but Gich was a "weigh the battles" guy, and he'd only confront her if it was absolutely necessary.

Gently, he touched her cheek. "I'm here."

She nodded, but didn't say anything. She didn't trust her voice yet. This man with his X-ray vision into her emotions was tough to be upset in front of. Trying her best to calm her chaotic feelings, she focused on happy thoughts.

SEALs had an uncanny ability to see the hidden.

Gich frowned at her. "Should I be kicking someone's ass?" A bit of anger was at the end of that question.

Shit! Does he know? Can he tell I just fooled around?

"Not yet," she said as calmly, coolly, and collectedly as she could muster. "But I might take a rain check on it."

"Uh-huh," he said, scanning his eyes protectively over her one last time before he allowed his gaze to roam the room. He seemed to be looking for somebody, but he never said whom, and she didn't want to ask. They took a turn around the inside of the establishment. When he seemed satisfied, the Commander walked her to her Dodge Charger and kissed her on the cheek.

"Good night, Laurie. Call me when you get home." He nodded at her. "Buckle up."

"You're such a mother hen, Gich," she replied with a half smile. It was important that someone somewhere in the world loved her. "Love you."

"I love you, too, Laurie girl," he said softly before he stepped back from the car.

She started the engine and pulled into the empty road. There was barely any traffic, and she doubted the trip home would be eventful. Regardless, if she didn't call within twenty minutes of leaving here, Gich would call her. Sort of nice… the actual feeling of being loved.

The image of Jack popped into her mind. She was tempted to ask Gich about Jack, but what would be her reason? If Gich learned about her… uh… moment with Jack, would he get angry, or would he be happy that she had fun—at least twenty minutes of it? She preferred that her personal life stay her own as long as it could.

Making out and fooling around!

As she turned onto the road that would take her over the Coronado Bridge, her mind spun. *If I could do it all over again, would I?*

The sensation of his mouth on hers... His strong arms around her... Those rock-hard abs... *Dammit! It felt incredible!*

Could I rewrite the ending?

Unfortunately, she didn't think there would ever be a do-over for her and Jack. Nope, that boat had definitely sailed.

Chapter 3

Sometimes it is entirely appropriate to kill a fly with a sledgehammer.

—Major I. L. Holdridge

"TODAY, WE ARE GOING TO BEGIN OUR GROUP THERAPY with a hug. Everyone put your arms around the person next to you and hug tight—squeeze your neighbor like he's a lifeline." Dr. Debbie "Dismal" Mucan was so proud of her activity that she embraced the person on the right. The fact she was stacked like a double-barreled gunboat was a plus for the guy grinning over her shoulder. Probably the best "feel-up" he'd had in months, too.

Jack sighed. Being here sucked! And he was not a hugger.

Fucking unreal! He wanted to utter the acerbic thought but used his great restraint to hold it in. The only expression he allowed himself to register was a slightly raised eyebrow and a frown. He was a man who could morph into anything that was required of him.

The guys on either side of Jack looked skeptical, too, shaking their heads and pushing their chairs even farther back from the group circle they all sat in. When the scraping of the chair feet and groans of the chair legs stopped, the ring of patients looked like a disconnected and oddly shaped trapezoid.

"Now, we're going to take the interaction to another level. Anyone who is *not* interested in participating or who is unable to contribute anything positive, you're welcome to leave," Dr. Mucan commented sharply, pushing her glasses back up her nose.

Six men rose instantly from their seats. Jack was out the door before the comment was even cold.

Hooyah! Get me the hell *out of here!*

He moved swiftly down the hall, over the steps, and out the door. He looked up into the hot San Diego sun, and for the first time in twenty-four hours, he smiled. Strike that, it had been twelve hours since he willingly grinned. Because at almost precisely that time last night, his cock had been almost inside the prettiest brunette he'd ever seen.

"Dammit! Why did I have to think about her? Probably a setup." He withdrew his phone to call Gich and ask him. But he just couldn't imagine the man sandbagging him that way. And she seemed too pretty, too reserved to do it... for money. So why did she come on to him so freely?

He looked in the mirror. No answers reflected back to him. He looked like... a dork.

The BlackBerry vibrated in his hand, and he almost dropped it. The screen said it was his shrink. If he didn't answer, the man would keep calling back. Persistent SOB.

He pushed the button and waited.

"I'm glad you answered. I can see you from my office, and I'd like to know why you aren't in group." Dr. Derek Johnson's voice was clipped. "We spoke about this in D.C. When you arrived back here, you would be required to go to group three times a week if you want to return to full duty—at some future point, that is, after you've gotten your memory back."

There was the rub. He would kill to be operational again. With the hole in his memories, no one would approve it, and "group" was a waste of his time.

He searched his brain for a loophole as he started toward his car. "Didn't you suggest that I seek other forms of healing—acupuncture, or something like that?"

"Oh, yes, physical therapy as well as biowave sound therapy and visual training have been shown to be extremely useful in memory loss and perceptual difficulty. Are you going to do that now?" asked Dr. Johnson with a note of surprise in his voice.

"Sure," agreed Jack, lying through his teeth. He could always make the call later in the day and arrange something, or perhaps he could poke himself with a few needles and call it done. There couldn't be that much to the acupuncture process.

"Well, that's interesting. I didn't expect this proactive behavior from you. I'm pleased to hear you are taking an active role in your healing process. Who is the therapist? Is he or she on the Department Of Defense approved list?" The sound of Dr. Johnson tapping his pencil on a pad of paper was a loud and impatient *thunk, thunk, thunk*.

Shit! Was she approved? "Laurie something. I'll have to get back to you, Doc."

"If you can provide me with her information, we can add it to your record…" began Dr. Johnson. "Oh, and don't forget our upcoming appointment. We have a lot of ground to cover, Petty Officer First Class Roaker." Using rank to remind Jack who was in charge of his future was a nice touch. Bummer, that he didn't particularly give a shit. He'd always be the master of his destiny.

"Uh, I'm late, Doc. I've got to go!" Jack entered the car in one motion as he shut off his phone. Tossing it on the seat, he spied the business card he had dropped the other night. Picking it up from the floor, he studied it.

Laurie Smith
Physical Therapist
Make appointments in advance.
Physical therapy takes your commitment.
619-555-5569

Sliding the key into the ignition, he shoved the gear stick into reverse, backed up briefly, and then quietly left, resisting the urge to peel out of the parking lot. No one would have access to his true state of mind unless he wanted it.

At the next red light, he dialed Laurie's office number.

"Hello, Laurie Smith, physical therapist, this is her assistant Frannie. How may I help you?" asked a clipped, authoritative female voice. She was also shuffling papers at the same time she was extending the greeting. "Hello, is anyone there?"

"Yes, ma'am. I'd like to speak with Ms. Smith," he said, uncertain of the precise words he would use to cajole her into giving him an appointment, but he thought the use of formality might help.

"She's booked up through next week. Did you want to make an appointment? Is Thursday morning okay?" Her brisk tone was not pleasant to his ear.

"No. Um, I need to set up an appointment today." He paused and an inspiration made him take a different tack. "I need to see her and apologize. My name is Jack."

"Oh, that sounds interesting. Let me check her schedule." The call was put on hold and Native American flute music with a new-age edge came wafting over the line.

The light changed and Jack flipped on his Bluetooth. *Connected*, the speaker said, and then the sweet-toned music was flowing into his car. As he reached the next traffic light, the man next to him rolled up his window to block out the melodic sound. *It isn't that bad*.

Just as another call was beeping in, the voice came back on the line.

"She can see you at five thirty p.m. You'll be her last appointment of the day." There was a click, and a dial tone blared on the line before the Bluetooth spoke to him: *Call ended*.

"Great job, boy genius. You were thinking on your feet, that Laurie was the lesser of the two evils. Now you have an appointment with a woman who you'd enjoy having in your arms again, but have no explanation for why you made such an ass of yourself. What next?" Jack followed the flow of traffic toward the bridge, letting his instincts lead him. The optimal action would be to go for a run, and that was precisely what he would do.

Amphibious Base, Coronado, California

Jack placed his military ID in a clear plastic arm holder and strapped it to his bicep, then tucked the keys under the front seat. He never worried about the car when it was parked on the base. He actually almost dared someone to take it.

Since his Jeep was surrounded by other cars better

looking and more expensive than his, it was doubtful anything would happen. Outsiders didn't have the balls to park here. This small fenced-in area was for his kind and their families. It afforded the military beachgoers an easy walk to the ocean or, for the men, a straight shot to the poles and climbing rope.

Today, he wanted nothing more than to sweat. This was the best therapy he knew. Working out, taking his body to the max, made all the demons go away.

Knowing his own limits had been a valuable lesson to learn during Hell Week, and since then he'd gotten even stronger. He could run twenty-five miles and then some with a full pack or carrying a body. Hefting them both at the same time was challenging, but he'd done that, too.

What he craved now was working not only his physical body but also his mind, setting them up to conquer the obstacle of his memory block. But how did he break that hard shell?

Without missing a beat, he pulled a warm Propel from his glove compartment and downed it in several gulps, then tossed the empty sports-drink bottle into the recycle bin. His feet knew where to take him. Having made this run thousands of times—it was definitely one of his favorites—he set off in the direction of the sand and waves.

The light jog along the path to the water felt good.

"Hooyah!" The shouts came his way from trainees. He nodded. Then he was on the hard-packed sand of the beach. The waves were crashing on the shore and he could see the tide pushing out to sea. He opened up his stride and was soon leaving the base—Gator

Beach—and heading onto civilian sand. Picking up speed, he stayed on the hard-packed sand of the beach as he passed the Coronado Shores and felt the familiar comfort of steps he knew by heart.

The wind smacked his face as he breathed in the fresh salty air. Exhilaration flooded his system and almost too soon he reached the rocks. He scrambled over them and veered toward the trampled sand in front of the Hotel del Coronado, which was busy with a fancy event, probably a wedding. Then his attention was back on the run—the chopped-up sand, the frothy water, and the thump of his heart as he dug inside and ran harder.

The world tuned out as his mind opened up, letting the air in and the issues out. This was how his mind worked, putting his body through the paces and allowing his concerns to unfold naturally. Solutions always came to him this way and he knew if he kept going that something would reveal itself as a clue.

The image of Laurie popped into his mind. The idea of her being a setup didn't sit well in his gut. She was too clean-cut for that, like a boat whose sails were just unfurled—too free and unfettered. There was no overt calculation; he would have seen it in her eyes.

All he remembered was Laurie's confusion. But how had she known Gich's name?

Shaking his head, he made the anger go away and concentrated on the memory of her hot, well-endowed body locked tight against his. It made him smile. Perhaps he had been too hasty in judging her.

Yeah, he could drum up an apology for the lady if it might help his cause, though it was doubtful she would forgive him. He'd been a pretty nasty asshole, accusing her basically of being either a prostitute or a froghog. In either case it was going to take a lot of fancy acting.

Was the "I fucked up" special still available at the North Island flower shop? It was colorful and supposedly worth the $99. Maybe he needed to go for the "don't divorce me" bouquet, which had three dozen long-stem roses, two red birds of paradise, and the large box of Godiva chocolates. Was it worth $200? A couple of the Team guys swore by it.

Abruptly, the Naval Air Station North Island NAS came into view. Had he run that far and fast?

As he neared the guardhouse, a strange tightness started to climb his skull with sharp icy pain biting stabs to the back of his head. It hovered over the spot where his wound was. Supposedly, the head fracture was mostly healed, but of late, the pain had gotten sharper and somewhat more intense. *What the hell do these docs know?*

Jogging in place, he rubbed gently over the spot. Pain washed away his mental gymnastics; a deeper jab—into his brain—forced him to stop.

Fuuuuuuuuck! It's like an ice pick!

A familiar voice made his head turn so fast, it felt like whiplash.

"You look like hell, my man." His swim buddy, Don, stood wavering in front of him. His BDU—battle dress uniform—was pristine; not a speck of dirt or blood was on the black cloth, and even his hair was slicked in place. There was an air of calm as if he'd just arrived at work and all was right with the world.

"You're not really here." Saying the words aloud made Jack feel better. His heart was racing and he consciously calmed his breathing. Training had taught him he could control practically every bodily function. Though in truth, he did feel slightly sick to his stomach. Oddly enough, at the same time, he was wishing with all his might that his swim buddy were really standing there.

"Nah, man. I'm here. Well, sort of…" Don said, still grinning. "I only seem to have a front. I can't turn around. Though, I guess it's okay. It's not like I'm going to do the hokeypokey or anything." His smile melted away. "Jack, how's my angel—my little girl—doing? I can see her, but I miss holding her in my arms. When can you visit, hug her for me?"

"I, uh, don't know." Jack was embarrassed that he hadn't seen Sheila or their daughter, but what could he say as an excuse? Nothing! His emotions berated him. "Man, I have to ask you, what happened?"

Imaginary Don shrugged. "It's my turn to say 'I don't know.' What's the last thing you remember?"

Looking down at the sand, Jack studied his shoes and allowed what he knew to come easily to him. The sensory data was crystal clear. "I can see my feet hitting the ground. Everyone was accounted for and had gone into formation, following the plan. Above us, bats were flying and the wind was picking up. Clouds blocked the light coming from the moon and stars. No one was around, but for some reason, I had an ache in my spine, which usually means there is something going on. I turned to look at you, and then… then… nothing."

"You've got to do better than that, my friend. Much better!" Don's image wavered. "I can't hang on. Time—for now—to split. Hang loose, bro."

"Hanging loose," Jack repeated, per their habitual parting.

The pain in the back of Jack's head squeezed tight. The ice pick drove its way even further in. He closed his eyes to block out the swirling images and he held the palms of his hands against his eyes until it subsided.

When he opened them again... he was alone.

Seagulls dove down in front of him, landing on the sand. *Screech! Screech!*

I'm fucking going insane. He put his feet back in motion. Pushing through the pain and the dizziness, he forced himself to run back to the Amphib Base. He set a brutal pace for himself, and sweat poured off his body in rivulets.

By the time he reached the base, his heart was thudding a harsh cadence and the back of his head was slamming with pain. Slowing his pace to a light jog, he calmed his heart rate and tried to convince the headache to go away, but the pain refused to leave.

He sat down on the beach, sifting grains of sand through his fingers, measuring and dumping the same handfuls until his breathing and heart rate were slower.

In front of him, the waves pounded the shore, showing their frothy whitecapped tops. The beaches were mostly deserted, except for a few individuals taking advantage of the waves and, of course, more Team types like him running or working out on the obstacle course. He knew this part of Coronado like the back of his hand—had gone through BUD/S here and could do sugar-cookie drills for days even now, not that he'd want to.

He flexed his hands, wishing he had a gun in them. This place should have reassured him. But it didn't. He had never felt so foreign, like an alien in his own body, and he didn't know what it would take to reconnect with himself and his world again.

~~~

Point Loma, California

A blast of icy cold air-conditioning slapped his face as he walked into Laurie Smith's small brick-covered office space with a sign proclaiming it was indeed Physical Therapy Central. The motto underneath said, "Healing begins with you."

He took one last look at his Jeep. Freedom was only a few steps away. He didn't have to do this, but there was other stuff at stake. The need to make it up to Laurie— for his impression of being a horse's ass—sat squarely on his shoulders.

Never once in his life had he backed away from a challenge, and he wouldn't start now. Though if someone had asked him if he'd rather have his gonads squeezed in a vise or apologize, he'd have to admit he'd take the former. Letting out his breath in a low, steady exhale, he closed the office door behind him and cleared his throat to displace the knot of discomfort growing there. "Hi. I'm Jack Roaker."

He could smell some mix of vanilla, lavender, and maybe eucalyptus. He guessed it was supposed to be calming, but smelly stuff was not his thing. Give him the outdoors and fresh air any day.

"A-a-achoo!" He couldn't hold the sneeze back.

"Bless you!" said the tiny older woman as she turned her attention to reorganizing the various items on her desk. She couldn't have been more than four feet four inches tall and she looked like a pixie or fairy or some kind of mythical creation. Finally, she found her appointment book. The secretary gave him a quick smile and then nodded at the bouquet of flowers he clutched in his hands. "She'll like those. Roses are her favorite. I'll let her know you're here."

Frannie pushed a button on the wall and motioned for him to have a seat. He took in the setting and the ambience. Sunlight streamed in through several small windows bordering the ceiling and the waiting room was überneat and orderly. Large plants held the corners, and the decor had an earthy feel.

Hey, he'd watched *This Old House*. His home might be as bland as a corn chip, but he knew what he liked. This place had clean lines and was personal as well as professional, with homey touches, too.

Along the wall, opposite the door, there were several benches and tables with books and magazines; next to the secretary's desk was a knotty oak bookcase overflowing with larger, more interesting-looking tomes. There was no other exit except the one behind and the door ahead.

He took several steps closer to the bookcase to get a better look at the books. Among the titles were *The Way to Vibrant Health*, *At a Journal Workshop*, *Forgiveness*, *Hands of Light*, *I Heal, You Heal*, and many more. The books definitely looked holistic to him.

On one of the shelves were bundles of sage wrapped in different-color yarn. He knew the stuff was supposedly to clear the air. To him, it smelled like pot, so he wasn't a big fan of the herb.

Another shelf held colored stones with tiny booklets sharing the *Art of Healing with Stones*. There were all sorts of shapes: hearts, circles, triangles, animals, and ones with holes in them, too. She must have been into all that woo-woo stuff.

He collected practically nothing. By his bed was a stack of gun books. Yep, he and Laurie were very different individuals indeed.

The door opened and a teenage girl came out. Her eyes darted all over the room until they settled on him. After a long moment of consideration, she must have decided that he passed inspection, because she paused in front of him for a few seconds and said, "Hi."

Laurie's voice drifted to him. "Come in, Jack."

Jack nodded to the kid and then stepped through the doorway. Teenagers were so often saturnine. He knew practically nothing about how to interact with them. Heaven help him, if he ever decided to procreate. He didn't know what he would do.

Dim lighting made him squint as he entered the room. His eyes grew accustomed quickly so he could see that this space was a much larger room than he had anticipated. The place was loaded with machines. The fire exit was to the left and the other closed door he figured must be a bathroom. His world was dependent on knowing how to escape. Though right now, he needed to deal with Laurie.

She was doing something in a dark corner. Ah, she was changing a lightbulb.

Flipping a switch, she flooded an area with light and then turned it off. Moving over to a therapy table, she pulled the sheets off and sprayed it down, handling it all

quickly and efficiently. He watched her deposit the rag
and used linens in a laundry bin and put the cleaner into
a cabinet.

As she washed her hands, he noticed the pungent
odor of the cleaner in the air. It was only there for a few
moments before it started to dissipate.

Her hips swayed gently as she stood at the sink. He
remembered the way her backside filled his hands, and
the feel of the muscles as he lightly squeezed. As if he
had summoned her gaze, she looked over her shoulder
at him.

"Do you want me to stay, Laurie?" asked Frannie
from the other room, her high voice cutting through the
distance like an air horn.

"No, I'm good. See you tomorrow, Frannie. Please
lock the front door as you leave." Laurie turned back to
the sink. The water cut off abruptly, making him more
aware of the silence. "Jack, please close the door to the
therapy room."

Why? We're alone now, aren't we? He decided
against arguing, and reaching behind him, he grasped the
handle and pulled it closed with a barely audible click.
He swallowed, suddenly a little nervous about speaking
with Laurie. Without the aid of beer or hormones, his
vulnerability came to the forefront. Fuck, he hated this!
But he was true to his word, and he was going to do it.

He cleared his throat. "I'd like to apologize." There,
he'd said it!

"Why?" Her tone had some serious attitude, not that
he blamed her. "You obviously think I'm some kind of
Loose Lola, like I hop into the arms of every guy who
smiles at me."

"No! I… I don't. Shit, I don't know what to think. But I should have given you the benefit of the doubt and allowed you to explain, without taking off so abruptly." His words were spoken in a cadence. "Um, because I thought you… well, I've had a few health challenges lately, and I inappropriately believed you had been part of a setup. I'm sorry I jumped to conclusions."

She whipped around to face him, stalking him like the goddess of vengeance. The light haloed her as she stood in front him, obviously not afraid to go toe-to-toe with him. He didn't like it, but he could respect it.

Her words were short bursts of emotion. "I don't know whether to be insulted or flattered. Though my first instinct is to say, 'What the hell made you think that?' I'm not a floozy!"

"I know. I mean, I know that now. Crap! I'm just putting my foot in deeper, aren't I? How do you know Gich?" he asked, letting go of the nerves and finding comfort deeper in the shadows of the semidark room. Some things were easier to talk about if no one could see his face—particularly the vulnerability he knew was there.

"Yeah, you are. He was my dad's swim buddy. They were in UDT 11 together and then later in SEAL Team ONE. Not that it is any of your business, Jack." Her words were acerbic.

"You're a SEAL pup!" The words tumbled out of his mouth. Dammit, what had he done!

He knew he deserved it. Learning that she was the daughter of a Team guy made his disrespect seem even worse. How was he going to make it up to her? Maybe he should just cut his losses and get out of there.

"Born and raised in the Teams. I cut my teeth playing on the Gator and SEAL beaches, back when you were still trying to figure out how to make a knot at your first Cub Scout meeting." She bent over to pick up two small bolster cushions off the floor, and his hormones rang in their opinion loud and clear. This lady had serious sex appeal. He needed to give this apology stuff another try and make it stick. He needed her, had to be kind to her, for the sake of the Teams and, well, himself.

"I didn't know. Gich was my BUD/S instructor and is a good friend." Shaking his head, he said, "He's my mentor, and he'd totally kick my ass if he knew we'd fooled around. How about you take pity on a Team guy and give me another chance? I'm very good, focused at what I put my mind to."

Color ran up her cheeks. Maybe she was thinking about their experience at Dick's Last Resort. He certainly was.

"Yes, he would slam you for it." She smiled, and then laughed. "It'd be a humorous scuffle to be sure. But…" Her eyes ran up and down his frame. "Maybe I won't tell. It depends on the next hour of interaction."

"I'm on probation, then." It didn't set well with him, but he understood her wish for it.

"I can totally envision you and Gich giving each other crap." Her laughter grew until she was holding her sides, probably imagining Gich and him chasing each other around like a couple of stooges. The apology, or that image, must have done the trick, because all of the tension drained from the room. Then again, humor always did clear the air.

When she was calmer, she studied him as if she was gauging him. "So you thought Gich sent me to you. Interesting thought. Has he ever done that before?"

"No. I just… I've had some stuff to deal with recently." He stepped forward and presented the flowers. "I *am* sorry. Please accept them." Using the word *please* was difficult for him, because it made him feel as if he were begging. But he had been wrong.

"Me, too. Thanks. Roses are my favorite. It's a stunning bouquet." She took the paper off, snipping the ends of the stalks and arranging them swiftly yet artistically in a white porcelain vase. He was glad he'd spent the $200, though the chocolates were in the car. He had a sweet tooth, too. "I'm not forgiving you, just contemplating your worthiness for it. And, uh, I'd like to be honest with you. When we met, I didn't put two and two together about who you were. But this morning I remembered. I've heard of some of your issues, via the grapevine, and I'm sorry that your military life has become so difficult. That's hard." She moved the flowers closer to her worktable, then opened her desk drawer to retrieve a pen. Giving her attention to the book in front of her, she scanned the pages and then turned to look at him. "I might be able to help you, if you would really like to have an appointment today."

"Was that a gun I saw in your drawer?" he asked, intrigued by what he saw. "It's not really pink, is it? It's so tiny."

"Yes, it came from Gich. It's a stainless steel pink polymer frame TCP Taurus .38. Of course, I keep the bullets hidden, but within reach. I can have a gun loaded, cocked, and pointed at you in less than five seconds."

She winked at him. This was a saucy lady, for sure! A woman with a significant amount of style was a pleasure to spend time with. "I'm protective of what's mine but not dumb enough to keep a loaded gun in a drawer where patients could access it."

"I agree, you have to be smart. I admire a person who can handle herself well." He gave her another half smile. "Okay, I might be interested in trying acupuncture or acupressure or something like that."

"Sure, I use some alternative methods—acupuncture or acupressure can both be transformative, and energy work and massage can cut healing time by half. So I'll use whatever techniques I have in my arsenal, holistic or standard. What level of healing are you open to?" Laurie's eyes traveled the length of him.

"Fully healed. Do whatever you have to." He rubbed his neck.

"Most head injuries have associated issues with neck and shoulders." She smiled at him. "My job is to identify problem areas." She pulled out a form. "You'll need to sign this so I can get access to your medical records and correspond with your doctor. The second piece of paper has a series of exercises I want you to begin that will loosen you up. Don't add weight to them until I clear you."

He frowned as he filled out the form and signed it. The other one he glanced over and then stuffed in his pocket.

"Don't worry, I only send updates on physical info, not mental."

"Huh?"

"I tape my sessions, just in case anything useful comes up that a patient might want to hear from their own lips. I keep them for two weeks and then I recycle them. No one else gets access but me. Got it?"

He wasn't thrilled with being taped, but there was a certain quality about Laurie that intrigued him. He couldn't identify it precisely, but they had already faced a hurdle and she had handled it well. Laurie didn't roll over and concede to his wishes. They'd gone toe-to-toe, and in the end, though she was tough, she was easygoing, too. These values were a must-have in his world. "Sure."

Most assuredly, he hadn't enjoyed apologizing, because it wasn't something he did well. Of course, he *had* made it work. He *was* still in the room and she had agreed to work with him. Several steps of his plan were happening correctly.

"Instead of attacking the history of your injury today, why don't we get started with an examination? Let me take a look at that head and neck," she said, putting clean sheets on the padded massage table and tucking the elastic part underneath to hold the cushy fleece heating pad in place. A top sheet and thin cotton blanket went on next. The mood of the room was much lighter than when he first entered. Laurie's gentle manner was soothing to his senses.

He raised one eyebrow. "Okay. What else?"

"I was thinking more about talking about your incident… with the therapy. This should encompass part of your psychological, emotional, and physical wellness. What do you say? Ready to get on my table?"

Automatically he shook his head. "I don't think so. I'm not ready to have someone mucking about in my head. I'm not a fan of that stuff. Though, you did say table? Maybe doing something physical, like massage, would be okay."

"Naturally, because you don't mind someone mucking about with your body," she teased.

"Nope." His smile widened and his eyebrows went up and down. "Have at it."

"Gee, thanks, Jack. You're such a guy. Cute, and I might have one or two soft spots for you, but don't take advantage of it." She gestured toward a table laden with crisp white sheets. "Okay, let's get started."

He was out of his clothes and on the table before she could say another word. A chuckle came from deep inside of him as he moved without hesitation to obey her command. "I'm ready."

"Guess I should have told you that you didn't have to be naked." As he started to sit up she pushed him down. "But since you're here. Let's get started."

Anything could happen in this room, and as that message telegraphed through his mind, several parts of him became very awake.

"Um, we're not having that kind of appointment." She said, pointing to his erection. "I don't do 'happy endings' or stuff like that. If you're here as a patient, then our job is to work, and you will be paying for the honor of my time. Got it?"

"Yes ma'am," he replied, hopping up on the table completely naked. There wasn't a shy bone in his body. "I'm at your mercy."

She smiled wickedly at him. "Yes, you are." Walking over to the other side of the room, she lit a cone of incense and the smell of salt and sea filled the room. Turning off the air conditioner, she guaranteed the frigid edge to the temperature would ease. She pulled a loose sheet over him, the one he had dumped on the floor. It was hard to provide modesty for someone who didn't have any.

Laurie moved her fingers gently over his neck and head. Probing expertly, she found several tender areas and then worked slowly down over the first four cervical vertebrae. "No extreme damage. A little swelling and tenderness, but your alignment is good."

"Do I get any rubbing with this?"

"Relax, Jack. Breathe deeply and let's begin." Laurie's hand lay flat on his chest, and he slowed his breathing to sync with hers. His mind was focusing on the sexy woman and being blank. When her fingers began gently tapping on either side of his temple and then over his heart and chest, it shocked him when anger filled his body like a raging fire. He'd gone from zero to one hundred and ten miles per hour in seconds.

The emotion was thick and combative, and he had to growl, "Stop."

Her hands froze and then lifted slowly from his body. "It's my turn to apologize. I should have prepared you. That form of therapy is called tapping, and it can bring some potent feelings to the surface. Would you like to talk about it?"

"No," he ground out. "Just give me a few minutes."

Laurie backed away from the table. There was a funny look on her face, but he couldn't think about that now.

Working to get his emotions back under control, he closed his eyes and used a SEAL technique. Granted it was rookie stuff—transforming an emotion into fuel— but he rolled the anger around in his head, making it turn from red to white and then forcing the energy to push through his shoulders and arms, torso and back, and then down his legs to his feet. When he felt himself come back under control, he opened his eyes and looked at her.

"I should have known better," she said, crossing and then uncrossing her arms. Finally, she came back over the table to within reach of him. "A client once swung a fist at me. I didn't think you'd have that much emotion hidden in there."

"What makes you think it's hidden?" he asked, though he knew it was there. The rest of the world was allowed to see the calm, affable Jack, but inside he was completely torn up about the death of Don and the loss of his memory. His life as a SEAL was at risk, and his greatest enemy right now was himself. Yes, he was certainly a volcano of issues and the lava spewed all day long, despite the redirection of the flow.

"Tapping is a gentle therapy that often unleashes a multitude of issues, and we should have discussed the method and concept beforehand. I can see you have a lot going on in those fierce eyes, and when you're ready, I'm here. Why don't we focus on something soothing instead, like massage and acupressure? Let's open the valve without emotion or words."

Relief filled him. She wasn't going to force him to talk. The session would have ended then and there, and on a distinctly sour note, because he wasn't ready to talk to anyone. Being pushed where he didn't want to go—like every other SEAL—shut down the chat function quickly.

"Next time we'll do a history and very frank physical exam before we start working."

He relaxed. He needed action. *Who am I going to*

talk to? Speaking to myself isn't solving the issue! The words echoed in his head. Were the therapists right? Did he need an outsider to walk him through his own mind? If it were true, he didn't want those medically oriented, note-taking sharks mucking up his record with their comments and the vast weight of his extremely personal frustrations. Some shit had to be personal!

Could he trust Laurie? Did this lady keep her mouth closed or would she be anxious to spread his inner secrets to the far corners of Coronado and beyond? He had dated someone like that, and it had been a painful lesson to learn.

"Jack?" Her voice was light, though he could hear the concern in it. As much as he didn't want to put his trust in her, Laurie really seemed to care. It was either her or no one.

He nodded, making the decision, and finally relaxing his muscles. The fight-or-flight reaction had been resolved. Staying was the right choice. He watched her like an eagle watching a mouse. "I'm ready."

"Okay, time for some deep-tissue relaxation." Filling her hands with a cream that heated with her touch, Laurie began by rubbing the soles of his feet. "I'm very good at this. Most of my clients fall asleep in minutes."

"I rarely sleep." The statement sat between them like a palpable creature.

"Why not?" Her words were gentle, yet he didn't want to answer. She did not give up easily, though. "Well, then, try *not* to sleep. For me."

The corners of his mouth lifted into a smile. She was funny!

His masseuse played "This Little Piggy" with his

toes, and the action touched something inside of him reminding him of his childhood. When she tickled the soles of his feet, he laughed outright.

Laurie's hands made magic. She was true to her promise. Her fingers pushed and pulled and dug until he felt a relieved groan slip from his lips. The tension and pain, which had been solid walls of ache, released slowly by degrees and then suddenly by layers. It was a strange sensation to hear his own voice sighing and know his body was lifting into her touch.

"Are you doing well?" she asked gently.

"Great," he moaned as he realized the predatory side of him had given way to the tactile joys of being touched. God, he wanted more of it!

"Yeah, I figured you could use it. I've never met a man who didn't like a good rub." Her hands were moving up his body, working his calves and thighs, pushing on places and digging deeply into other spots. "I'm adding some shiatsu massage techniques, too. Very few souls get to feel this."

"Why? You're amazing," he said, though his body was beginning to feel like mushy oatmeal.

"The physicality takes a lot out of me," she replied. "It tires me out. This is the end of the day, though, and you did apologize to me, and—well, as a person with a healing spirit I feel this is what you need. So, enjoy your reward."

"A helluva gift. Thanks…" His words felt distant as the layers of relaxation took hold, and for the first time since his accident, he started to really let go. The room seemed to slip away, replaced by a feeling of distance and floating.

Syllables and images slipped from his lips as he drifted. "Maybe you can find the hole."

"What hole?" she asked, whispering in his ear. The tips of her soft breasts rubbed against his skin, and he could feel the nipples even through her shirt. He wanted to respond to ask her to get more intimate, but he was being pulled away.

His exhaustion dragged him further under. The last conscious thought he had was of his own voice murmuring, "It's a setup, Don. I think one of us is going to die."

Chapter 4

I have not yet begun to fight.
                —John Paul Jones, aboard the *Bonhomme Richard*

"I TOLD YOU FROM THE BEGINNING WE SHOULDN'T BE doing this Op. Something is seriously fucked up with the Intel. None of this is sitting right in my gut. Don, are you listening to me? You've got to explain it to the others." Jack's words were hard, forceful.

His shoulder muscles tensed beneath her hands. His words were low and gravelly. "Shit! No, I'm not being superstitious. Remember: Swepston's Rule of Three has already gone into effect—count them. One, be alert to the first hurdle—it can be a feeling or an actual object blocking your path. This is your first clue there's a problem. Two is the second action gone wrong—reassess the mission or path, immediately. Three is for seeing the truth—the third screw-up has occurred and it is time to wrap up and go home, because the fourth incident will most likely have us boxed in and dead."

Spit flew out of his mouth as he yelled, "This is FNG shit! We're not fucking new guys. We need to abort. Don! What the hell! *Don!*"

His body shook as if his entire being was having convulsions. Then, as suddenly as it started, the movement stopped.

Crap! This guy didn't just have a heart attack on her table, did he? Jack was deathly still and very pale.

Hurriedly, she placed a finger against his neck and found his carotid artery. The beat was strong. She sighed. "Jack, thank God!"

His lips expelled one long intense exhalation. Then his breathing became ragged, slowly smoothing out, until it once again became regular and easy paced.

Laurie could hardly believe her ears. Had Jack just said that they were going to die, and what did he mean that there was something wrong with the Intel? Softly she spoke next to his ear. "Tell me more Jack."

"Argh." He only grunted and then fell silent. His body tightened and twitched now and then. Otherwise, if the sounds of his snores were any indication, this man was very much asleep.

Thoughts swirled in her brain. This guy had some major issues. As her hands moved over him, she realized with each touch, she only wanted more. Maybe he'd be a bed buddy, a lover. That could work for her. If they just had sex now and then, she wouldn't have to worry about the girlfriend thing, the marriage and family stuff, and her concerns about the military aspect could just wash away.

A liaison with Jack could be a "hit it and quit it" proposition, and oddly enough, the candor of it could fit her life right now. Concentrating on business was important, because it was beginning to thrive, and being with Jack wouldn't distract her. She wouldn't have to worry about them when they weren't together. Her inner core was all SEAL ideology. Early in life she'd learned that "not getting caught" was terribly important and so was living by your instincts. Jack showed up on her radar in twenty different ways, and she had to know more.

She smiled. Her reasoning worked for her. Her moral measuring stick would be used to gauge how she helped him heal. Using every trick and technique she knew, she would do her utmost to give him what he requested.

Straightening, she continued to work her way down his back. Her hands gripped the muscles, working over the contours and dipping in between the ridges. There were old scars in places, and she gently traced them with her fingers as she pondered his body wrapped around hers.

Jack intrigued her. His body. His situation. His determination. And the wrap of his steely hard arms around her had been pure heaven. If he weren't unique, she knew she'd never risk her peace of mind and possibly her heart in this situation. His body was loosening up.

She felt a calcium deposit the size of a baby's fist lodged in his right hip and her fingers pushed and probed against it, working the edges until the lump broke and dissipated. A feeling of accomplishment surged through her.

Sweat beaded on her cheeks and she wiped them on the bottom edge of her T-shirt before moving down his body. The heavy lines around his face encouraged her to continue her path of healing. Her instincts told her that Jack was severely stressed out and needed the rest, so she kept her word—pounding and pushing on as many kinks and knots as her own body could handle eliminating.

When she had sweat so much that her clothes were

completely soaked, she knew she was getting close to being done. She could only exert as much energy as she was willing to sacrifice. Her number one rule was always to keep some energy for herself. It was basic emergency-responder doctrine—take care of yourself or you won't be able to take care of either your partner or the patient.

Stepping back to look at him, she put her hands on her hips. *Why is it that men look so angelic on the outside when they are sleeping? Also, what is the circumstance or reason that pulls all of that sweetness back inside when they wake? What is the mystery, the lure?*

His snores reverberated in the small office with a deafening refrain and made her smile. It reminded her of a very cherished memory—Josie. She'd had a Labrador dog that snored like that. The sound was sheer comfort to her. Of course, Jack might not appreciate the comparison, but it automatically put her at ease. She bet he'd like that part.

Her hands gripped his buttocks, working the muscles—pushing and pulling on them as if they were bread dough. Another part of her anatomy kicked up interest, and she had to talk her sexual desire back into its box.

For now, Jack was a client who sought healing and she was going to give it to him. Though her libido called dibs, having had first contact—well, kisses—she still wanted to be true to her work commitment. Yes, she was walking a fine line—doctors didn't get involved with their patients—but physical therapists didn't have the same type of code. It just wasn't… seemly.

Of course, his interest in pursuing treatment

seemed dubious, too. She wasn't going to give up the opportunity for the most incredible pleasure she'd ever experienced in her life because of an inkling of doubt. Especially when it had been ages since her last "involvement," or rather, love interest. But if she had to do the client/therapist gig, she supposed she could put her feelings on hold to provide Jack with all of her mind energy.

Her body wasn't thrilled with the notion, but her sense of duty and professionalism appreciated the nod.

All of that was future-casting. Right now she was living in the moment and being present in the here and now. The heat got to her. Grabbing the bottom of her T-shirt, she peeled it off her body and dropped it in the laundry hamper. The service washed everything.

Looking at Jack, his body glistening with oil, she shook her head. He was drop-dead handsome and her body craved him as if he were a caramel-filled Godiva dark chocolate. Both made her mouth water for a bite… or a binge.

Walking across the room, she flipped the switch and stood in front of the air conditioner, silently begging it to pump out cold air faster. Even the Arctic wasn't cold enough for her, though, and she cranked it up another notch. As the machine began to whirl louder, the motor kicked up to a higher gear, drowning out the sound of Jack's snores and her own worries.

Placing her hands against the wall, she let her head fall back and allowed the cold air to draw away her looping thoughts. The noise roared in her ears as air whipped over her body, teasing her senses and making her nipples harden. She welcomed the blissful cold relief and partially surrendered her body's tremendous heat.

"Hello, sweet Lilac Lady. How do you do that… smell so damn good," said a voice into her ear.

Laurie practically jumped out of her skin. When she was steady on both of her feet again, she looked over her shoulder at the sexiest man she'd ever seen naked. It was hard to keep the smile from her lips. "I didn't hear you move," she replied, putting a little sass into the tone. She knew she should feel a little self-conscious, but she was too aroused to care. "And it's called soap."

He laughed, but his eyes glistened with a darker inter-est. "I'm glad you didn't hear me," he said as his lips gave her a very sensual smile and then kissed a path around her neck and shoulders. "I'm trained to do that. Surprise people."

"Oh, do you mean surprising women by shocking them out of their skin, so they have to stay on their toes?" she teased back.

"Yes, I rather like you on your toes. Your pussy is almost even with my cock," he said slyly. "And yes, we learn control. I can control everything. Watch me." He pulled her body against his, and she could feel the outline of his cock against her buttocks. Giving into the wicked side of her nature, she wiggled against him.

He sucked in his breath and then turned her in his arms. Looking into her eyes, he said, "Sexy lady." Then he grew serious for a moment; his eyes lost part of their gleam. "Laurie, thank you for the massage. That's the first deep sleep I can remember having in a while. According to your clock, I was out cold for three hours.

I'm grateful." Before she could say anything else, he kissed her.

The emotion and tenderness of his kiss was so captivating that it reached into the inner recesses of her soul. This man gave a part of himself to her in that moment. She wanted to comment, say thank you or share what it meant… but the kiss turned hungry, rousing the lioness in her that wanted to mark him as hers.

Opening her mouth, her tongue darted in and out. She licked at the thick warmth of his lips and fed on his heat as if it were food from the gods.

When their tongues dueled, skyrockets of desire burst through her body as she locked her arms tightly around his head and drew him closer. Time was lost to the multitude of sensations shooting through her body. One minute, he had scooped her up in his arms and was walking with her, and the next, she was stretched out on the massage table and he was on top of her.

When he broke the kiss, her breath panted out and she couldn't keep the smile from her lips. "So, what's your next move, Jack?"

His grin was wicked. "I'm going to show you why they call me Red Jack."

The gleam in his eyes made her shiver. "Will I like it?"

"You tell me," he said softly as his eyes devoured her. Then his hands and lips were blazing a trail of heat along her skin. Deft fingers released the bikini top that she wore for quick dips in the ocean, which was right off her patio. As he released the knot, her skin prickled with the cold air, making her shiver in his arms.

"Laurie…"

She couldn't stop her body from moving, lifting into

his touch. Turning and sighing, she was undulating beneath his ministrations. "Jack, please."

"Please, what?" He asked with one eyebrow raised.

"You're going to make me beg, aren't you?" she asked, needing his cock inside her with a desperation born of pure chemistry and attention.

"No," he said softly as he made his way back up her body. When he was gazing into her eyes, he spoke with his eyes and mouth. There were many messages there. The words she heard were, "You only need to ask." But his eyes spoke volumes: *Lose yourself in me. Let me lose myself in you.*

"Plea—" She didn't even get to finish the word, before he moved. Grabbing his pants, he fished inside, withdrew a condom, and sheathed himself. Within seven heartbeats, he was primed between her legs and prepared to push in. His cock teased gently between her slick lips, causing a shivery ride of mini orgasms to zip along her body. Her eyes started to close as she began losing herself in the sensations and the moment.

"Look at me. Keep your eyes on mine." Jack's tone was deadly serious.

Laurie's eyes sprang wide open and the surprise at his tone must have been evident, because he softened it.

"Please look at me." The tenderness of his words was like a caress.

She nodded and then kissed him, closing and opening her eyes quickly before she pulled back. Kissing with her eyes open had never been an art she could master. It just made her dizzy. But making love gazing into each other's eyes would be a new one.

"Ah." The sound came from deep inside her as Jack

bumped the top of her cervix, sending a riot of feelings through her abdomen. He was so deep, she could hardly breathe.

He balanced himself on his elbows, keeping his weight from crushing her and at the same time retaining his ability for full control. Poised above her, he just stared at her. It was too much!

Bucking against him, she wanted him to move, but he was in charge and there was nothing she could do to change that. She finally stilled beneath him, deciding she could live with it—let him have this one. A small part of her objected, but she conceded control.

"Ready, lovely Laurie?" The evil rogue was back in his eyes. He whispered in her ear, "Red Jack is in charge."

"Right, like I need to be… ready," she said, half joking with him, but the other half was unsure and slightly nervous. She squeaked out, "I'm—"

Then he moved, ever so gently bumping the top of her cervix at the same time his fingers found her nipple. A hazy fog filled her brain as she became lost to the crazy play of sensations. Her sheath gripped his cock tighter and tighter until she spilled a massive climax of satisfaction on him. She sighed as her body shook and convulsed, milking him.

Her hands and nails raked and tore over his flesh, forcing him to move more.

He took the cue and began thrusting in and out of her with ravaging heat that went beyond anything she could imagine. Pulsing with need, her body built to another climax until she cried, "Jack!"

He rolled her on top of him. Yes! She was in charge now, riding him like a wild dolphin surfing the waves.

Power surged through her mind and body as she watched him. The honesty was bold in his eyes. He liked her. Admired her. And wanted her body. "Cum with me," she gasped between thrusts.

He gave a slight nod and then gripped her hips, guiding her into a short, hard rhythm that had her coming again and again. She was lost on the waves of pleasure.

"I'm going to cum." With those words, he pulled out, lowering her onto his thighs. Pulling the condom off in one swift motion, his seed spewed out, hitting her breasts and belly. Before she could even react, he was pulling her completely down on top of him and wrapping his arms tightly around her.

Closing her eyes, she gave into the safety and warmth and thought about the vulnerability she'd seen in those last moments. Even through the haze of her pleasure, she'd witnessed this fierce, tender part of him. It was like looking into his soul. It touched her deeply, and she had no words for what she wanted to say to him about it. Maybe saying nothing was better.

"That was like some kind of fantasy scene." His words were loud in her ear as he hugged her close.

Unwrapping his arms, he released her slowly and reluctantly. "Are you okay?"

"Yeah," she said. "I'm going to jump into the shower real quick."

"You have a shower in this place?" He seemed surprised. "Wait, is there an apartment in back, too?"

"Yep, I've got a lot of perks going on here." Her body was sore in places it was hard to comfort, and as she passed the full-length mirror she paused to look at herself. Why did she feel different?

Shit! What are those red spots? "Are these hickeys?" How could a man put that many marks on her body… and without her realizing it?

"That's why they call me Red Jack," he said smugly as he put his hands behind his head and stretched his legs out, obviously making himself more comfortable.

"Don't give me that load of crap. I grew up with the Teams. You probably got the label for some dumb-ass reason during training." Her hands were on her hips and she meant business. She pointed a finger at him. "Tell me the real reason right now."

He laughed and then rolled on his side to face her. "There were three guys named Jack in my training class. Gich was into wearing those colored bandanas, and he gave me the red one, another guy a yellow, and the last guy a blue one. Yellow Jack eventually became known as Streaker, mainly because he liked to run around naked. Blue Jack became known as Blue-balled Jack, because he kept pissing off the ladies and Gich. And me, well, I turned red as a lobster during the first week of training—before I got my tan—and kept the tag Red Jack. I also have a propensity to make the ladies blush." A wink and salute came her way.

She laughed. "Oh my, you are full of it, aren't you?" Walking slowly toward the bathroom, she put a little extra swing into her hips. When her hand was on the doorknob, she said, "Well, are you coming?" Looking over her shoulder, she gave him a wink. "I could use someone to scrub my back and perhaps a little lower, too."

They'd just had sex, and she wanted him again. Hell, the truth was, he just made her feel seriously sexy and very feminine, and that felt very good.

His body moved like lightning. This man definitely had good "quick twitch" muscles. Within seconds, he was standing before her and she was looking up into his eyes.

"You are fast, aren't you?" She grinned at him.

"Only when I want to be," he said wickedly. "Let's see what I can do to help you, uh, in the shower."

Chapter 5

He who knows others is wise. He who knows himself is enlightened. He who conquers others has physical strength. He who conquers himself is strong.

—Lao-tzu

DARKNESS PAINTED THE NIGHT SKY AND ONLY A FEW stars peeked out now and then. A heavy marine layer was hovering above the sand and water, trying to decide if it was coming farther onto shore. Jack had been unable to resist rising at three a.m. Part of him had wanted to stay in bed with Laurie, have a cup of coffee, and eat breakfast, but there was too much weighing on his mind. Getting to the obstacle course early to take advantage of the quiet was his number one priority. Exercise forced the demons out, or at least helped him make sense of them.

He'd tried to work out on the O course yesterday, but reporters had surrounded the base, attempting to get pictures of SEAL training. Everyone wanted to get snapshots, given the way SEALs were lighting up the news channels. Their successes were splashed around the globe.

Jack wished they would go bother the Teams on the East Coast. There were Team guys there, too.

Didn't the news people understand that if their

identities were known throughout the world, it would be hard to operate? Being stuck behind a desk was worse than death for a SEAL; it was torture, one excruciating report at a time.

Whipping through the course, he pushed himself to climb the rope ladder faster and faster, until sweat poured off his body. When his hands were aching from use, he turned his attention toward the beach and did his usual grueling run.

Turning his mind off, he allowed the thud of the whitecapped waves and the hard wind to keep his mind blank. People were already dotting the beach, securing blankets and canopies to stake out their favorite spots. A few Team guys were enjoying the surf and had obviously dragged their wives with them.

Dogs ran free, barking and chasing the seagulls. The owners would get fined if they were caught, but it was probably worth it. There was never a cop or lifeguard on duty this early. Who cared anyway?

It was like that uproar several years ago. "Stop the dolphins from pooping in our oceans. They are polluting our water. Do you want your kid to swim in waste products?" Then some kid had replied, "Don't we do that already? The dolphins live there. What do you want to do, put a diaper on them in their own homes and make a greater mess? Poop is biodegradable; nature is smart about such things." The rebuttal had gotten so much laughter, the issue had been dropped.

Why didn't people realize that the planet is the way it should be? Animals are wild and people are, in most cases, unpredictable. No matter how many regulations are set, someone or something will always be unhappy or uncomfortable. Jack's philosophy was "get out there and live—the world is whatever it is." His job was to make it safe and never get caught.

That's why the group therapy bugged him. He felt like he was being punished, which made him clam up even faster. None of that psychobabble was going to help him.

Opening up needed to come about naturally. Like last night, after he and Laurie had showered, they'd eaten and they talked. The organic unfolding worked for him. It was even better when she'd shared the tape of his session. According to her own set of procedures, she taped every client session, and hearing his own words had impacted him. The sleep had helped, too. In just a few short hours, this woman had done things the shrinks could not.

Maybe he needed to try that other earth medicine—hoodoo stuff. Mulling over the how tos, he reached the fence of Naval Air Station North Island, turned around, and headed back. His mind was methodical. He weighed the pros and cons, and though his sense of control wasn't spanky-happy, the alternative—doctors and group therapy—was worse.

It seemed to him, if he could get the answers without the whole horrific medical experiment being documented on his permanent record, it would be worth taking the leap for Laurie's methods. How bad could it be?

Besides, this woman acted as if she cared about him, and she definitely enjoyed his body. The image of her mouth working over his skin made him harden slightly. Yep, going down Laurie's road felt right.

He visualized cleaning his gun—piece by piece—to

make the issue "stand down." As it began to take effect, he gave himself over to the serenity of the morning run.

The sweetness of the air was spectacular, and the early morning sunbeams, as they poured across the sky, sending a rainbow of colors to announce the dawn, held his attention. A snapshot of this moment would have made a spectacular painting. Even this brief perfect moment in time would eventually fade.

Nothing was permanent, though he sometimes wished he could freeze time, just to appreciate it longer. He had never been very skilled in art, though it appeared relaxing. One of his heroes, a retired SEAL from Team ONE, had learned to use watercolors after a car hit him. The devastation to his body had been tough, but art had helped him gain mobility in his hands and arms.

Jack wasn't sure he wanted to wait for something tragic to happen before uncovering any hidden talents. When he was a kid, he'd spent hours performing daredevil stunts on his bike or drawing with his colored pencils. Back then, he'd considered being an architect, but after his parents died, he hadn't dared dream.

The SEAL bug had found him when he read in school about Thomas Rolland Norris—SEAL Medal of Honor recipient—the special-operations man who'd led a mission into Vietnam to rescue two pilots caught in enemy territory. Half of the men were killed trying to reach their goal, and Tommy helped the wounded, mounted a counterattack, and saved the pilots.

Norris spent three years recovering from injuries and went on to become a member of the FBI despite his disabilities. The man had serious strength. He never quit.

Jack knew what his goal was after learning about

Tommy. The SEAL continued to be an enormous influence on him, too, though he probably never knew it.

UDTs were bad-asses! He thought about the Underwater Demolition Teams, which were the SEAL roots. The World War II guys were unstoppable, and the Vietnam-era guys made it through some of the hardest traumas of their life even as part of America condemned their commitment to the fight for freedom. They didn't give up. SEALs were made to keep on giving back to their world, their communities, their families, and each other. Honor, courage, and faith were supposed to radiate from their pores, even when tasks seemed monumental. Those were the footsteps he had to follow. *Dig harder. Run faster.*

Stretching his stride farther, he felt his heart rate kick up a notch. His aim was to push himself to the brink.

"They never said die, and I will never give up," he panted. His life—his entire career—was depending on resolving this memory issue. "I will find my answer."

Waving briefly to the on-duty sailor watching him from the guard shack, Jack leaped over the line that separated the civilian world from the Amphib Base and made his way toward the middle of the beach. Finally, he slowed his pace.

Dependents—military wives, husbands, and children—dotted the expanse. A small sign stuck in the sand read Child Development, which was a mommy or daddy and children-five-and-under playgroup. Weaving in and out of the kids, Jack slowed his pace so he didn't step on anyone or anything. His eyes focused on the pregnant bellies, the mommies in tiny bikinis, and a woman breast-feeding her baby.

"Uncle Jack." The label froze him in his tracks. His eyes worked hard, quickly scanning the kids around him until he zoned in on his target. Sunlight was shining down on her, blinding him for a second, and then the clouds pushed together and he could see her. Kona.

Jack sank slowly onto the sand, panting. His heart felt like it was going to pound out of his chest.

Don's daughter sat on the ground before him. This innocent, charming child humbled him. He took a deep breath, resisting the urge to pull her into his arms and hold her. Too much pain and too many tears would come from doing that. Instead, he reached for his tactical cool—the soldier part of himself. "Hi Kona, how are you? Is your mother here? You're not alone, baby, are you?" Emotion was a thick knot stuck in his throat and the words felt tight as he spoke around them. "Where is she, honey?"

"Behind me. Sitting near the sand hill," said Kona as she smiled at him and then went back to her work. Systematically, she filled her shovel with sand and then dumped the contents into her waiting bucket— pink with giant gold trident stickers on it. Decorated, undoubtedly, by Don. She must really have liked that bucket, because she protected it from the water—lifting it so it stayed dry.

Then she placed it back on the sand and diligently scooped sand until her child-size container was full. Flipping it over, she made a house, making smaller mounds around it to create a tiny village. When it was complete to her satisfaction, Kona spoke. "I like things that are full. Empty stuff makes me sad, and quiet time, too."

Jack's eyes scanned the child's face and then the surrounding men, women, and children. There was nothing here to harm her, and yet he still felt as if something could. Maybe, it was him. Keeping himself away from her protected the child.

Changing his aim, he sought her mother with his eyes. A curvy mocha-skinned woman smiled and then waved at him. Sheila had been watching him—of course. Don's wife was the protective type, though her appearance was welcoming.

He nodded and waved back, but he couldn't make himself smile. Shit! He should have gone to see her sooner. Running into each other here was hard. Maybe he could just get up and continue his run. No one would fault him for training. This was the way of Navy SEALs—exercise was a way of life. He didn't have any answers to give her yet.

Someone was tugging on his sleeve. He gave that charming little one his full attention.

"Kona, I... I'm so..." began Jack, then he stopped. He couldn't complete the apology. Finally, he said, "I loved your dad."

The pretty little girl nodded and then she went back to her sand piles. She looked the way she always did—sweet and kind. He'd always wanted a daughter like her. The thought took him by surprise. As a terminal bachelor, he shouldn't have been thinking these thoughts.

"My daddy died," she said in a matter-of-fact manner. "Mommy takes me to sand therapy at school, but I like being at the beach better. The waves are pretty, the air smells yummy, and... there is no one looking over my shoulder, asking me questions. I know what they're doing. They want the answers in my head. That's called shrinking. Daddy didn't like it—he told me about it—so I don't like it either."

Misery chilled his blood at hearing those words. "You're a pretty smart five-year-old, aren't you?"

"Yeah," Kona said, looking up at him. "Uncle Jack, why can't Daddy come home from heaven? He came home from other places. No one will es… explain it to me."

"Kona, did Mommy talk to you about heaven?" The sweat on his back was cooling on his skin.

"Yes, Mommy said, 'Heaven is in the sky.'" She gazed at him wide-eyed. "Would you go find him for me, Uncle Jack? Grab him when you wear your parachute. It won't be hard for you. I want my daddy to come home." Her tiny fingers scratched at the tip of her nose. "Mommy cries a lot and that makes me sad, too."

There were no more words. She just stared at him.

He had nothing to say to this beautiful child who was shredding his heart. His eyes darted back and forth over the sand as his mind searched for an appropriate response, something he could push past the knot in his throat.

A shadow fell over them, blocking the sunlight. If only it would rain and save him from this moment.

"Hi Jack." The soft, dulcet voice of Don's wife brought gooseflesh flying up the skin on his back. He craned his neck to see her face. The sun outlined her body, making her look ethereal. Her skin was clear and creamy, and there was only a smudge of darkness under her eyes. She was such a gorgeous woman, made even more beautiful by the bulge of her pregnant belly.

"Hi. I'm sorry I haven't been by. There have been a few complications that I needed... to take care of and—"

"Don't. No excuses. Whenever you're ready, we're here. Kona, it's time to go home and get ready for school." The wife of his swim buddy and the best friend he'd had in this lifetime extended an open hand to her daughter, and the little girl obediently stood. The link between them was palpable.

Dumping the sand out of her bucket and placing the empty shovel inside, Kona grabbed the handle with one hand and reached for her mother's hand with the other. Sheila looked at Jack for a few seconds, and then she leaned over and kissed his cheek.

The wet smack felt hot on his skin as if he'd been branded. He swallowed the pain of emotion down deep inside of him. "Bye, Kona. Have a good day at school."

"I will, Uncle Jack. Come see me soon." Her little girl voice was soft. "I miss you, too, Uncle Jack."

He nodded. A fixture in this child's life from the day she'd been born, Jack hadn't considered that he had taken himself away from her. The want to be there, for her and her mother, was raw inside of him. "I'll come see you soon. I promise."

"I'm packing. We have four and a half more months before we need to be out of the house." Sheila said firmly. In other words, *Get your ass over before we go!* If Kona hadn't been there, would she have said it... called him on his avoidance?

"Where are you moving to?" asked Jack. Shit! He hadn't considered that regulation that they would have to leave the base after Don's death. The idea of them going was too final—they were part of him, too. "You could have my place. I'm never there."

"That's kind of you, Jack, but a one-bedroom apartment won't work for us. We need three bedrooms, with the baby coming. I'm heading back to my parents' house in Riverside, Connecticut. They'll help me until I can do it on my own again."

Nodding, he stood and looked her in the eye. "I'm sorry to see you go."

"I know you are. We are, too." Sheila started to walk away and then stopped. Turning back to him, she said, "Don't be a stranger. You'll always be family to us, Jack, and we want you in our lives now and in the future, too. Got it?"

"Understood," he said. Too much emotion came through in that one word and he had to clamp his lips tight so nothing else slipped out. A litany of pain, excuses, and troubles was on the verge of exploding out of him, but none of it was appropriate—this woman had lost her husband and the father of her children. There was no greater pain on the planet, and she had her hands full already. She didn't need to hold his burden, too. What he needed to do was figure out how to lighten hers as he handled his own.

※

Sitting on Laurie's office couch while she rummaged around in her desk drawer was not how he'd visualized his day. *Tough luck!* He'd made his decision when he'd seen that child on the beach. Whatever it took to find the answers, he would do it.

This sexy lady might be his best bet. "Laurie, can you run through what we're going to do?"

"I found it." Holding up a somewhat crushed chart, Laurie's smile said it all. "This is a chart on neurological physical therapy. It's perfect for what we need to do."

"Which is?" Jack wanted to do this right. He didn't want to flip out on her the way he had with the tapping. Okay, *get frustrated and angry with her* might be a bit more accurate.

"Get you to relax and let go. Basically, this involves your head, neck, and shoulders. As I massage a specific quadrant, it helps you let go of tension, frustration, mental blocks, and so much more. If there is a problem associated with an area, it surfaces and you should be able to vocalize it. So, are you game? Speak now or…"

"Yes, yes," he waved his hand and stood. "How do you want me to lie on the massage table? Should I get naked?"

"Hell, no, that would be more of a distraction, right now." She grinned at him. "Don't look so disappointed. Just take off your shirt and sit in the massage chair. Your face goes on the paper O."

She stretched her fingers as he sat down. "All that is required of you is for you to pay attention to my fingers, where they are and what they're doing."

"I could say the same thing," he teased.

"Jack, hush up! Do you want to do this or not?" she chided.

"Yes, sorry," he said somewhat contritely. "How can a man complain about being rubbed?"

"Good grief! Let's get started." Her fingers dipped in a small clay bowl warming over a candle. It was a mixture of rosemary and lavender oil—for memory and stress relief—and then she placed her dripping fingers at the base of his neck. Slowly she rubbed the warmed oil in small circles.

"Mmmmm…"

She felt the muscles of his neck give, relaxing by inches. Tightness melted into supple, pliable flesh beneath her fingers as she moved upward to the base of his skull.

"Tell me the first thing that comes to mind," she whispered next to his ear.

"Besides having sex with you?"

"Be serious, Jack," she chided. "Come on. Now, if anything pops into your mind as I work over spots, let me know, okay?"

"Sure." He sighed. "I guess. Could you make triangles instead of circles?"

"Jack, you're a pain."

"You have no idea," he said with a soft chuckle.

"I want you to do those neck and shoulder exercises—three sets of each—today, okay?"

"Sure."

"It'll help you with blood flow and movement." Her fingers moved over his skull, rubbing, pressing, and invoking. They asked questions of him as they gently prodded the areas near his scars… and yet no words came.

Laurie glanced at the clock on her desk, almost the top of the hour. She'd been at it for nearly forty minutes, with no tangible results.

"Jack, it happens to everyone. Don't worry about it." She was discouraged, but she didn't want Jack to know.

He'd responded so quickly to her last session that she expected too much. The SEAL psyche was not giving up any of its secrets today.

"Do you have to say it like that? It's not like I didn't perform," he teased. "Next time."

"Sure." She smiled briefly. "Listen, I've got another client in five minutes. Would you like to use my shower and then go out the back?"

He nodded. "Sounds like a plan. Thanks for, uh, fitting me in."

"Get out of here!" she laughed. The man was all puns and bad humor. She watched him leave and then she stripped the paper off the headrest of the chair. Perhaps she was too vested in the outcome. If she let go a little more, maybe it would help. Or was the personal approach the way to go? Whatever it was going to be, she had to switch focus to her next patient.

~~~

Jack stood beneath the shower, reveling in the pounding hot spray as he reviewed the session. When Laurie touched the small scars on his head, he had felt something. It was foggy, indefinable, and yet hanging there at the edge of his consciousness.

Turning off the water, he reached for a towel and rubbed it over his body. Securing it at his hips, he entered Laurie's small apartment and helped himself to a beer. He took a long draw from the bottle and looked around at Laurie's personal space.

Jack had seen her apartment the other night. It was on the small side, yet he liked it.

A queen-size bed was pushed into one corner and

there was a working wood stove with a small wood-bin next to it. The kitchen consisted of a single counter along one wall with a medium-size fridge and a small two-burner stove. A television was mounted on the opposite wall, with a beat-up leather couch and a couple of chairs perched in front.

Stacks of books in milk crates lined the walls in colorful disarray, and piles of movies were on the DVD player, which was balanced on an antique sewing desk. Knitting needles and yarn were stacked in a basket alongside it. A sweater was three-quarters completed with the needles poking out, waiting. Maybe he'd ask her to knit him a gun cozy.

Grinning, he lay down on the bed. Resting the bottle next to him, he picked up one of the tiny recorders Laurie used for her sessions. He turned it on, placed it next to his beer, and then stretched his arms over his head and closed his eyes. "Hey, Laurie, you're probably only going to get several hours of my snoring, but I'm giving this alternative stuff a try, so you'll just have to suffer."

Using a trick he'd learned in training to block out the world, he counted *one*—breathing in through his nose—and *two*—breathing out through his mouth. Over and over he did it until his breathing steadied and he stopped counting altogether.

Chapter 6

A leader is a man who has the ability to get other people to do what they don't want to do, and like it.

—Harry S. Truman

LAURIE'S DAY DRAGGED BY AT A SNAIL'S PACE. SHE had looked at the clock a hundred times, and she finally admitted to herself that this was one of the rare times she longed to have the workday over. She loved her job, and each client was a personal investment of time, research on his or her case, and careful guidance. Today, though, she was anxious to have the appointments complete so she could prepare for Jack's session tonight. It had been hard for her to kiss him good-bye and watch him leave just a few hours earlier.

Funny that she thought of it as a session and not as a lover who needed help. Was she kidding herself about crossing the line between therapy and involvement? Probably, but he definitely needed professional assistance. Brought on by an actual head injury and emotional trauma, acute psychological suppression was nothing to sneeze at. A patient could suffer from the memory block his whole life. The good news was that there were many ways to work with the patient, from the benign to the controversial, but the bad news was that Jack seemed reluctant to take advantage of the team of medical doctors available to him at Balboa. It shouldn't have surprised her, though, because a SEAL is a different breed of man. This particular one seemed to prefer a hands-on approach.

Being a SEAL pup, Laurie had a few extra insights on the warrior mentality and additional tricks up her sleeve on how to handle one. She felt certain she could make a difference in Jack's life. As long as he was game, she would give it her all. Though she wasn't sure if she would able to keep him from infiltrating her heart. That part made her a little nervous. For her, keeping her emotions solely on the friendship level would be the first and biggest hurdle. Her healer's spirit drove her to make a positive difference in any wounded individual's life, but with Jack… He was already pinging her stability.

"L-L-Laurie," Clarissa, the young teenager who had come to her for a jaw and neck problem, stuttered. "Do you l-l-like him?"

"Who?" Laurie asked. She was suddenly jarred out of her mental wanderings by her client's question.

Silently, she chastised herself for letting her mind wander while being in a session with a client. Clarissa was one of her cherished favorites, and the teenager's success had been extraordinary, especially over the past few months. "I'm sorry. I owe you an apology."

"N-n-no. It is o-o-okay. I felt that way about a boy o-o-once. His family moved away and I never g-g-got to tell him." She half smiled and then started speaking rapidly. "I-i-it's th-th-the m-m-m-man I s-s-saw th-th-the o-o-other d-d-day."

"Remember to slow down your speech pattern,

especially when you get excited. Pace the words. Count silently in your head, if it helps. I, one-two-three-four, like, one-two-three-four, you, one-two-three-four." Laurie gave the comment gently, so it wouldn't sound like a criticism, and then she grinned. "Yeah, it's him. How did you know?" Reaching across, she laid her hands on the teen's jaw and slowly worked her fingers over the muscles. It was hard to be serious when the girl was grinning at her.

As she moved her fingers into the teenager's hairline, Clarissa said, "He's a hunk! V-v-very. Handsome. If I were old enough, I w-w-would date him, too."

"Clarissa!"

The teenager pushed Laurie's hands away. There was only so much interaction a teen was willing to bear. "I'm d-d-done. C-c-can we c-c-call it q-q-quits, p-p-please?"

"Show me your exercises first."

The teen demonstrated the simple jaw, mouth, and tongue exercises, and then moved into the complicated ones. Laurie was proud of her. Clarissa did them with ease.

"Great job, Clarissa! I'm really proud of all the progress you've been making. You are obviously staying loose." Her compliment made the teenager beam. Laurie wanted her to feel good about herself. She was concerned that this was the only place where positive reinforcement was given. "How do you feel? Is it helping your overall jaw movement as well as your stutter?"

"Yes. It helps a lot. I'm delightfully delicious and decidedly delighted." Clarissa had spoken each word perfectly, and both she and Laurie clapped at the well-done pronouncement and the excellent jaw movement.

"Glad to hear it. Well done, Clarissa! Let's call this the wrap-up for today. I hope you have a terrific night." Laurie watched the teenager gather her schoolbooks and purse. "See you next week."

"Okay. Don't be t-t-too s-s-smitten," she teased.

"Oh, goodness. I'll try. Hey, if you need me before our next appointment, you have my cell number." Down deep, Laurie worried that *smitten* was the last word the girl would speak for the whole week. Kids could be pretty competitive and very cruel.

Clarissa's school guidance counselor was a friend who had asked Laurie to take the case pro bono. Laurie would do anything to help a kid in need and was pleased that the hard work had paid off. Clarissa was finally speaking to her. She had worked with kids who stuttered before, but Clarissa's issue had at first been complicated by recovery from a broken jaw. She still didn't talk at school or home, but so far her progress had been astounding.

"Yes. Bye." Clarissa waved, opening the door and letting sunlight into the room. Framed by the fuzzy yellow sunlight, she glowed. The halo of light made her look angelic and far too vulnerable. Laurie hoped there was someone special watching out for that sweet girl.

There's never a quick fix, Laurie thought. She sat at her desk and let her worries swirl around in her head. Long shadows climbed the corners as the sun slipped away to set on the horizon. Too soon, it was only she, alone and surrounded by four walls.

Her eyes wandered to the picture of her and her father. They were standing next to her first telescope. The size of it dwarfed her, but her dad would cradle her in his arms as they examined the heavens. All those constellations… He'd whisper the myths into her ear, sharing those special secrets and transporting her imagination to another realm.

Closing her eyes, she tried to hold on to the precious memory. Slowly, though, it drifted away. The warmth and happiness were replaced by anger and frustration. His neglect and her childhood fears rose momentarily like bile in her throat.

"Nothing is ever easy with SEALs." Her words barely rose above a whisper, but they eased the pain like an ill-fitting bandage.

Turning her attention to the file on the desk, she made a few notes in Clarissa's file. Nagging doubts taunted the edges of her mind, worries that she wouldn't be able to fully heal Clarissa or Jack. They were both so solitary, as if the whole world were a series of grave threats to be faced alone. *Jack needs more help than you can give him. Wake up, ducky, and let go of him.* She steered her eyes to her little apartment door.

But what if I'm all either of them has?

Someone jumped on the bed, startling Jack out of his dream.

He swiftly flipped the figure onto its back, pinning down the intruder's arms to their sides. He opened his eyes wide and stared unknowingly at Laurie's startled face for a few seconds until recognition dawned. He finally loosened his grip and she wiggled free. "Sorry," he murmured. "I'm not used to being surprised when I sleep."

"Yeah, I wasn't thinking about that. I'm good, though. All in one piece." She wrapped her arms around him and kissed his worried lips. How had she forgotten that SEALs were loaded weapons and it was better to throw a pillow from the safety of the doorway and duck for cover than it was to try to wake them with a simple touch like a normal human being? Perhaps he'd get used to her presence over time. "Let's start over. What a lovely surprise to find you in my bed. I am a very lucky Alice."

"This is some nice digs, but it isn't a wonderland. Also, I hate to break it to you, but you're thinking about Goldilocks."

"So, you're what… a bear?" She laughed. He was too quick for her.

"Yes, but I'd rather be the wolf. The better to eat you with," he said, and then he rolled her underneath him. There was something in his eyes, a serious quality that held her attention.

"What were you dreaming about?" Touching his chin, she rubbed her fingers up his jawline. "Jack, do you remember?"

"Yes." He rolled off of her. They lay side by side in silence. The minutes stretched between them until finally he answered. "My childhood.

"When I was six years old, my father woke me up at five in the morning. He wanted me to sit with my mother so he could run to work. He said he would only be an hour. I remember hearing the door close and the lock slip into place. I got out of my bed, bringing my favorite blue blanket with me. It had soft stuff on the edges. My mother made it for me for my third birthday…"

Jack took a deep breath and continued the story. "The air was cold. My feet were covered in footie pajamas that made a slapping noise on the wood floor as I walked. I always thought the noise sounded neat, so I would run hard, trying to make it as loud as possible.

"My parents' room was at the end of the hall, which seemed very far away this morning. Mom had been sick for most of my life, but lately she was worse. She hadn't gotten out of bed for a long, long time.

"When I walked in the room that morning, the smell was funny—sour. I crawled up on the bed and sat watching my breath cloud in the cold morning air.

"But I didn't want to crawl under the covers. The smell was just… wrong.

"I asked my mom if she was okay.

"Jackie, she called me. 'Call 911, Jackie.' We had one of those old rotary phones. I don't remember much of what I said, only that I insisted Mommy was very sick. The operator wouldn't let me hang up the phone, so I laid the receiver next to Mom's head and pressed the other side next to my ear.

"It must have taken a lot out of her… to push the phone away…

"She looked me in the eye and whispered, 'I love you, John Matthew Roaker. Remember that, my Jackie. Do something important with your life. I want you to know you were the most important thing I ever did.'

"My mother died after those words. I remember the room was so cold, empty, and without her there, I was so alone. When the ambulance arrived, I was still sitting next to her body. I told them she wasn't inside. They were too late."

Tears streamed down Laurie's face. Her stomach was twisted with the pain in his voice.

He held her, and together they wept for that small child. When the tears passed, she asked, "Was this a vivid memory or a dream, Jack?"

She heard him swallow. Reaching over, she grabbed the beer sitting on the nightstand and handed it to him. He drained the bottle. "Thanks." Sitting up, he resettled her in his arms. "It was a memory, one I had buried deep. I hadn't tapped into those events since I was little. Too painful."

Laurie sat up, excitement racing through her veins. "You know what this means?"

"My childhood sucked?" He raised his eyebrows and stared at her.

"No. I mean, yes, your childhood was hard and you're remembering things. Jack, your brain is going through the motions. It's healing." She grabbed his shoulders and shook him slightly. "Do you get it?"

"Yeah. You're pretty strong for a girl," he teased.

"I'm pretty strong for a guy," she replied. "I pound on people all day long. It's better by far than a gym." She wiggled closer to him, shaking the bed. A basket hooked on the other side of the headboard fell off, spilling its contents.

"Is that knitting? Do you work the needles? Man, I haven't seen someone do that in ages." He laughed.

"Stop laughing, and maybe I'll knit you a bag for your bullets." She leaped off the bed and gathered the contents back into the basket. Placing it on a stack of romance novels by the foot of her bed, she sat down beside him. "Gich taught me." Her eyebrows lifted. "It's one of the few domestic things about me. I find it relaxing."

His surprise was clear. "Gich? No kidding? I'm going to have to ask him about that."

"I wouldn't poke that grizzly. He might bite you." She kissed him and then gave him a little push in the direction she wanted him to go. "Come on, Jack, go back to the topic we were talking about."

He rubbed his nose, but finally acquiesced. "What makes you think I changed it?"

She grabbed his hand and hauled him out of the bed, guiding him out of the small apartment and onto the patio. "Because you're slippery. Evasion is one of the first thing SEALs are taught. You'll find it's hard to bullshit me."

"Did you ever think, maybe, that's why I like you?"

The words were a nice little shock. She smiled to herself, and then whirled around. Her eyes held his. "Thanks."

Pushing up onto her tiptoes, she tenderly laid her lips on his. The kiss was sweet, a caress that held passion and hunger behind it. But there were things she needed to say before she allowed herself to be swept away.

Stepping back, she took him to a double lounger. They sat down on the giant cushion. She was grateful he sat silently, because when she finally looked up, her eyes were moist again. "Jack, I'd like to say I'm sorry to learn about the circumstances of your mother's death. I never knew mine. Sometimes it hits me with an emptiness I cannot fill. I somehow take on the aspects of this missing piece of me and try to mother the world."

Taking a deep breath, she let it out slowly. "Can I ask what it was like… to have a mom?"

She hoped he could hear the earnestness in her voice, triggering the private part of him to unfold further. The need to know, to understand, was burning in her.

He nodded. "I remember a feeling of comfort and safety, initially. Things changed, though, from her caring for me to my father and I caring for her." Jack shook his head. "I guess I learned more of this information later in life. When I was younger, I didn't understand her pain or the issue. My mother had cancer. My father worked those long hours to help pay for her medication and treatments. None of the medical procedures worked, so she just had to endure the pain until she died."

His voice sounded strained, as if he spoke through a mountain of pain. "At the time, I was a child and had only that perspective. I couldn't understand why my father wasn't there or why my mother found it painful to hold me. I was devastated when she died. I was angry at everyone and everything that crossed my path." He coughed and then she watched him breathe slowly, drawing in the fresh ocean air. "My father died six months after my mother, from a stroke. He was only forty-one. I never got to know him. So much of that year is this red haze of uncertainty."

He took her hand in his. "That is… until my grandfather brought me home. He taught me normal things that parents teach kids—coping skills, honor, courage, values to be proud of, and the ability to have faith in myself and achieve. After I finished high school, he passed, too." *Crap! That fucking hurt, talking about Granddad!* "I have cousins on my mom's side. We've never been close."

"What was your grandfather like?"

"Old, crotchety, funny, fair, and kind. Every day, I learned more about him and grew to respect him even more. It was a rocky beginning, but I grew to understand him." He rubbed his eyes. "He was a Navy veteran. I miss him. Damn, I haven't thought about him for ages.

"I'm done." He squeezed her. "Your turn in the hot seat. What about you? Tell me more about your life."

The words tumbled quickly from her mouth, as if she had said them a million times before. "My mother died giving birth to me. Neither of my folks had any living relatives, so I was passed around from Team house to Team house when my dad was deployed. For the longest time, I believed I was related to everyone. In a way, I was and still am."

"There's more there. Spill it."

She sighed. "I learned to keep my emotions to myself. To take care and share my basic needs, like food, clothing, et cetera, but to hide what bothered me and deal with it on my own terms. No one wants a child with problems. If I was happy, then I could hide behind the smile and let my mask speak for me."

"Laurie, you know you can share with me, right?" He was so supportive. His voice with those honeyed tones eased through her defenses.

She shrugged. None of what he had said meant that she would tell him right now. Though it was precious he had been so forthcoming and open. Never in her life had she spoken her secret aloud; in many ways, she knew she must actually trust him.

"Okay, enough grilling. Tell me something funny."

A smile grew slowly on her lips—that, she could do.

"Did you know Gich gave me my first beer? I was four years old. He said, 'If Laurie can open it, she can drink it.' So, I did. It astonished everyone, and then after five gulps, I threw up on him. He's never let me forget it, either."

"Four! That's crazy young."

"Yeah," she smiled. "He made a lot of mistakes with me, but I had him and he had me. Having someone is all that matters, you know?"

"I never really thought of it that way. I suppose it could be true."

She pinched him.

"Ouch!"

"Just like a SEAL to be noncommittal. You've lost me now! I'm going for a swim." She was up in a flash, peeling her clothes off. "There are advantages to living on the water. Skinny-dipping in the dark."

"You're not going anywhere without me," he replied, leaping off the lounger and chasing her to the edge of the patio.

"God, I love this place."

She assumed that Jack meant the best part of the whole building was her inviting garden. Filled with orange and lemon trees, roses, and other beautiful flowers, this was a place tended with a great amount of loving attention. Laurie had tried to stay in tune with the needs of the foliage, but it didn't look like she had much of a green thumb. A few weeds that looked pretty were sneaking through and choking some of the plants. She'd have to deal with that at some point.

"It's really great out here. Did you do all of this?" he asked as she perched on the short wall, preparing to slip over to the other side and into the ocean.

"No. The former owners planted everything. I do the best I can to keep it maintained, though Gich comes by now and then. He truly has a green thumb." She stretched, letting the moonlight bathe her bare skin.

"This is terrific."

"Yeah, I really lucked out when this place opened up. John Hatchett used to own this place. His wife had a small craft store up front. When she died, he wanted to buy an RV and travel the country. Gich told me about it, and we made a deal on the spot." She waved her arms around in a circle. "I'm sure I got the better deal."

"What happened to Hatchett?"

"According to Gich, Hatchett bought the camper, drove to Virginia, where his wife was born, and scattered the ashes in a field of daisies where she'd played as a child. Then he settled in a rental only a few miles from the spot. He passed within six months of her. I heard his neighbors sprinkled him in the same place. He must have loved her very much," she said wistfully. Did all women want to find a man who would love them that much? Would he be able to do it? Would the idea make him uncomfortable?

"I'm sure he was just as happy with the deal." Slowly, he walked toward her. "The community is good that way. I've seen it. We take care of our own."

She watched his movements; he seemed ready to play. She still wanted to talk, because there was a lot she wanted to know. "Yeah. Speaking of which, I never hear you talk about your Teammates… what's up with that? I remember my dad and Gich talking almost non-stop about their Team, especially when Ops went sideways." Her blunt comment stopped him in his tracks.

She studied his face, the angles looking somehow more shallow and sharp.

"Things aren't that easy right now. When it first happened, when I took some shrapnel to the head, I spent most of my time in ICU. I tried to go see a couple of the guys, but they were bounced around to different places. Couple of them won't answer my texts, but I've heard from one or two. Nothing major. Just stuff like 'Hey, you're alive!' and shit like that." He shrugged. "The guys know I want to touch base. They'll connect when it works. In the meantime, everyone's walking around on eggshells with me. The doctors chat the tough-love line—be in therapy or you won't go operational again. That group crap doesn't work for me. I'm not great at opening up to strangers."

"Am I a stranger?" Laurie looked from beneath her lashes, intentionally flirting with him, attempting to ease the tough topic.

"Not unless you let all your patients chat from between the sheets." The corners of his mouth turned up and slowly, lazily, pulled into a smile. His pupils were large and dark. In the moonlight he was such a handsome rogue. She knew his teasing was a sign of respect and adoration; it was how SEALs communicated. She could handle him and actually liked the banter, too. "I'm going in," he announced.

"Don't get lost. I can lend you some floaties, if you'd like them for your arms. Or maybe you'd like a life vest." She watched him turn away, hop over the short wall, and run into the water, changing into a dive at the last moment.

As he emerged on the surface, he shouted, "Wiseass!"

"Ready or not, here I come," she yelled with a laugh. Then she jumped the two-foot wall and felt the sand squish between her toes as she hurried down the tiny wedge of beach. When she reached the water's edge, her steps slowed as she made her way forward into the gentle waves.

The water was warm from the heat of the sun. Walking into the ocean always stripped away her concerns and worries, as if there was only room for the sensation, and she relished those first baptizing steps.

"Mmmm," she murmured. She could feel his eyes on her, watching her every movement. She didn't care. She was in no hurry, now that the waves were lapping her skin.

Too soon, only her head was above the surface. Her body relaxed in stages as the salt water enveloped her, a familiarity that eased her even as it surrounded her in buoyant bliss. The ocean definitely held a healing magic.

Pushing off from the sandy bottom, she swam. She spread her arms wide and drew the water under her until her flawless breaststroke had her moving quickly and silently. Her eyes sought his—Jack, her macho tough guy—and he was coming toward her, joining her in the darker recesses.

He caught her to him. His arms wrapped tightly around her, drawing her body against his. Their wet bodies slid along each other. He kissed her, dragging her farther into the depths of the ocean, away from land.

"Let's explore," he murmured in her ear.

Kissing his ear, she replied, "Yes."

His hands held her close as he rolled onto his back.

She balanced on top of him now, like a queen riding a dolphin. Still, he swam, keeping her perfectly balanced.

She ran her fingers down his chest and watched him shiver.

His eyes were almost black in the darkness, but she could see the glint of mischief.

Spying the bank on the far shore, she knew he was going to a small alcove where they could make love. It was perfect.

Jack was a puzzle, one she enjoyed. But how prepared was she to accompany him into the unknown? More willing than she realized...

Chapter 7

All right, they're on our left, they're on our right, they're in front of us, they're behind us... they can't get away this time.

—Lewis B. "Chesty" Puller

JACK WOKE WITH A START. STANDING NEXT TO THE courtyard door, he had both hands on the door frame and his body was covered in sweat. His muscles were tense and his body was ready to fight or flee.

"Jack, can you hear me?" Laurie's voice came to him from afar as if she were shouting down a tunnel. The tone, with its beckoning sweetness, lured him.

Mentally, he drew himself toward her, bringing himself closer and closer until her voice was clear. Turning to her, he sucked in a deep breath and tried to get it together.

He shook himself. His eyes were wide and it took a few seconds for the images in his head to reconcile with the reality around him. Lowering his arms, he turned and looked at her.

Patient. Quiet. And with a look of concern that filled her eyes.

He walked over to the bed and pulled her into his arms. He couldn't find his voice, not yet. The visuals were bombarding him, and he couldn't make sense of it all yet.

"I'm here," she whispered, wrapping her arms tighter.

He nodded. Stroking her hair, he held her for a time.

Then he looked over her shoulder at his hands. The place he had to see. Relief eased through him. His fingers were clean. In his mind—in those raw images—he had seen them covered in blood. His best friend's blood.

"Hey, answer me, Jack. Are you with me?" She prodded him.

"Yes." The word felt strange—alien—as if it were something entirely separate from him. Dammit, he needed to snap out of it! "Just give me a minute. Okay?"

"Sure." Nodding her head against his chest, she quieted down.

What had happened? It must have freaked her out, too. He didn't have any reasonable explanation… other than that he was sleepwalking. Going where, he didn't know.

Pushing her back, he held her by the shoulders. Her skin was pale. "Did I hurt you?"

"No, of course not."

"Why are you so shaken up? I know why I am." He didn't want anyone else lying to him, and he always felt like the doctors were skirting the truth about his situation, reluctant to share the actual issue or stakes in play. "Give it to me straight."

"Have I ever given you reason to distrust me?" She looked earnest as she spoke.

"No." His hands dropped away from her. "You're forthright with me. Stay on that track."

She nodded her head and then reached for a mini audio recorder on the bedside table. "I reset this last night, before we went to bed."

"Should have some racy stuff on it, then." He grinned, knowing it was a sad effort to ease the tension. Grabbing his pants, he pulled them on.

Maybe he should just leave. Where the hell were his socks and shoes?

"Jack, please, let's sit down. I'll make coffee and we can listen to it."

The recording from last night might hold the key he was looking for—but was he ready to unlock those memories?

Laurie placed the recorder on the table and went about the process of making coffee. His eyes kept straying to the small silver digital recorder. He wanted to listen to it now, and get it over with, but made himself wait. Coffee would ground him, wake him up, and give him something to steady his nerves. *Christ, I hate feeling this way!*

Placing two steaming cups on the table, she sat down across from him. "Are you ready?"

He took a few sips of the hot brew and then settled his hands on the outside of the blistering mug. The pain was grounding. "Hit it."

She pushed the button. For a long time, there was nothing, just sounds of their combined breathing. Jack felt frustration start to mount. Then it began... a word here and there.

Don. Blood. Bomb. Helo. Head.

His own mind searched through the cabinets of experiences he'd locked away. When he located it, he tried to open the file, but it was stuck. He wanted that trip down memory lane, but in dossier form, in order of action. Then, as if his subconscious from last night had heard him, his own voice began to speak from the recorder.

South America. Intel. CIA. Don's pregnant wife.
Drop zone. Hike. Rain. Factory was fucking ghost town.

His hand reached for the recorder. He clicked it off
as the images rearranged themselves in his head. So
many times he had searched his mind for the memory of
that last mission… this time he didn't want to come up
empty. He opened his mouth to speak, praying the words
he wanted would come out. "I remember…"

Just as suddenly as he started speaking, the memories
flowed like a movie to him. He could see it, down to the
last detail and tree. Or at least part of it was there. He
was thrilled that there was more than he had previously
had. "It worked, Laurie. I remember the planning, arriving there, and…"

"Jack—"

He held up a hand to silence her. His first priority was
that the pictures come together. He was almost there;
then he saw it. He spoke, slowly letting the memories
out. "The brass wanted us to go to South America to get
some Intel that had been stashed. The CIA had tried and
several agents had died, so they had gotten in touch with
the Navy. Supposedly, this info would provide details
on drug drops and the various relationships between
political leadership and the cartels.

"This wasn't the first Op we'd done with the spooks,
but command insisted it be a solo deal. That we go in
alone, get the info, and bring it back. SEALs are better
trained—yada yada. So, the orders were signed, the details were sent, and then we worked with our Intelligence
Officer to develop the best plan.

"Don was distracted. His wife was pregnant. They
had a lot to do to get ready for the baby. A bigger house.

Her parents would want to stay with them. Listening to his father-in-law talk about being a lawyer, and how stable and steady it is…

"The helicopter was dropping us off pretty far from our destination—fast-roping, of course. This was meant to confuse any pursuers, as there were a number of hot spots in the area. I was itchy and felt in my gut that things weren't right. I spoke up, but no one listened. They blamed it on nerves. But I wasn't scared—something felt wrong to me somehow. I just couldn't put my finger on the problem.

"Well, we headed up and over the mountain, which could have been dicey but was pretty easygoing. Seeley kept stepping on snakes. He hates reptiles in general. Amused the hell out of Don and me, the fact Seeley had to slice their heads off before they bit him. That was his Achilles' heel, but as a SEAL, you end up facing whatever you fear a lot until you are mightily desensitized to it.

"When we got to the top of the mountain, we saw the factory. Didn't look like there were any guards, and it was mostly deserted. Obviously, there had been a bad fight there—bodies were strewn about and there were a couple of burned-out jeeps and trucks. I suggested two of us scope it out.

"Everyone wanted to stick with the plan, so we all pushed down the mountainside. Working our way down was tricky—there were IEDs (Improvised Explosive Devices)—but we easily entered the factory grounds. The place was a fucking ghost town. Nothing was there! Didn't even see a rat, which is unusual for a place like this. Usually cats and rats are everywhere."

Jack looked at Laurie and grinned, happy that the memories were flowing.

"I was going to break radio silence and say, 'Nobody has been here in weeks,' when we saw lights on in the factory—down in the basement. Methodically, we made our way in. Don and I stayed outside to guard the rear, but Pickens called us in. So, we went in the door—" The memory cut off abruptly, making him physically jerk. Jack started coughing and his throat began to spasm. Standing, he rushed to the sink and turned on the faucet, cupping water in his hand. He scooped the warm water into his mouth and coaxed it down until the spasm stopped.

Bracing his hands on the sink, he reviewed the chain of events. "It's correct. This is how it all began. I fucking remembered!" He turned to her. His eyes were bright.

Lifting her out of the chair, he held her tightly in his arms. "I did it. I have more information. Thank you!" The emotion was clear in his voice, but he didn't mind her knowing how much he valued her. He trusted her, and for the first time in a long time, he trusted himself.

———

Walking into the Team ONE Quarterdeck with high energy—or at least an energized hop in his step—felt great! Jack realized how he had been going through the motions of daily living without connecting to anything positive until now. For so long, he'd lost his joy. Now, with the help of Laurie, a part of his memory was finally falling into place, and he could hardly wait to talk to his CO (Commanding Officer), XO (Executive Officer), and Teammates.

As he walked through the corridor where portraits of heroic brethren, fallen in battle, or acts of heroism and achievement had been documented, he couldn't help feeling humbled. Whatever he had done in his life, these men had done more. They had willingly gone the extra mile, though he could honestly say his passion and desire to be in the fight was as great as their own.

The first time he walked in here, he had spent a great deal of time staring at the photographs, considering these men and their lives. Only the exceptional knew what it meant to be chosen for the Teams; the ones who made it through Hell Week and deployments were eager for an ever-increasing challenge. He was a SEAL Team ONE guy, and short of retiring, he wanted to serve for as long as his body held out.

The offices on the second floor of the Quarterdeck were unusually quiet. The daily bustle of activity was lacking. *Crap! Is there some kind of event I don't know about?*

A couple of Intel Officers entered the hall. They nodded at him.

He nodded back, but neither of these guys was the one he sought. He actually wanted to talk to the XO, and seeing his empty office did nothing to help Jack's cause.

Screw this! I'm not waiting around.

He walked down the hall. Fresh ocean air flowed in from the open back door. At least it didn't smell as bad as the ST1 (SEAL Team ONE) Platoon Area. Where the cages were, that place usually smelled like feet and sweat, and the stairwell was worse.

Checking his watch, he read 0639 and was relieved to see that he was on time to meet a few buddies. *They should be strolling in here any minute now. C'mon guys!* The email that shot into his phone at midnight had made him feel like heaven was smiling on him when he read it. With a few more pieces of the puzzle courtesy of his buddies, he might be able to put this whole damn puzzle together.

Turning around, he double-timed down the hallway and exited down the front stairwell and through the front door of the Team ONE Quarterdeck building. He headed for the ST1 Platoon Area.

Entering the building, he climbed the stairs two at a time, going straight for the third floor. Briefly, he considered stopping on the second floor to pull some gear from the cages. The discomfort of keeping someone waiting kept him moving. As he hit the top of the landing he saw a familiar soul enter the Platoon 1-Alfa room.

Jack pulled the door wide and jogged down the hall, hitting the room at a dead run. He considered tackling Gerry, who was now seated on a couch with his nose buried in a manual. But that man was built like a steamroller, and Jack didn't need his nose rearranged, so he stopped short a few feet.

Towering over the human "man-wall," he shouted, "Hey Knotts!" Jack knew his smile must be at least a mile wide. God, it felt good to see a brother!

A corpsman from Bravo shut the door between the rooms, shaking his head at them before he laid the barrier in place. *To hell with him!*

"Red Jack, you slacker, what the hell are you up to?" Laughing, Gerry Knotts said, "If I were on medical leave, I'd be in Hawaii on Oahu, surfing along the North Shore, instead of hanging here." Knotts dropped the manual on the couch, got up, and closed the gap between them. The guy was wide like a linebacker but all lean, hard muscle as he grabbed Jack and hugged him, giving him a painful backslapping embrace. "You missed the rest of the guys by an hour. We got back at 0530."

"Shit! You lily-livered fish, I thought I'd made it here on time," Jack said, mirroring his buddy's gestures and then taking a step back. Man, seeing Knotts was like manna for the soul.

"Cell service sucks on base. We got pulled into an impromptu meeting. You know how it is…"

"Yeah." Nodding his head, Jack didn't know what to say or where to start with his next comment. His brain was a jumble of opinions, thoughts, and questions. "I need to… I wanted to…"

"Talk about what happened. Yeah, that'd be good. Fuck, you were a freaking Hercules, the way you tossed bodies into the helicopter." Moving past Jack, Knotts went to the top of the landing and looked down. Confirming all was clear, he came back over. "Did you just see anyone on your way in—like the XO?"

Jack shook his head.

Pushing one of his hands into the other one Gerry kneaded them together, a leftover nervous gesture from their boot camp days. He spoke softly. "Dammit, you need to know this, Jack—we've been ordered *not* to talk to you about the Op, until you remember something yourself."

"I get it," said Jack, disappointed. "They're covering their asses."

Gerry's cell phone beeped. He withdrew it, smiled, and then pocketed it.

Patting Jack on the arm, he said, "Listen, I gotta go. That's the third page from the wife. If I'm not home in five minutes, she'll come here armed to shoot bear, or just me."

"Yeah, uh, Gerry. Could we, uh, get a beer later?" Jack couldn't let go of this golden opportunity to fill in the blanks. He needed Knotts to help him. His swim buddy was dead, two more were still in the ICU and had been put into comas "for their own protection," and the others had been routed from San Diego to Virginia for debriefing and other stuff no one would talk about.

Being in the military meant operating in the dark to some degree, though Teammates had always found a way to help each other and watch each other's back. He had to know what had happened and what was truly going on.

Gerry Knotts nodded. "Let me meet-and-greet and then I'll hit the pond. Say… two hours. Wait, better make it three."

"That works," said Jack. They shook hands, and then Gerry disappeared down the stairs.

Congregating covertly in the ocean was significantly less conspicuous than aiming for a chat downtown. The only creatures that would be able to overhear them would have either feathers or fins.

Looking around the room, he contemplated what he could do for three hours. Going down to the cages to organize his gear would only make him long for deployment. So would target practice. There was no one he really wanted to talk to, and going back to his apartment to stare at four empty walls just plain sucked.

Setting his sights on the couch tucked against the far

wall where Gerry's manual lay, he strode over and sat down. Picking up the book, he looked at the title. It was the latest updated manual on their grenade launchers. "I bet you still shot them off-target, Gerry."

Tossing the manual aside, he lay down. Pain spiked the back of his skull, and he dug a pain pill out of his pocket. He hated the stuff, but if he could go horizontal for a short time, it might be worth it.

He closed his eyes, forcing his body to relax. The pump of adrenaline that had been surging through his body eased off an inch at a time.

Stretching his legs out so they balanced over the far armrest, he laid his forearm over his eyes and told his body to go to sleep—a SEAL trick that usually worked, though as of late…

His training had taught him how to conquer a lot. He could do it all, except fill those memory holes… so far.

—————

The images were hazy. He squinted at them, the SEALs that had passed from this earth were gathered on the beach before him. Chills raced up his spine.

The day was stormy and the ocean was tumultuous. Waves crashed hard on the shore, sending up massive amounts of foam to bathe his legs and feet. He stood on the curling cusp until his toes were icy and goose-flesh climbed his legs. But he'd endured worse on this spot—Hell Week—and he was capable of doing it again. Lightning arced overhead like a fireworks display, showing the faces of men suddenly standing before him. There were gaping wounds on some of the bodies and frozen expressions on faces. These cracked dolls were otherwise perfect, and yet not uniform. A couple of guys were dressed in whites, their ice cream suits bedazzled with medals, and on top of all that glory was a shiny trident. It practically glowed on their chests.

Others were wearing black BDUs. He preferred those… so he could fade into the nighttime shadows. A few wore the old blue Navy digital fatigues with the horrible nickname of blueberries. They'd get slammed for being out of uniform, since the SEALs now had their own Special Ops digi design and everyone was supposed to have switched over.

But blood seeped through the fabric, spreading like some ghastly nightmare. He rushed toward them, to aid these men somehow.

"We are gathered here to weigh the crimes of our brother, Red Jack. What say you?" His CO's voice, the one who was killed by a drunk driver a few years back, boomed over the area. The man had been an extra dad to them all, and had been known as Jiffy, because no matter what, he arrived quickly.

What did he say? Oh Fuck! Were they here for him? He stopped in his tracks.

"Roaker, I'm sad for you, son," said Jiffy. Then his voiced boomed out, "Attention!"

Jack's back went arrow straight as his whole body responded to the command.

Thunder boomed as lightning cracked again, showing all the great and decorated men before them multiplying into an even larger force. So many faces, and yet he knew in his heart that these were the heroes of the Teams.

A fine mist fell from the sky, making it surreal. This had to be a joke! No one did this. Yet the intensity was almost blinding as his SEAL brothers pulsated with color. Their faces contorted into masks of ferocity. Bolts of lightning sliced across the sky as they stepped toward him.

Jack did not move—though he knew he'd been singled out.

Standing parallel was the CO, who was reading from a sheet of paper. The edges fluttered in the wind and seemed to stretch on for at least a mile. The drone of Jiffy's voice went on forever. Words such as unworthy, traitor, failed your Teammates, dishonor, *and* coward *made Jack's neck move with whiplash speed.*

Had he heard the words correctly?

"In all our years as a Team, we have had only rare occasion to do what we're doing today. You will be stripped from our ranks. Petty Officer John Matthew Roaker—Red Jack—today is the day you died in our eyes. We are disappointed in you and your dishonor."

The CO ripped the trident from Jack's uniform, and then he opened Jack's shirt and plunged his hand into his chest, dislodging the symbol branded on his heart.

The gaping hole spilled life from his chest and there was no way to close it.

"Say good-bye to the civilian," ordered Jiffy.

Jack's mouth was open, the horror holding him in shocked silence.

As one, his brothers turned away and began to fade.

God, he would rather be dead then this... dishonor. His spirit was draining out of his body. He was losing himself one chunk at a time. "I'm disappointed in you son. Good-bye, John. Matthew. Roaker." And then Jiffy was gone, too.

Tears streamed down Jack's face, falling unhindered into the sand. They disappeared in the hundreds of grains below him as his world lost cohesion. The SEALs, they were his entire world—

The final warrior, standing tall and strong, was Don. He knelt beside him and grabbed his shoulder. "I love you, my brother. I know it's not your fault. It's up to you to fix this. Solve it before it's too late."

Waking abruptly, Jack sat bolt upright and then stood. His body was covered in sweat and his heart raced. He scanned the area, looking for threats. What had awakened him? No one else was inside the room. He checked his watch. It was almost time to meet Gerry.

"Shit!" he said to himself, remembering the nightmare. He rubbed his hands over his face and eyes, and then over his stubbly head. "Screw the pain pills."

Fingers found the healing injury at the back of his skull. Like an optimist rubbing a lamp, he silently prayed he would find the rest of the answers to his memory block, and that it wouldn't show dishonor. "Tell me it's not fucking true!" But doubt was a ravenous creature and ready to devour his sanity. He couldn't allow it to take a foothold.

The room suddenly felt incredibly stuffy and smelly; he craved fresh air and sunlight.

He kicked at a pair of shoes near the couch. "Damn foot odor." Yet it was oddly reassuring, too. The smell was his and everyone's in Alfa. This was home, and it was hard to escape that fact. The best thing he could do was concentrate on the tangible.

Undoubtedly, everyone was out on the O course, in the gym, or home reuniting with his family post Op. It was time for him to leave the nest, too. This was just an empty room with the memorabilia on the walls marking memories of men like him who walked the journey and lived their best for the Teams. They had courage, fortitude, and never gave up. Neither would he.

In a minute he was out the door, down the hall, and to the stairwell, where he took the stairs two at a time. Then he was through the front door and outside.

Heat and salty air smacked his face. Turning away from the wind, he felt tiny grains of sand pelting the back of his head.

Stopping at his Jeep, he pulled his shirt over his head and dropped it on the backseat. He fished around on the floor and found a pair of dry swim shorts and a towel. Like a thousand times before, he unlaced his boots. Ditching the leather, regulation-issue size elevens and his socks on the backseat, he wrapped the towel around his waist, dropped his pants, and pulled on his swim shorts. Laying the towel over the passenger seat to heat in the sun would guarantee a toasty wrap upon his return.

Once that was done, he headed for the pond, relishing the gritty sand beneath his feet. His body longed for the ocean, the waves, the buoyancy and freedom of movement.

Pushing into a light jog, he headed around the buildings, pumped a couple of salutes as officers passed, and then opened his stride when he hit the long strip of beach. Digging into the sand with his toes, he bounced up, gaining his rhythm. Pounding through the heat, he welcomed the sweat as it glazed his body with warmth and chased away the demons.

Knotts was already standing on the sandbar, waiting for him. It looked like the man was doing some kind of water ballet with his arms. Jack had to hide his smile as he made his way to him.

Jack reached the ocean quickly. His feet smacked the cool water and he kept running until he saw a wave, and then he dove into it—aiming his body downward and missing the undertow. He knew this stretch of seafloor like the back of his hand, and unless something had changed drastically, there would be a nice deep groove here where he could swim straight out and gain the far sandbar.

Everything was exactly as he remembered it. The water was clear and happily free of seaweed. Popping up on top of the water, he took a breath and then swam easily to where Gerry lingered.

"Took you long enough. I'm missing my beauty sleep. Though I had a very nice homecoming." Gerry winked and then laughed. His legs were moving as he treaded water and then stood. Give a SEAL a choice between standing and moving, and action would always be the choice—activity birthed options.

Jack quipped back, "Beauty? Let me look closer. Yep, your skin has never looked so pasty."

"Funny, Roaker." The man had seen some hospital time and was pale as linguine. But Gerry had been in and out, and then shipped to D.C. and Virginia for chats with the Admiral's Staff and a bunch of other people. That much he knew. Everyone wanted the details on the last mission. Only fuckups and great successes got this much attention. Either way, he felt screwed.

"I didn't know that the prune texture was my look."
Spitting a mouthful of water in Jack's direction, Gerry
said, "Shit, this needs to be beer. I'd give anything to
bathe in a vat of beer for a week. Do you think we could
talk a local microbrewery into letting us do that? Maybe
Karl Strauss or Coronado Brewery—I can drink a ton
of it. Hey, they could write it off as a tax donation to
the troops."

"Sounds good to me. It'd keep spirits up." Jack's
comment made both the men laugh.

When they were both quiet again, Jack said, "Hey,
thanks for meeting me."

"Yeah." Gerry looked away, his eyes scanning the
beach and water. "Surf sucks. We haven't had any good
waves for a while."

"Nope. Look, Knotts, what happened? It's not too
late to give me the highlights." Jack dunked his head
under and then shook it free of water. *Damn, it feels
good to be in the ocean, like Momma's womb*. He was
hoping it made Gerry relax, too. Might be too wishful a
thought. The man could be immovable when he wanted
to be.

"What part of 'I'm not supposed to talk to you' don't
you understand? Not so fucking bright, are you? The
brass will *not* take lightly to a beer and barbecue social
with a side of Intel." Gerry winked at him. "That being
said, let me say this quick."

Relief surged through Jack. He knew he'd be able to
count on his friend Gerry Knotts.

"I remember opening my eyes and seeing you lifting
Duncan into the helicopter. Next you hoisted Chalmers,
Billings, and then I saw you grab Seeley and Pickens.

You did me a solid by helping my ass and getting me to cover. Fuck, you saved us, Jack. You are a fucking hero! Bullets were pinging against the helicopter, and then we're all in and the door's slammed shut. The copter took off and everything went black." Blocking first one nostril, then the other, Gerry blew snot out of his nose and wiped the excess with his fingers.

"Here are the shits! The brass is trying to figure out how we walked into an ambush without seeing any signs of the trap. I've told them about a hundred times, all I know is you got us all in the whirlybird safely. Blood's dripping out of the back of your head, and everyone's pretty much laid out flat."

There was no usable data in that info dump. Could he prod Knotts to go further and share more with him? Jack urged his buddy to elaborate. "What else? Any details?"

"It was so fucking dreamlike! I remember the sound of RPGs whistling through the air and not striking that close to us, which, given the cloud the copter was kicking up, they couldn't have missed. Aim right here, you assholes!" Gerry turned his head to the side and knocked water out of his ears.

Gerry nodded. "Details... Shit! I remember their bullets hit metal. They connected with the helicopter. Luckily, they didn't strike anything vital."

Jack lifted his hands in frustration and then smacked them on the water. None of this was striking any familiar chords.

Gerry just kept on chatting, though. "Given the dust I had difficultly pinpointing where they were firing from. I just needed a few clear shots and those suckers would have been gone."

Knowing Jack was going to have to dig through his own knowledge to get Knotts talking again wasn't very comfortable. Staring into the water, Jack gave it his best and continued. "Gerry, I remember seeing blood on my hands. Don's blood. I wrapped a pressure bandage around him and held him tight, trying to keep him alive, and then I got him on board and rigged a weight to keep it all in place. I got out, but I knew in my heart he was…" He rubbed his hands over his face. "Christ! Then there was an explosion and I was on my tail, seeing stars.

"When I rallied, I cleared the kick-up and saw you guys exiting the factory, which was on fire. Fuck, Gerry, there are too many blanks." Jack scratched his head gently. "Wait, what about before the helicopter—at the beginning of the Op?"

"What about it?" Gerry lifted on a wave.

Jack pushed. "Come on, that can't be all the information you have."

"Jack, I don't know, man. I don't want to be your memory on this. It's too important. If I tell you what I know, it might change something for you. The planning I'm sure you remember. In the helicopter, Don and you were bitching at each other like two cocks of the walk. You kept saying something 'felt off' and he was ragging your ass to shut up."

Splashing water on his head, Gerry shook the extra drops off like a dog. His bald spot looked like a bowl of strawberries. "Man, you were right. There was something screwy about the setup. What do you remember?"

"More than I did. I remember the ship with the hot crew women and then the helicopter. Fast-roping into a clear zone between the trees. The snakes, and there was cloud cover moving in, but the ceiling was high, so flying was no problem. It was a long hike, quiet in the beginning—eerily so, and then it started raining like Noah and the flood." Abruptly, Jack coughed. "The terrain was tricky on the way down to the factory. We spotted a couple of IEDs. We cleared them without problem."

Jack cleared his throat. "When feet hit the ground near the factory, lightning lit up the sky like a motherfucker! Everything looked empty and neglected, like the compound was possibly ditched in a hurry, with open car doors, broken windows, and half-filled bottles dropped randomly. And then, when we finally reached the factory door, the thunder was booming, the rain was soaking us, and gooseflesh was climbing my back and neck like a baby Komodo dragon seeking its mommy. Everyone was way ahead. Don and I were holding the rear when Seeley and Pickens called us in. I entered the building last. That's all I've got! I'm missing a gap of time between entering the building and the helicopter." Jack wiped his finger over his face, sluicing off excess water. "You were point man, what did you see?"

Gerry looked away, deep in thought for a few minutes or maybe considering what he was willing to share. Jack wanted every fucking kernel of detail. Sighing, Gerry said, "The details are sort of fuzzy. Your version jives with mine, so that's good. The rooms had full-grown dust bunnies living in those corners at the far end of the factory. No one had been there in months.

"According to the Intel, the layout of the building was right, but I agree, this Op went sideways fast. We stuck to the plan and made our way to the cellar. I remember seeing stacks of crates and boxes along the wall. We followed the path all the way through and there was nothing. We were called to the front of the building. The explosion happened right after I stepped outside. I smelled smoke and then fresh air, and then you were helping me onto the helicopter." Gerry shook his head. "Thing is, I don't really know the exact events either. Obviously, some kind of explosion blew the factory— with serious accelerants—because that place was spitting colors as it burned. I remember that."

"I've got too many fucking blank spaces... Why can't I remember any of this crap?" Jack swished a mouthful of salt water, relishing the familiar salty taste, and then spit it out. He needed answers and Laurie, bless her sweet heart, had helped him fill in some of the holes, but a significant amount of the picture was still missing. Too much. Maybe she could help him do more to bridge the gap.

Frustration laced through Jack. Meeting Knotts had not been very useful. "I need to know the truth. Where was the goat fuck in this chain of events?"

"I don't know," said Gerry, looking at the waves. "Listen, I'm going in. I have to go be Dad for a while." He splashed water in Jack's direction. "Hey, don't give me that look. I'm looking forward to it. I miss them! Seems like they grow an inch every time I leave. Someday you'll get it."

"Wait, Gerry, what about Seeley and Pickens? What did they say?" Jack asked as his friend started to swim away. Neither of those guys had returned his texts. At least Gerry had the balls to say shit to his face—whatever it would be. To him, that was a friend who went to the mat.

Gerry shook his head. "I talked to them at the hospital, and they went to Virginia after me. Jack…" He looked away, pausing for several heartbeats, before staring Jack again in the eye. "They said there were guns and drugs there. That you triggered something and that it set a bomb off."

Jack felt the blood rush his head like a giant explosion of noise. "What?"

"Man, I hate to even say this to you, 'cause their stories vary from what I know."

"I'm responsible?" None of this rang a bell! Frustration and disbelief flooded him. Had he really been the one who endangered the Team and killed his best friend? "Shit! I can't believe it. Why the fuck don't they say that crap to my face? Call me. Talk it through."

"Here's the thing, Jack. My gut's shouting that this is not the whole picture. Those guys act like short-timers, just want to do their stint and get out. I'm not disrespecting them. It's only that our explanations aren't in sync." Gerry's face was tight with anger and frustration. "Give it time. The details will surface."

"Great," said Jack, disheartened. God help him if it were true, and he'd fucked up!

Knotts swam over and put his hand on Jack's shoulder. "I believe in you, man. Whatever was going on, I know you saved me and the rest of the Team. I know it's what we do—just know that I'm grateful. Jack, you saved us all that day, and Don would see it that way, too. His body came home."

Knotts looked at his watch. "Oh fuck! I've gotta go!

I've got to pick up the kids soon. Daddy duty is serious stuff. You're gonna be okay, right, Jack?"

Jack nodded. He wasn't, though. "Catch you later, Gerry."

Every sense shouted it was highly unlikely he would be okay ever again. His worst fear was coming true. He was responsible for the death of his swim buddy, and a portion of the team agreed.

"Yep! Just don't let anyone know we talked. I don't want to leave you hanging, but I don't want to get hung out to dry either." Gerry nodded and then swam toward shore. They'd been trained to use either the sidestroke or breaststroke as the preferred movement through the water. Conserving strength and being stealthy was important. Gerry used both to get him back. The man did look seriously tired and there were some new scars on his body. Nothing major, but definitely not pretty.

Jack stayed locked on Gerry's form until his friend was safely on the beach, then he turned away from shore and swam toward the center of the Pacific. The urge to be as far away from the base as possible was pushing him. He moved from the breaststroke to the crawl, punching as much energy into the motions as he could. But the tide was coming in, and all it did was give him a losing battle to fight.

His arms ached and his belly groused. The loop of criticism in his head was like an overplayed song that he didn't want to hum anymore. All he wanted was to stop... to find some kind of solace or peace.

Cumulonimbus clouds moved in overhead, threatening to storm. The winds picked up, throwing choppy waves up to splash his face, and a few raindrops began to pepper the surface. After the dream he'd had on the couch, the sign of the gathering storm actually ran a chill up his spine.

In the distance, he could see fins and birds. Had to be dolphins feeding. Though usually, where they were, so were sharks. Perhaps facing toothy predators would solve part of his problem, especially if he died right here. It would be messy, but with the headspace he was in right now, what would he even care?

Death. The idea played in his mind. What would it be like to die? SEALs were always prepared to live or die in action, but to consciously choose death? That was a forbidden corner of his psyche he'd never chosen to visit before.

Jack's emotional energy was waning. The iron will he'd used to avoid so many dastardly situations was flagging—wavering to the point of being almost on empty. If he had been responsible for his buddy's death, how could he survive it?

"I need answers, dammit!" he yelled at the top of his lungs.

Nothing.

Rage, frustration… and fear… built inside of him until he thought it would explode like a bomb in his brain. He needed to stop. So he cut off the emotion. He took a deep breath, stopped swimming, and just floated on his back. His ears filled with water and there was silence. Finally.

What it would be like if I just let go?

He visualized it until he felt his eyes close. His body bounced aimlessly on the surface of the sea.

With an act of conscious determination, he folded

himself into a ball and dove to the shelf. Making his hands into scoops, he dug through the current until he reached the bottom. Then he picked up the heaviest rock he could find and held it.

Sitting on the bottom of the ocean with the rock in his lap, he made himself become part of the sandy floor. He knew his limit for holding his breath, but he wasn't ready to give up his burden.

Experiences—those vivid and intense memories that made him who he was today—flashed through his brain. Training before Hell Week, running with his buddies, holding rocks like the one in his lap to learn how to control his heart rate and breathing.

Other images—relationship ones—popped into his mind, too. Laurie. Sheila and Kona. Gich. His Teammates. His dearly departed grandfather.

Then there were things he still wanted to do: fly a glider; make love to Laurie on a deserted beach in Hawaii; mountain bike, like everywhere—he had only been to a handful of places in California. Have kids.

Shit! I don't want that! What the hell am I doing?

Get your shit together, Roaker! There was a lot to do, and he couldn't achieve any of it if he were dead. His lungs ached, burning with a need for air. He struggled with the rock, feeling the burning sensation in his chest growing.

Who will clear my reputation, or at the very least figure out this whole damned issue, if I don't find out the truth? Didn't he want to know what really happened to him, Don, and the rest of his Teammates? He couldn't die with so much still unknown. Giving up wasn't who he was! This route—ending this way—wasn't the right decision. Not for him. He liked choices. There were always many of them, and right now he had to get going. *Fuck this shit!*

Jack released the rock and kicked off, pushing up and up. The air bubbles left his mouth in short bursts. Arms dug through the water, legs kicked, driving him toward the surface. He popped through, back to the world of the living.

Eagerly, he sucked air between the falling raindrops until a sharp pain spiked at the back of his neck. He grimaced, growled, and began swimming toward the shore. The current had swept him farther out than he wanted to be and it would be a long haul to get back to the Amphibious Base.

"Good decision! What if Kona had found you? She might never have recovered from the shock." Don's voice came from behind him.

Jack spun around and was face-to-face with his dead swim buddy. "Shit! This is worse than the hallucination in the sub."

"No shit, Sherlock!" laughed Don.

That mission had taken them on a series of subs. The no-sleep factor and rather stubborn bout of flu and fever had really played with Jack's mind during that one, but he'd kept it together—mostly. The Team watched out for each other. They had snatched catnaps now and then, but it had still been taxing. "As for your daughter finding my chewed-upon corpse, she'd probably dissect it. Didn't she take apart that octopus on the beach last year? She was so excited! I'd be just another curiosity."

"Possibly! She's a strange one, but she'll be strong like her papa." Don grinned at him and channeled the conversation back to the glory days on the sub. "Hey, I know that look! You're thinking about those mermaids from that Op. You kept talking about them and how you wanted to open the hatch and go swim with them. Damn, you were hilarious!"

"No, you wanted to go with the mermaids. I was fantasizing about a king-size bed at the Del with room service—steak, potato, and fresh asparagus, with apple pie for dessert. Probably because I couldn't keep anything down and I was starved. Fuck! A steak really sounds good right now." Jack licked his lips. Hunger bit into his "need" scale and it was hitting a ten-plus. The last time he'd eaten was yesterday. "Hey, are there any boats out here that want to give me a ride back?"

"You look like hell, Jack. You need to take better care of yourself." Don swam closer.

Jack held his spot. "What happened, Don? Did I kill you?"

"No, man. What the hell makes you think that?" The anger on his friend's face at the comment was real. "You're my best friend. What the fuck?"

"Knotts said…" Jack began.

"What the blasted hell makes you think Gerry knows anything! Or any of those other guys! Didn't he say that Seeley and Pickens were unconscious and you loaded them into the chopper?" Don asked. "Look at the facts, Jack. They might be responsible and are using you to cover their asses. I've never trusted those East Coast pukes. Or maybe there was another factor at work in there somewhere."

"Uh, yeah." Jack agreed somewhat reluctantly. "Being East Coast has nothing to do with it. Don't start the East Coast versus West Coast rivalry. There's just something hinky, I can't put my finger on it."

"Hinky! Yes! So, then how can they know what really happened? Listen, keep doing what you're doing—well, not the thinking about dying crap! Only sheep give up. Got it? You're a fighter—not one of the herd—and you're going to find the answer." Don spit out the words and then he pointed his index finger in Jack's face. "Be strong."

"Or die living." Jack chanted their mantra back to him. Then he moved in to hug him, but the illusion disappeared instantly like a puff of smoke.

The image had been enough of a wake-up call. The answer to his mystery was out there, and he would succeed in his quest.

Turning toward shore, he swam for home. A steak wasn't far from his mind either. When a wave lifted underneath him, he stiffened his body and surfed his way toward the beach.

The dolphins he'd spied from far away joined him. They were riding the waves, too. They chirped at each other as they dove and rode the surf.

He took a mental snapshot. This was nature, how life was meant to be—riding alongside the dolphins. He was in sync with the elements.

It was a rare pleasure. There was something about being in the water with them, the way they played and their sense of happiness at such a simple action, that encouraged him to smile.

Closer and closer the shore sped toward him. As the sand began to slap his toes, he waved at them and they turned back, heading back out to sea, deeper water, and greater waves. If only life were that easy: find a joy, live it, and then go get another one.

Swimming in alone, he knew that whomever he brought into this battle would have to believe in his cause. There was no room in his life for naysayers. Ultimately he would have to walk this path to wherever it would take him, and each step would be made with honor.

Every action changes us. Isn't that life's plan? I'm the result of my experiences. He licked the salt off of his lips. *I am not at the mercy of any issue. The hurdle is my choice.* "Life and learning are a salad bar," his granddad had always said. "Take what works for you and leave the rest. It's all fuel for your learning. No regrets."

As he gained the beach, he looked around. Granddad was right. *Where else would I want to be? Only here.* Coronado was home.

He walked the familiar path to the parking lot. Somehow, he felt lighter as if he was meant to be on this journey. He'd rather know the depth and breadth of an issue than to stay in the dark. Living in the shadows and working in the inky night might be his gig, yet there were times he needed to be able to walk in the daylight and see everything the brightness revealed.

He reached and entered his car. Flipping his phone open, he dialed Laurie. She had become more than a means to an end; there was something extra special about his lady, especially as she helped him find the truth. He just could not let go of her and whatever was happening between them.

Laurie answered her cell phone on the first ring.

"Hello? Jack? I was just thinking about you." There was a smile in her voice, and he felt his lips rising to mimic her mood.

"Hi, Laurie. Would you like to have dinner? Nothing too fancy, but good grub. Can you meet me now at the Hotel del Coronado for a steak? Or, would you rather go to the Coronado Boathouse? Whatever we do, I'm craving a steak."

"Sure. Let's do the Boathouse. I love sitting outside and throwing bread to the ducks," she agreed with a laugh. "I can be there at five. That's seventeen hundred, super SEAL."

"Great! I have a lot to tell you," he said before he closed his phone. He'd be able to grab his gear and get a hard weight-lifting workout in at the gym before he hit the shower.

Scratching his chin, he felt the stubble. Not as dire as Gich's woolly mammoth whiskers but sharp enough that he didn't want to damage Laurie's soft skin. Crap, did he have the right clothes for a date with his very sexy lady? *Damn, I am a blessed man! Guess that workout is going to have to be quick.*

A dozen peach-colored roses wrapped in white paper were sitting on the table. Their reflection in the antique glass made them look like part of the Coronado Boathouse's design.

He checked his watch for the tenth time. She was late. Point Loma to Coronado was not very far, though the I-5 freeway and bridge traffic could be terrible if the Naval Air Station North Island base was changing shifts. A ten-minute drive could turn into an hour in a blink of the eye. *She's a local. She would have compensated for that.*

A 1967 Mustang pulled into the parking lot with a screech, and Laurie waved at him from behind the wheel. She was wearing a skin-tight red dress, he noticed right away.

God, she's gorgeous. He had an urge to kiss her immediately.

Laurie moved toward him, all sensual movements and curves. The spiked heels made her legs look even longer and that hearty appetite he had for steak began to morph into another kind of primal hunger.

She obviously knew the layout, because she took the side path that brought her directly to his table on the outside deck.

"You look amazing. I'd stand, but, uh, it might embarrass us both," he said with a hint of discomfort in his voice. "Crap! I feel like a schoolkid who's just gotten his first boner."

Laurie laughed and seated herself across from him. "Do we play spin the bottle first or go hide in your parents' game room and neck?"

"I'll vote for the necking, but after we eat. I need refueling." He took a sip of water. "After dinner, I'd like to stop by my place, before we go to yours."

"What's wrong with staying at yours? Is there a live-in girlfriend you don't want me to meet?" She poked at him and her expression said she enjoyed the banter. "Of course, if there's a wife, then I completely understand. There isn't, is there?" Worry crossed her eyes. "You're not that type are you?"

"What type?" he inquired angelically.

"All cock and no depth," she mouthed in a whisper so the neighboring tables wouldn't hear.

He smiled at her. "I'm not married. When I give my word in terms of loyalty and fidelity, I keep it."

"Yes, I believe you would. I've been the recipient of your undivided attention, and I can happily say I like it." She took a sip of water.

"Damn, you only *like* it! I need to do better." Leaning over the table, he whispered back, "I'll make it my mission to knock your panties off."

"I'm not wearing any," she confessed, with a blush rising up her neck to cover her cheeks.

"I need some ice water." Jack gestured for the waiter.

They both ordered steak, potatoes, and broccoli. Foregoing dessert, they lingered over coffee and threw chunks of bread to the ducks and birds hanging out on the railing and in the water just a few feet from the boathouse.

Laurie had been quiet during dinner, listening to him. She seemed preoccupied by something.

"Is there something bothering you?" he asked.

She nodded. Putting her hands on the table, palm up, she said, "I owe you an apology. When you woke up and were standing at the door, I realized how little I am equipped to deal with your PTSD. I think you should talk to the specialists about it." The tension drained from her face as she spoke. "I hope you can forgive me for saying this. I just, uh, don't want to be the person who misses an important sign or lets you down."

"Laurie, you're better than you give yourself credit for. Now, if you're ditching me, I won't forgive you."

He leaned forward. "But if you really feel you're in over your head, I honor the courage it took to speak up. Just know, Laurie, I have retained everything we talked about, and more details have fallen into place. What we're doing is working. Please. I need you to keep helping me. Be with me."

"It's working because you're relaxed, Jack. Getting laid and doing extra nice things for your mind and body opened those floodgates. I didn't do anything special." She toyed with her napkin.

"Look at me." Their eyes locked together. "You're important, Laurie. I couldn't have done this without you. Sex with just anyone wouldn't have brought me happiness or given me my memories back. It's you, Laurie. You're walking next to me, taking this journey alongside me, and you and your dedication are making all the difference.

"You've been around the Teams long enough to know each member is only as strong as their Teammate." He took a long drink of water, leaving fingerprints in the condensation to decorate the glass. "If there had been problems, I would have let you know immediately. With you, I don't hold stuff in. I say it exactly as I see it. Might not be a popular way to handle life, but I like honesty and a challenge."

"Me, too," she replied, heat flushing her face. Pleasure lingered in her eyes. "And I want to get to know you better. Can we talk like two people on a regular date?"

Jack nodded. "I'd like that. Let's forget about missions and memory loss for a night."

—⁓—

"You really like the movie *Evolution*? Me, too!" They both laughed. Jack liked learning that they had more in common, and it felt good spending time together.

He wiped his mouth with his napkin. The dinner had been outstanding. The food melted in his mouth and the company was great. Later on, this luscious lady was going to be his dessert.

"Are you ready to leave?" he asked.

She smiled. "Yes…well, no. One more question. The minute I saw you I was drawn to you." Laurie laughed. She lowered her gaze to the table where she fiddled with a fork, then finally placed it aside. She raised her head, locked her wandering fingers in her lap, and looked him in the eye. "What changed for you? What made you take that leap to get know me better?"

Her vulnerability was clear in her gaze.

Oh, crap! That was something he definitely did not have an easy answer for. He sighed. "I felt you could help me, and my instincts told me that you were special, besides being killer in the sack."

The horror on her face was instantaneous and intense. God, he was terrible at fancy talk! His lady had gone from charming and happy to downright furious in the space of a heartbeat. He guessed most women had that button somewhere in them. This was one of the reasons he didn't date and relationships didn't last for him. He sucked at the male/female social etiquette interaction.

Laurie's tone was frosty. "Gee, should I thank you for calling me the 'Fuck of the Day' or be excited that you want to 'use' me to get better?"

Help! Why can't women come with instructions? Why isn't there a speed-dial service for this eventuality? He sighed; he really did not want to screw this up! "I really like you, Laurie. In every way..." Shit! "I don't know how to say the right words to fix this."

"I didn't know it was that hard to be with me. That you had to find the 'right' phrase to get me back into your bed and fixing your shit." She pushed away from the table and stood. "Thank you for dinner, though I guess that's my pay for all the good work I've done." Shaking her head at him, she looked so disillusioned.

"Laurie." He couldn't let her leave this way. Grabbing her wrist as she passed, he tugged her to a halt. "C'mon. Give me a chance. Don't fly off the handle because I'm not a sweet-talker. Wouldn't you rather have a man who's honest, even if he isn't smooth and full of it?"

"Yes," she said softly. "I know the difference between those two types. I'm listening."

"I'm an idiot, miserable at explaining myself. I want to be completely honest with you. I've never... You make me feel like no one else has. I have strong feelings for you. Emotions I've never had with anyone else. Shit! I don't play games—just give me a break here." He mustered his best sense of apology.

She didn't break his hold and run away. Of course, she didn't sit either. The fact she was still standing there was a good sign. Her voice sounded more neutral. "Go on."

He took a deep breath and gave it his best shot. "My relationships have always been miserable from the second date on, so I don't have them. The night I saw you, that first moment, something about you... your energy drew me to you. The chemistry was electric. Again, no female has ever captivated me like that. Then when I went to you for help, you listened to me—gave my apology a fair hearing—and did it with kindness and generosity. You're special, Laurie. There is a readiness and easiness about you. I mean, there is something amazing about being with you… that I respect and enjoy. Shit! Why isn't this talking stuff hard for you, too?"

Her lips turned up gently at the corners. "It is. I get it." Her hand touched his cheek. "Thank you."

She sat back down at the table. She still clutched her purse tightly as if she was ready to escape at a second's notice if need be, though her features had softened. He supposed the male equivalent was a guy holding his car keys. If he's flicking them or jingling them, get out of his way. If he's grasping them loosely, it means the chances of his staying are sixty-forty.

"Yes, it's hard for me, too. I'm glad you bought me peach roses instead of the don't-divorce-me special. Though, it *is* a pretty bouquet." Laurie laughed. He couldn't believe the woman had the audacity to speak those words and chuckle. Where the hell were his keys?

"Remind me never to date a military brat again. I won't be able to slip anything past you, will I?" He drank more of his water. "Come on, share your experience."

Sighing, she said, "Yep, I'm aware. My dad used the flower trick on many live-in type girlfriends. Also, it's hard being the person waiting for a military family member to come home. Add in the fact my former boyfriends have not treated me well and the cards are greatly stacked against the next man I choose. Sorry to admit it, but it's the truth." Her eyes held his in a steady gaze.

"I'm not one of those idiots." He rushed to say the

words he knew she needed to hear. The good part was, it was the truth. "I respect you, Laurie, and I like you… a lot."

"Thanks." She fingered the stem of her wineglass. "I like you, too." She couldn't seem to get the words out and then finally they fell off her tongue. "The problem is, I should treat you and not have sex with you."

"The fact you can't keep your hands off me, and vice versa, sounds like a hard problem." He winked at her and then finished with a grin of pure male satisfaction.

"Yeah, yeah, thanks for teasing me on such a sensitive topic." She grinned back at him and placed her purse on the table next to her empty dinner plate. Her shoulders relaxed as she sat back in the chair. Was it greedy of him to want both her body and her mind? Those were two of the assets that made the duet of a perfect woman.

"Okay, you're fired! Now, would you like to order some dessert?" he asked.

She laughed. "Gee, thanks, that helps a lot. No on dessert; I'd rather enjoy a walk." He took her hand and held it, his fingers toying with her fingers. Her smooth hand laced into his. Both of them squeezed tight. God, he had to have her.

"Do you think I'd let you go that easily?"

"Unlikely. But I'm not forgiving you that quickly, either. At the bar you jumped to conclusions, and just now, too, with this whole 'lack of communication' business. You have to speak to me, make everything crystal clear and clean. Got it?" Her tone brooked no argument. Either he agreed or they parted ways. "I won't sit here and keep track of fuckups, because I don't believe in that, but I will call you on your crap."

He laughed as she gave him a glare. "I'm not laughing at you. I'm chuckling over something my swim buddy said about women—the right one will have you toeing the line so tight it feels good, and the experience will be mutual." He knew there was fire dancing in his eyes. He'd put all of his emotion and desire into that one look. For better or worse, this was who he was—a passionate guy with a dedication to duty.

She bit her lip for a few seconds and then finally admitted, "Unfortunately, it is. You've been yanking my strings as much as I yank yours. I guess we're evenly matched. But what are we supposed to do about the double-edged sword—your quest for answers and my need to rip your clothes off?"

"Ms. Smith, let's go tour my apartment. I'll show you my stellar dedication to making sure that no pleasure goes unexplored." He smiled, allowing the wickedness of the promise to tease her. "What's your answer for Red Jack?"

"Why, Petty Officer First Class Roaker, I do believe I'm owed some pay. Maybe I'll allow you to, uh, take it out in trade." She winked at him.

"What I'd like to know is—"

A bellow shattered their calm. "What the *hell* is going on here?"

Chapter 8

*Anyone can just go in there and kill someone, but you can't
get information from a corpse.*

—U.S. Navy SEAL saying

"Gich!" Laurie squeaked. Gich towered over both
of them, blocking the light. His shadow threw jagged
lines on the table, and he was definitely angry.

For the first time in her life, Laurie felt like she'd
gotten caught doing something naughty in front of
Daddy. But he wasn't really her biological father. He
was better—they had adopted each other.

Of course, his being a SEAL made it tough to get
away with things, and she had been known to keep a
secret or two. In many ways, though, this meant he was
even more protective of her. "I, uh… This is Jack."

"I know *who* the hell *he* is! What I want to know
is what *you* are doing *together*?" Gich bit out the final
word so loudly that several waiters and the hostess came
over to the table.

"Commander, if you'll let me explain…" Jack began.
Laurie nearly smiled at Jack's expression.

"You shut up!" Gich pointed his finger at Jack. He
paused and then looked at Laurie. "You speak. Now."

Jack was digging bills out of his pocket and placing them on the table on top of the check. Then he was

standing and facing Gich. "If there is a problem, talk to me, Gich. I was the one who seduced her."

Laurie watched Gich's temper ratchet up from a six to a ten-plus. She had to head this off. Jack was trying, but he had definitely said the wrong thing to her adoptive daddy. "Uh, Jack, why don't you wait in the parking lot. I'll be there in just a few minutes." Heaven bless the man, he hesitated. "Please, Jack. Go." He looked even more reluctant now. She knew she was right to take some of the wind out of Gich's sails before they faced off.

"I will be within eyesight," he said as he slowly walked away. It was obvious that he was not happy about leaving.

Laurie and Gich watched Jack depart. He didn't go far, though, standing about fifty feet away with his arms crossed over his chest and staring at them from the parking lot.

Gich turned his back to the man as he took Jack's seat. She knew his habits and watched Gich deliberately pluck the unlit, well-chewed cigar stump from his mouth and stare at it. Damn, that was one helluva pacifier Gich had, and it wasn't working either. Finally, he pulled out his lighter and held a flame under it until the top glowed. Only at the Boathouse could he get away with it, because familiarity breeds favoritism and the original owners had been SEALs.

Blowing out a smoke ring, Gich finally spoke in a steady voice. "Laurie, what did I say about getting involved with a SEAL? Haven't you listened to enough of our stories, your dad's and mine? What the hell are you thinking?"

Ah, crap, maybe that I needed to learn my own life

lessons. She pursed her lips, thinking about how to begin. In truth, it was terribly sweet that he watched out for her. Honestly, she liked it, for the most part, but she also wanted to make it clear that *she* was an adult and the person who made choices in her world, especially with relationships.

"Bastard! If he dishonored you, I'll…" Gich was winding up for a helluva lecture. Laurie had to cut him off at the pass. If she didn't, he'd be railroading her into what he wanted.

"This isn't second grade and me wanting to wear a bikini to school. I'm a grown woman." Placing her hand on his, she said firmly and gently, "Gich, it means a lot having you in my life as a dad and a friend, but—"

"I can't help it, Laurie. I've been watching out for you most of your life. When your dad died and I adopted you, I took and still take being your dad seriously. I never married and never will. You're the only kid I will have, and I won't fuck this up."

Her heart melted like butter at those words. He really cared. "I love you, too, Daddy G." She hadn't called him that since she was a little girl. "I am old enough to know what I want and need, Papa Gich. Why would it surprise you that I'm with a man like you?"

His eyebrows shot toward his hairline. "Me! Fucking A, you can do better, Laurie!"

She smiled despite his comment. "Gich, you need to let me make my own choices."

He sighed, then signaled the waiter who was hiding behind the doorway. "Give me a Stella, young man, and put some snap into it."

Laurie nodded at the waiter, and then she said, "I

want you in my life, always. Please get on board with me dating Jack—I really like him."

"He's a mess, that's why you like him," Gich stated firmly. The beer was placed in front of him and he gulped the entire bottle down in several swallows. When the bottle was empty, he placed it gently on the table and tucked a ten-dollar bill underneath it. "Listen, his life is in flux and I don't want you to get hurt. SEALs will do whatever is necessary to be operational. I don't want you to be just the springboard that rockets him back into the world and have you get crushed when it happens."

"I'll be fine, Gich. I'm walking into this relationship with my eyes open. I grew up in this stuff. I know the pitfalls. This is the first time I've ever fallen for a SEAL, besides you, that is, and I want this experience with Jack regardless of the fact he's a Team guy." Saying the words aloud made her realize that she really did want to explore the relationship with Jack further. She still had reservations about the whole thing, but she already had feelings for him.

She scanned the tabletop and then she sought Gich's eyes. She knew her own mind very well. "Shit! I really want to do this, don't I?"

"Guess so, Laurie. Be careful. And I'm here if you need me. Okay?" He picked up her hand and laid a loud smacking kiss on the back of it. "I love you! Damn, stubborn kid. I just wish you had adopted at least one of my qualities when you became my daughter, like taste." His words were gruff.

Laurie stood up, and so did he. They hugged. The bearlike warmth was very comforting and for what seemed like the zillionth time she said, "I love you, too, Daddy G." And she truly did. "My papa."

As they pulled back, he gripped her arms. "Promise you won't keep stuff from me like this again. It's not good for my heart."

"You have the heart of a bull. You're fine! A girl has to have her secrets, Gich." Laurie was teasing him.

"Love me less, girl. And remember you promised me once that you'd try to let me know about the important decisions. This is a big one, got it?" He pointed a finger at her and she batted it away before she kissed him on the cheek.

"I'm telling you now. Are we square?" she asked, hoping he let her have this one. Over the years, there had been moments she and Gich had gone toe-to-toe. Maybe that was the reason Jack didn't faze her. She could dish back whatever he gave her, and drawing a firm line was easy to do. Having Gich as a dad had forced Laurie to become her own woman, know her mind. Those were awesome gifts, whether he knew he'd given them or not.

"We're round, or maybe triangular," he laughed as he backed away. "Now, give me five minutes with your *boy*friend before you come out." With that, Gich was hauling ass down the narrow passage that took him off the boat and to the parking lot. The boat reverberated with the force of his running.

"Oh, shit!" Laurie, seeing the expressions on the people around her, said, "Sorry. A family tiff."

An older woman in her eighties said, "Not a problem dear. Most of us in this restaurant are Navy, and we know love when we see it." She glanced in the direction of the parking lot and her eyes widened. "Heavens, dear! You'd better go save your beau. I think he's getting beaten to a pulp in the parking lot."

Sure enough, when Laurie looked up, she could see Gich landing some solid punches in Jack's gut. "Dammit!" She grabbed her purse off the table.

"Thanks! It was a great meal." She yelled back to the waiter, or whoever was listening, and then she was running down the passage as best she could in stilettos. It was doubtful they would be welcome at the Coronado Boathouse again.

The sound of traffic grew louder as she neared the fight. A few people honked horns and shouted as they passed by. She prayed no one stopped his or her car to join in. This was a military town and people pulled that stunt here.

"Stop!" she yelled at the two men. She knew that physically getting between them would be a bad idea. Of course, she was going to do it anyway. No part of her could let her papa or the man she cared about get hurt.

Running full force into the fray, she grabbed Gich's arm and was the recipient of two punches coming together, one from Gich and one from Jack. Only one landed. She wasn't sure which one, because all she remembered was the pain and the world going black.

———

Ow! Ow! Ow! Ah, there is nothing more horrific than waking up to the glare of red and blue lights shining in the eyes.

Laurie groaned. *What hit me? Ow!*

A police officer leaned over her. "Are you all right?"

Her jaw hurt like a ten-ton weight had landed on it. She blinked her eyes quickly, trying to make the haziness go away. The world had fuzzy edges and there were bright lights hurting her eyes, too.

"Shit! Laurie, are you okay?" Jack was yelling at her. She wanted to tell him to take it down a notch but she was scared to move her jaw.

"It's your fucking fault, Jack," accused Gich. "Why didn't you man up and ask me for permission to take her out? That's what an honorable guy would do."

The blaring of ambulance sirens drowned them out briefly.

How did I get into this mess?

"Laurie's her own person, above the age of consent," shouted Jack. "Besides, I didn't know she was yours, Commander."

"For good reason! I don't want anyone sniffing around her." Gich said through clenched teeth. The gleam in his eyes had Laurie worried. She had seen that look right before he laid her father out flat after a drinking binge.

"What is she supposed to be, a nun? Laurie doesn't look like she's ready to be fitted for a habit." Jack took an aggressive step toward Gich.

"You're not under eighteen, ma'am?" asked a police officer with a tag that read Officer J. T. Lightmore.

Slowly, she shook her head in the negative. Ouch! Was her jaw broken? She'd kill both men if she had to get her jaw wired and drink through a straw for months on end. But as her eyes focused, she knew she'd need to put her powers of persuasion into effect because her two favorite guys were in handcuffs, leaned up against a police car, yelling at each other. Posturing was probably the better description, as they pecked at each other like two peacocks.

EMTs started fussing over her, taking her blood pressure and demanding her attention.

Refusing the chem pack for her jaw by force of sheer will, she slowly moved her jaw and found it was still happily hinged together. There was no doubt in her mind that this was going to leave a serious bruise.

Watching them all hover, the need to speak outweighed her pain, but rest assured, the guys would pay for the frustration. She'd make sure of it!

"I'm fine. Give me whatever paperwork I have to sign, and let me go."

"Are you sure we can't change your mind?" asked the shorter EMT, who looked slightly annoyed to have already pulled the gear out.

"Yes," she said in a flat voice.

"Ma'am, is there anything we can do?" The other police officer, Henrix, had hair that was buzzed tight and he had the air of man who had just come out of the Marine Corps. Jarheads and Squids—the terrible slurs the Marines and Navy had for each other—did not get along very well. "Help me to my feet, please." To her own ears, her words sounded like she had cotton in her mouth. *Perfect!*

Laurie put her hand out and the officer hauled her to her feet. She staggered for a minute before she steadied herself. "I'm okay, I just got my bell rung. Give me a minute." She took a few shallow breaths and when she was sure she could handle it, faced the wrath. "Officer, can you please let them go? That's my

adoptive dad and my boyfriend. I will not be pressing charges. Let's just call this a misunderstanding,
if possible. Please."

"The older guy smells like beer. We could have him
booked on a drunk and disorderly. That would hold him
overnight and sober him up," said Officer Henrix.

Gich said, "Young man, I am *completely* sober."

"I'm a therapist," said Laurie. "And the daughter
of a SEAL. They are both SEALs, and I can take care
of this. I'm sorry you were brought out here. Please,
could we wrap this up? I'd like to get some ice on
my jaw."

The police officers studied her carefully. If she had
been drunk, they would never have agreed. Something
in her demeanor must have given them confidence because they agreed to abide by her wishes.

When the cuffs were off him, Gich put his hands on
the ground and did a walking handstand for five minutes.

Everybody watched, while Laurie wondered if she
could die of embarrassment. When she was a little girl,
that move had delighted her, now it was just pissing her
off. Mentally, she was adding to the list of things she
needed to talk about with "Papa Gich."

But Laurie was relieved the cops had let them go. It
wouldn't help Jack's situation if he were thrown into the
slammer on a domestic-disturbance charge. The legal
system was tough on military personnel. SEALs were in
essence living, breathing, walking, and talking weapons.
She'd been through it all before with her dad. No, Jack
didn't need anything bad hanging over his head, and
neither did Gich.

"Just take them both home," the cop said when Gich

was done making a fool of himself. "I don't want to see either of them driving," he said as he and his partner got back in their car.

"Understood," she said. "Thank you, Officers." As she turned to the two men, she rubbed her jaw. Damn, it hurt! Her voice boomed out as she barked out her orders. "You two. Get. In. The. Car. Move!"

Oddly enough, both men trotted obediently to her vehicle and got inside. She smiled to herself. Wow, she didn't think the order would work, but even if it was temporary compliance, she would take it. "Well, gentlemen. Where do we go from here?"

Both men had crawled into the backseat and it looked like they were going to brawl again. "Don't even think about it!" she warned. Laurie turned on the ignition and pulled out, then turned onto Orange Avenue and headed into the main part of Coronado.

Stopping at a traffic light, she stared at the two men in her rearview mirror. What was she going to do with them? What should she say?

The cops went the other way, and as their lights revolved, shining blue and red, and their siren sounded for another call, Gich popped out of the vehicle.

"Gich!" Laurie yelled, incredulous. "What the hell are you doing?"

"I know where you live," Gich said to Jack pointing his index finger. "Be good to her." That was such a Gich action. To her he said, "Call you later, Laurie girl." Then he was trotting down the street toward his car. Nobody told Gich how to live. He had his own rule book and every rule related to his protection and pleasure, except perhaps when it came to her.

"Well, that went better than I thought," said Jack as he hopped into the front passenger seat.

Openmouthed, she stared at him. "Are you kidding me?"

"Nope," he said with blood running down one side of his mouth and obviously nursing the right side of his ribs. "You better close that mouth, before I take it as an invitation."

Chapter 9

Dulcis domus (sweet home).

—Latin phrase

NESTLED IN A ROW OF IDENTICAL WHITE AND BEIGE units, Jack's apartment was only minutes from their location and the base. The keys were barely out of the front door before he had her in his arms, slamming the door with his foot. It closed with a bang, and then he slowly lowered her to the floor. "I can't wait."

"I want you, too." The words were breathy as he kissed her tenderly and then nuzzled and licked his way toward her breasts. Their clothes were barriers to what they both needed—skin-to-skin contact.

A haze of sensations filled her mind as his hands caressed, lifted, and moved her into the perfect position. Her nails scraped down his back, trying to gain purchase, as his fingers sent an orgasm shivering through her body. "Jack."

"Yes," he said, and then he was pushing into her.

Her voice caught in her throat. She was holding her breath as he filled her, and then her body was convulsing around his length and width until his name squeezed out of her throat, coming out as a sigh. "Jaaaack."

Laurie woke up slowly, wrapped in Jack's arms. Her body was warm and relaxation swept her senses. Raising her head, she was surprised to find that they were still on the floor. She must have nodded off right after...

A smile pulled at the corners of her mouth. Jack could seriously transport her.

Looking around the room, she was prepared to compliment him on his decor, but there wasn't any. Calling it ordinary might have been an insult to those individuals who strive for the mainstream. Jack's home was just... impersonal. Not that her place was an advertisement for *House Beautiful*, but the thumbprint of her personality was firmly in place.

Would a whistle echo in here? The idea of actually doing it seemed rude, so she resisted the urge. Also, she didn't think her jaw would comply.

"You hate it," he said, watching her. She froze, not really knowing what to say. Then he slowly withdrew his embrace, stood, and walked into the small kitchen. He pulled out a bag of frozen peas. "For your jaw."

"Looks that bad?"

"A little bruised. I'll give you some potassium." He handed her the peas.

She sucked in a startled breath as the cold stung her skin. Regardless, she held it firmly in place, hoping it would help bring down the swelling and take away the concern in his eyes.

He offered a hand to help her up, and then grabbed their clothes and took them into the other room. The bedroom had to be through that doorway. It was the only logical choice.

"Jack, I, uh, well, we could go to…" She didn't know what to say to him. Actually, she did kind of hate the apartment, because she couldn't find any evidence that he'd settled here, made this place his home. What message did it convey if a man never put a nail in the wall? For her, a quiet place of her own was crucial. Somewhere she could let her hair down, take her makeup off, be in her own head without interference, or just plain walk around without clothes. All that was vitally important.

"Give it a chance, okay?" he said with a frown, standing in the doorway. "It's not a palace, but it's where I live."

"Sure," she replied. Her quick smile to reassure him was blocked by the bag of frozen peas. She gave up on comforting him, or even mitigating her faux pas. Instead she concentrated on healing herself.

"You won't find any dust," he joked.

"Yeah, I remember the Navy is very spick-and-span." The kitchen had white cabinets, white walls, and a white linoleum floor. The rest of the apartment was off-white or beige. The furniture looked like it had come with the unit: glass table with bamboo chairs, a beige couch, glass coffee table and two matching chairs. All the surfaces were empty. Not even a speck of dust was present.

Huh, maybe men don't nest.

Searching for a sign that he actually was living there and this wasn't some elaborate hoax, she went into the bedroom, and there she found evidence of the man. Stacked along a whole wall was gear: fins, masks, oxygen tanks, scuba suits, surfboard, cross-country and downhill skis, parachute, gloves, cases that looked like they held guns and ammo, books, and a ton more stuff.

The closet stood wide open. Lining the floor was a shoe holder with highly polished shoes. On the racks were uniforms, seven shirts—from Hawaiian to button-down—and two formal suits, all in clear dry-cleaning bags. Were those hangers an exact distance apart?

Crap! She and Jack were very different. He was a neat freak and she had clean clothes piled next to her dresser to be worn, put away, or just stepped over. He'd even put their discarded clothing in a stack.

Taking herself into his bathroom, she noted his toiletries: moisturizing shampoo, shaving cream, razor, deodorant, Tylenol, and baby oil were lined up on a small plastic tray with an ornate sailboat underneath it. Nothing was in the medicine cabinet, and only toilet paper and bath-room cleaner were stashed underneath the sink.

Towels and washcloths were folded neatly and stacked in a wicker stand next to the shower. The place was spotless.

"Do you sleep here every night?" she asked, not be-lieving anyone could be *this* neat.

"Pretty much. Do you always snoop in people's bed-rooms and bathrooms?" he quipped back with a smile on his lips.

"I just needed to make sure you're not Clark Kent and this is your supersecret identity," she laughed.

"I admit it. I'm Batman." He answered.

"Wrong comic universe. You'd have to have a bat cave. Seriously though, I'm looking for signs of life." The words popped out of her mouth before she real-ized she'd spoken them aloud. For a second he looked shocked and somewhat taken aback. Wounded. "I'm sorry. I didn't mean to be so…"

"Critical. Callous. Harsh," he said, completing her sentence. "What are you looking for?"

"You." Her comment was definitive.

Pushing past him, she walked out of the bathroom and sat on his bed. He stood in the doorway, staring at her.

She laid the peas on the nightstand and then pointed to the pile on the floor. "This looks and feels like you. The rest of this place is blank. Empty. None of your personality resides anywhere but here."

"It's a rental." He shrugged. "Besides, I only come here for quiet, and to sleep. Nothing else happens here. Well, rarely happens here."

"Do you even have food in your refrigerator?" she asked, seeking further insight into the tacit walls that Jack built to make his boundaries. The protection it provided and convenience was obviously created from necessity, a type of self-preservation. The military shuffled its soldiers all over the world, and it rarely made sense to get attached. She knew this fact from personal experience, but she had never seen someone with such overt behaviors.

Also, the arm's-length factor was common in many people who trained themselves to live only a portion of their lives at a time. Jack obviously existed as a single label to fulfill his work. He was a SEAL, and that was his only definition of himself. Psychologically and physically, it wasn't healthy. This kind of focus usually meant that there were emotional factors held at bay. Few were eager to confront the reason they wanted to live only one part of their life, because if things were rolling along harmoniously, why bother? A compartmentalized life cannot last forever, and Jack would eventually need to expand beyond his professional box. "Yes. Please note the frozen peas." He nodded in the direction of the nightstand.

Her gaze swept up his rock-hard body. *How many unknown areas do you have hidden away, Jack?*

He rolled his eyes. The silence must have gotten to him. "Give me a break, Laurie. I'm on the road most of the year. There's frozen vegetables, a couple steaks, and soup, dried fruit and cereal in the cabinet, and beer in the fridge. What else do I need?"

"Nothing," she said. *Me! Shut up, brain.*

"Man, I can't believe I'm allowing myself to feel like a dork because I didn't buy a plant or pin an Eagles poster to the wall." He sat down next to her. The bed sank and her body shifted toward him.

Her nostrils flared. The scent of his skin and the heat from his body were drawing her closer. The urge to kiss him and feel his muscles tense beneath her fingers was making her wet.

He was looking at her with those terminally gorgeous eyes, and her objections were quickly flowing away.

"Laurie, it's difficult being this close to you, and not... kissing you, touching you, and feeling you exploring me."

Her mouth was moving closer to his. There was no way she could keep her distance. What the hell was she going to do? An antisex shot had not been manufactured that would make her immune to his chemistry.

"Yes," he said before their lips locked together.

"Ouch!" she exclaimed, pulling back from him.

"Your jaw?" he asked, looking embarrassed. "I'm really sorry."

"Which one of you hit me?" Laurie finally asked.

"Gich. I pulled back. Your body weight on his arm set him off balance. It was sort of too late." He looked sheepishly at her. "My apology is still valid, though."

"Yeah, okay. That was a 'pulled punch'… damn." She watched him draw a bottle out of his pocket.

"This is Vicodin. I've gotten punched in the jaw plenty of times, and this is good stuff. I'm not much on pills, so there's a lot of it."

Normally, she wouldn't have taken it, but she needed something to take the edge off. She swallowed two pills dry. It wasn't long before the drug's effects started to make her feel better. "Let's try that kiss again."

Their lips met. Her jaw ached only moderately, and then abruptly the pain was gone. All she felt was his tenderness and the beginnings of her own hunger.

The kiss transported her, taking her on a magical journey that ignited her senses. She drew her body on top of his. They rolled on the bed—kissing and mashing their bodies together like teenagers.

She suckled his fingers, tonguing the palm of his hand until his mouth opened, and then laid tiny licks along the tender flesh of his wrist, his elbow, and inside his arm. Jack tasted of soap, a faint hint of salt water, and himself, such a clearly definable sexy male musk, too.

Thankfully, there was no rush. Not even a tick of time to push them along. Nothing was claiming their attention besides each other.

She took advantage of it and him, planning to explore every part of him from the tops of his ears to the soft spots between his toes with gentle caressing strokes. She didn't get the chance.

Jack had other designs and he took the lead, teasing his fingers along her skin—not quite tickling and still not satisfying her.

"Jack."

"What?" he gasped, apparently surprised and intrigued at her frustrated stare. "Did I do something wrong?

"Gich taught me to wrestle for my sixth birthday." She hooked a leg, shifted her hips, and flipped him on his back. Pushing his arms over his head, she pinned him. "I'm good. Very good. So, get to work, or let me play."

"I have no doubt Gich did a great job, but… ah," he said as his hands played over her skin. She arched as he cupped her breasts. Then she leaned down and kissed him. "Could we keep his name out of our more intimate discussions?"

Their tongues dueled.

"It's a bit of a mood killer."

Wiggling her hips on his rather exposed body, she felt his cock stir. "Aye, aye, sir."

"I am enlisted. There's no officer here," he said before leaning up and capturing her lips. "Get it right."

She smiled as his hands settled on her hips, urging her back a few more inches. She could feel his cock moving against her, but she wasn't ready to give in to the temptation yet. There was a lot more exploring to do.

Slipping out of his grasp, she padded barefoot into the bathroom and found the baby oil. Turning the water on hot, she put the bottle underneath and felt it quickly grow warm. When it was as hot as the water could make it, she grabbed a towel and sprinted back to the bed.

Jack was still lying sprawled on top of the bed. His eyes crinkled when he saw the oil.

"Don't look at me like that. You're going to have to work for your satisfaction, too."

"Hey, I'm ready. I don't walk from a challenge," he said. The comment sat well in her gut. She knew he was the step-up type—most SEALs were.

At this moment, Jack was lying buck naked on a bed, reaching his arms out to touch her, hold her, and make love to her. What woman could deny that invitation?

Uncapping the bottle of warmed baby oil, she drizzled it along his chest and stomach. Then she abandoned the bottle for those welcoming arms.

Her body slid along his as she fit herself against him. His lips locked to hers as they rolled around the bed, rubbing the oil back and forth onto each other. Strong fingers rubbed the slippery stuff deeply into her skin before moving to her sensitive areas.

She relinquished control and allowed him to lay her on her back. Watching him lift her arms above her head, she relaxed back into the pillows and enjoyed his caress of her neck, her shoulders, her arms, and finally her breasts.

Her back arched off the bed. His tongue teased the sensitive tip and then his lips wrapped themselves around her nipple and he began to suckle… hard then gentle, fast and then oh, so slowly. Watching her reaction until she was on the verge of coming, he released the tortured flesh and moved to her other breast.

As his lips rained tender kisses along the tip and areola, his fingers caressed a path downward. Her legs opened to him, wanting him to touch her. Strong fingers tenderly parted her vaginal lips and then landed squarely on her clit, stroking firmly and rhythmically. Pleasure and heat flooded her body.

Laurie could barely contain herself as she lay under him. She bucked against him, wanting to move more, but his weight and strength kept her pinned to the spot.

"Cum for me, Laurie. Cum with me holding you tight." His words poured over her like a life-giving elixir, and she blossomed, giving into his breathy wish.

The climax built—one layer after another—and still his fingers worked her, forcing her body to climb higher. When she couldn't stand the rubbing, his movement, everything, for another second, her body tightened and she came, screaming his name. "Jack!"

His fingers stopped moving against her clit and instead pushed inside of her, catching the intense splash of warmth. He lifted it to his mouth and tasted her essence. "Sweet and savory, like you."

She shivered as her body gave another mini climax and then she wrapped herself tightly around him. Drawing him closer, she drew in the intoxicating smell of his spicy masculine warmth and then began nibbling on his ear.

"What's that, that thing you're doing?" he asked.

"What do you think it feels like?" she inquired, smiling as she ran her tongue along the top of his ear and then suckled the lobe.

"I, uh, like that," he said softly. His voice was low and the tones drenched her senses like dark melted chocolate. "You're so sexy!" His hands played over her skin—intimately stroking and rubbing her back.

"Thought you might like it," she replied as she continued to tease his ear before moving to the nape of his neck. Licking under his jaw, she lingered on his chin and then kissed him. The rest of the night could have been spent delving between those well-rounded lips and dueling with his devilish tongue, but she needed sex, to feel the length of him pulsing in and out of her.

She was going to make it unforgettable for him. "Can you get on your back?" As she whispered, she blew tiny puffs of breath along the rim of his ear.

The earlier enthusiastic romp had brought them teetering on the edge of the bed. It probably was not the ideal place for seduction. *Should I say something or just move? Why are the beginnings of a relationship so awkward?*

Jack must have been reading her mind. "Yes, ma'am," he replied, lifting her in his arms and moving her back to the center of the bed, and laying himself next to her. "I'm ready. Are you?"

"I'm a woman, Jack. There's nothing you can do to shock me." Her smug words brought a gleam in his eye. Ah, challenging a Navy SEAL was like dangling bloody bait before a shark. Someone or something was about to be devoured. Though she wanted to be in charge right now.

Turning the reading light on, she adjusted the neck of the lamp, shining the bulb on her body. Then she kneeled over him. Shadows danced on the walls. Their lovemaking was performance art.

Her goal was enlightenment. She wanted them to see each other, the pleasure and the wanting and the needing of these stolen moments.

Her hands played over his skin, tracing the valleys and peaks of his muscles. He watched her, his entire SEAL focus on her. She could feel the force of his heat and the depth of want and desire coming from his gaze.

Repeating the pattern with her mouth and tongue had him moving into the motion of her lips. As much as she adored those big biceps and the rock-hard six-pack of his stomach, she wanted his cock deep inside of her. First, in her mouth, and then she wanted to ride him as if she were surfing a wave.

Teasing the fragile skin around his cock, she let her hair sweep over him again and again without actually taking him into her mouth. The heady smell of him was intoxicating, and she had an overwhelming urge to lick up the beads of precum, those charmingly salty tears of pure male essence, but she had another plan in mind for him right now.

Pressing between his cock and bottom, she found a spot that could bring more tears weeping. Sucking first one ball and then the other, she rotated back and forth until he was begging her to touch him.

Hands reached for her and she batted them away. Finally, deciding she had gone far enough, she looked at the engorged cock. It was almost purple with want.

Crawling on top of him, she lowered herself slowly onto his throbbing member. His cock stretched her as it slid into her warmth. When she was completely seated, she had to pause—the length and breadth of him was almost too much at this angle, and yet she couldn't bear to lift up and let him go.

Slowly, she rocked forward. Sensations waylaid her, pleasure spikes that had her reaching for some kind of stability.

Her flailing hands found his open waiting ones, and

her eyes locked onto his gaze. They began to move, together, just rocking back and forth gently. The electricity grew, spiking in her like bolts of lightning.

Her climax caught her by surprise, making her cry out. Her body posted on Jack's cock—up and down—drinking in his heady masculine seed, and before she could finish, his hands caught her hips.

"Please," he said softly. The look in his eyes was pure need.

She couldn't speak through the haze of pleasure. She nodded her head.

Instantly the rhythm changed to one of long deep penetrating strokes. Her body came again and again as he found the beat that worked. Their bodies slapped together as the friction built, the wet splash growing thicker until it felt as if her body were coming apart. The edge of pain and pleasure mixing together—where one minute it hurt and the next it was sheer inexplicable joy. Just when she was about to tell him she couldn't take anymore, his body spent its final drops.

His shout was loud and harsh as his hips ground into hers. Laurie's body felt as if it had blown apart and the pieces, along with her ability for conscious thought, were floating in space. Never in her life had she imagined such a feeling existed.

Jack lifted her hips and withdrew his cock before he laid her gently next to him. Then he pulled the edges of the comforter over them, cuddling her close.

Light snores that were already coming from his mouth made her grin. The sound was comfortable, and even her aching jaw couldn't distract her from sleep.

Relaxation invaded her mind's wanderings. The whole world slipped away into a blissful and very peaceful darkness.

———

Laurie's legs felt like limp spaghetti as she tried unsuccessfully to stand on them. She landed on the floor, toppling several stacks of books in the process.

A head popped over the edge of the bed. Jack grinned at her. "Are you okay?"

Heat bloomed in her face. "Yep. My jaw is starting to ache again, but nothing else is hurt." She laughed at herself, then grabbed a book off the floor and looked at the title, *The Art of War*, by Sun Tzu. Grabbing another book, she read the title aloud. "*Team of Rivals*. Isn't this a biography of Abraham Lincoln?"

He rolled onto his back and looked at her upside down. "Yeah, I'm a biography hound, especially for philosophers, political or military leaders, and inventors. I like to read about the way people outthink others, using quickness of mind or other resources." As she stretched her arms farther, she dislodged a stack of boxes.

"No," he said, trying to stop her from upsetting them. Quickly, he moved off the bed, but her body and the spill of books caught him in their wake and he half fell on her.

"Ouch," she said as his shin connected with hers.

"Sorry," he said, moving off of her and lying on the various objects to his side.

"What are you hiding?" she asked, craning her neck.

"Nothing," he replied with thin lips, but the mischief in his eyes was practically killing her. She had to know what he was hiding.

"What? Are there porn magazines or photos of ex-girlfriends in there or something? You're not a serial killer and those are your trophies?" Laurie teased, but there was a question in there. How much did she know about him? Shouldn't she know more?

He sighed and then leaned forward, revealing his secret. Games! The man had a huge box full of board games.

"Clue! You like Clue! I loved this as a kid!" She laughed. "Is this your deep, dark secret?"

"One of them," he admitted with a half smile. "I played them with my grandfather. My parents didn't really do games. Come on, let's get back in bed," he said to distract her.

"Jack, you haven't really mentioned your dad that much. What was he like?"

Jack looked at Laurie's pretend pout and caved.

"Don't give me that expression. I'll share. Sheesh, women!" Quick as a rabbit, he was on his feet. Then he scooped her up and placed her in the center of the bed, crawling in beside her. Jack opened his arms to her, and she cuddled close to him, laying her head on his chest.

The sound of his heart beating was soothing. Feeling his chest go up and down as he breathed was oddly reassuring and, well, nice.

He cleared his throat and began speaking. "After my mother died, my dad tried to hold it together, but child services kept coming to the house. It wasn't violence necessarily that was the toughest issue. According to the social worker, the problem was neglect. He would forget to feed me, wash my clothes, fetch me from school, and general stuff like that. One day, the social worker came to the house because the school reported that I had missed three days of class. She found me locked in my room. I vaguely remember her helping me take a bath and then taking me to the hospital.

"I stopped speaking then. Didn't really have anything to say to anyone. My dad saw me once more, to say good-bye, but I didn't know what to say to him. He cried and grabbed me from the bed and held me, but I didn't want him. I wanted my mother, but I knew she was gone and wasn't coming back.

"My grandfather—my mother's father—came to the hospital a few days later and took me to San Diego. That was my first plane ride and everything that followed was very… very surreal. He had a small house in a cul-de-sac near the beach. When I walked in the front door for the first time, I saw an enormous brass clock. He told me it came from the ship he'd served on in World War II. The floors were wood and everything was neat and clean.

"Giving me the room that had been my mother's was nice. I could feel her there. But it wasn't quite right for a boy—too much pink and too many flowers." Jack grinned.

"But I wasn't willing to speak up to complain. I didn't say a single word for that first week. My grandfather wasn't a man who gave up, so he brought down every board game they had stored in the attic, and we played until I 'loosened up.' I hadn't had much fun in my life until then," Jack admitted.

"Your grandfather sounds like a special person," Laurie said.

"He was. And he had this great laugh, almost a guf-faw. The first sound out of my mouth with him was laughter. Because he was laughing, I did, too. Talking came next, and once I began, I couldn't stop. I told him everything that had happened since I could remember. I rambled on and on. When I finally realized the effect of my words, how they made him sad, I stopped again.

"He wouldn't let me walk away from myself, though. He forced me to converse and encouraged me to reach beyond my own limits. 'Never run from the truth. There is honor in facing life head-on. Be brave.' I've always lived by those words." Jack squeezed her tight. "So, that's the story of me and my board games."

"Precious memories, Jack. Thank you for sharing them with me." She swept her hair over to one side. "Have you ever told this story to anyone else?"

He considered the question for a few seconds and then shook his head. "No. You're different… easy to be with and to talk to. You speak your mind. And you're not afraid to stand up to me. I like those attributes."

"I'm doubly honored, then." She threw her hands up. Another concern surfaced that she was going to face immediately. "Though, you must realize, Jack, I'm a physical therapist. Of course, you're comfortable with me. There's a certain amount of trust given to someone who puts their hands on your body."

"Perhaps to some degree, or even for a short while," he said seriously. "You're mistaken in thinking that's the reason. It's you! I show you the inner me, because you're… special, Laurie. I dread doctors and I hate having to talk about myself." He scratched his head. "Crap! When we're together, I feel… like you're my friend." He shrugged one shoulder. "I guess you are. Huh?"

"Yeah," she said, somewhat deflated. She didn't

know what she'd been trying to get at, maybe some crazy declaration of love. A commitment would only have complicated things. The best plan of action was to enjoy what they had for as long as it lasted. Sometime in the future, she'd have to face the fact that this man would be operational again and he'd be out the door like a bullet. Nothing would stop it.

"We are friends, right?" he asked, drawing her away from her brooding.

"Definitely," she said with a rallying smile. "Highest compliment a SEAL can pay a woman." She kissed the palm of her hand, slapped his knee, and then stood. The right thing to do was to change gears and flip the switch on her mood. He hadn't done anything wrong, though if she stayed on this current train of thought, she would be going down a dark and winding road. He deserved better, and so did she. Doubts had no place here. "Do you mind if I hop in the shower?" Soap and hot water were reliably useful in washing away worrisome mental patterns.

"By all means, hop away," he said. His long eyelashes shaded his light eyes, but she felt them track her to the bathroom. They gave off a heat signature that seemed to linger on her bottom.

A part of her felt good that he liked the way she looked, but her romantic nature still wanted more—more wooing, more verbal gushing, and more time spent together outside of the bedroom—and she wasn't sure if that would ever happen.

Were some things just standard—men never wanted to commit and woman always wanted the gold ring? Laurie felt like she was out of her depth. If her mother were alive, would she have been better at this stuff? The reality was, there was no one to ask but Gich. Given their last encounter, she was not anxious to ask him anything about love, sex, or men. She'd just have to muddle though.

Buck up, baby, and concentrate on the happy things. Jack is making you pretty blissed-out… for the most part.

The sweat and oil had congealed on her body and a wish for a squeaky-clean body was her first priority. The rest would undoubtedly sort itself out.

The showerhead was one of those high-tech ones. As she turned on the spray, she tried to figure out how to get it set to her height. "Jack!"

An arm stretched past her and adjusted the water. On its way back, fingers pinched her.

"Eek!"

She looked over her shoulder and there he stood. Naked. Sexy. And oh, so desirable. He was wired for stealth, even at home.

He grinned at her with boyish charm.

"Hey, gorgeous, let me adjust the water for you," he said with that wicked gleam shining again. "Just so you know, I'd be happy to wash your, uh, back, too. I'm a full-service guy."

"Such a gentleman," she replied, silencing her internal sound track and preparing for a little more fun. "Do you have any references?"

"I don't like to rely on others for my praise. Let me show you my talents." His grin had her smiling back. The spray came out strong, but soft—as if they were caught in a rainstorm. He adjusted the heat and then drew her close, running his hands over her shoulders and arms.

"Oh, boy," she sighed as he kissed her. She couldn't stop the shiver—it was half anticipation and half excitement—and it only made him draw her closer until their bodies were rubbing together. Skin on skin, and tantalizing every nerve ending.

"Not quite, honey." His hands pushed her hair over her shoulders and his lips caressed her neck. "I'm all man, and I'm all yours."

Wrapping her arms around his neck, she wiggled in his embrace. His touch drove her wild and his teasing words touched her heart. *All mine*.

Chapter 10

Nuts!

—General Anthony McAuliffe,
surrounded in Bastogne, Belgium

JACK DROPPED INTO HIS CHAIR WITH ONE MINUTE AND fifty-three seconds to spare. Being in the psychiatry department of Balboa Naval Hospital made his stomach clench, though he'd never reveal the depth of his discomfort to any of the men in white. Some day these guys would learn to lose the office and meet their patients at the beach or in a pub for a chat. The doctor's secretary poked her head around the door and said, "The doctor will be with you in a moment, Petty Officer." Then she was gone.

He took a deep breath and let it out slowly, going over his strategy for the session. The best method would be to act calm, cool, and collected, which in all truth was the exact opposite of how he felt. Show him a guy who was comfortable talking about his emotions, and Jack would be amazed. He'd rather have bamboo shoots shoved under his fingernails, and since that had actually happened to him, he knew how torturous the pain could be.

His preference was for *this* appointment to be his final visit. He had a sinking feeling that he was not that lucky.

Heavy footsteps approached. Had to be the doc—sounded like he carried the weight of the hospital with him or perhaps a mega-sized ego to go with his know-it-all attitude.

"You're here." Strolling in with a pile of file folders in his hand, the doctor sat down at his desk. "I had my misgivings, especially given how many sessions you have actually made. Glad to see you didn't violate your orders, Petty Officer First Class Roaker. Now, where should we begin?"

"Officially, I only rescheduled them," commented Jack with a single raised eyebrow.

"On that topic, let's clarify the rest of your attendance issues. When last we spoke, you had walked out of group," Dr. Derek Johnson, the chief headshrinker, began. The man smelled of rubbing alcohol and cigarettes. Seemed like this doc had at least one bad habit and probably a few issues, too. Who was he—or anyone else—to judge?

"Correction, I was *excused* from group by the doctor, as were many other participants. With all due respect, there is a difference," Jack replied in a monotone voice. He could maintain his blank expression forever, if necessary. It was too bad, really, that the doctors had become the enemy to him.

The clock on the wall ticked loudly. Only two minutes had passed. "Yes, of course, that particular group leader will not be providing that option next time around. I see your next group session is on Tuesday morning. I believe the topic is love and relationships and the importance of creating balance in a soldier's and sailor's life. I'm sure it will be fascinating."

Good Lord, kill me now! Jack used every bit of control he had not to groan in misery. He would rather spend a month in a mosquito-infested jungle than talk about his interest in Laurie and the uncertainty about the future.

Wasn't he allowed to keep anything private?

Tick. Tick. Tick. The clock pronounced each grueling second.

"Patients with acute psychological suppression and/ or post-traumatic stress disorder can exhibit a number of symptoms, including but not limited to paranoia, persecution complexes, anxiety, mood swings, depression, and…" Dr. Johnson's words droned on. Jack had heard the litany several times before—at the hospital when he first woke up and every time he was in group therapy. He had even read the pamphlet on PTSD and had no interest in tuning in to the lecture again.

Jack needed to redirect the topic and get this guy and the rest of the psych team off his back. "I was thinking about the breakthrough I had. You know, the missing information. I've been able to fill in some of it."

Dr. Johnson looked surprised. He pushed his glasses up and leaned forward. His voice held a hint of excitement, too. "Excellent news. What have you learned, and how?"

Jack held his smile in check and began his buildup. He leaned in the doctor's direction and used his hands to illustrate the experience. "I'll begin with the how. As you know, I'm a down-to-earth guy, and I am partial to a natural approach. I went to a physical therapist who has been using a number of alternative therapies to help me dislodge the barriers."

The head doctor was hooked. Now, control of the conversation was in Jack's hands. *Ha ha ha! Come into my crosshairs, Doc Johnson!*

"Together, we have succeeded in piecing together several of the steps in the Op." As Jack spoke, the doctor scrawled hurried notes. When he reached the end of his narrative, the doctor continued writing for at least ten more minutes. Was that a good sign or a bad one?

Then Dr. Johnson looked up and asked, "Is that it?"

"For now, yes. Doc, this is what I wanted, to know the details of what happened. I have more work to do, and I know this is an excellent beginning." Jack grinned as he leaned back in the chair. His arms settled on the chair's armrests.

Taking his glasses off, the doctor studied the nose guard on his glasses. His body language suggested that there was going to be some kind of heavy-duty chat about something. When he put the glasses back on, the doctor's eyes were hard and dark. "This therapist you speak of… was she on the approved list for working with the military personnel?"

"I don't know. Maybe. I didn't check her out, if that's what you're asking me." Jack crossed his legs. "Why?"

"We have very strict rules when it comes to civilians working with military personnel, especially when that sailor has Top Secret Clearance." Dr. Johnson's words were clipped. "While I am pleased to learn several of your barriers to memory have been removed, a physical therapist is for body movement and healing, and a psychoanalyst or psychiatrist is for mental recuperation. Do you understand the difference?"

Is he kidding me? "I'm not a child. I get it. But what does it matter how I found answers, as long as I have them?"

Johnson looked angry. "Because you're missing important steps. You have to walk each one! It's important. Otherwise, how did you learn the answers?" He sucked in air greedily and continued. "Were they told to you? How can you be sure these are your words and memories? By going through our system, you will be exploring your own mind in controlled circumstances. What if you have a break from reality—are you taking into account that you are a lethal weapon?"

"Why are you doing this, cross-examining me? Making me feel like a bad guy for finally learning the truth?" Frustration flared inside of him, but Jack tamped it down.

"I'm not making you feel anything, Jack. Emotion is a choice, and you are choosing to be upset by this conversation." The doctor spoke very evenly and softly as if he was speaking to a child. Looking down at his pad of paper, he made a few notes. "How are you feeling now, Jack?"

"A little pissed off, Doc, because it seems like the fact that I didn't find the answers while I was sitting in *this* chair or out *there* in group therapy means that the information is less valuable or accurate. Am I right about you... feeling threatened by *your* lack of success, Doc?" Jack's temper was rising, though he was trying desperately to hold it at bay. Unfortunately, he was losing the battle and his usual steady finesse was gone.

Jack continued. His voice was growing quieter and more stoic. This was pure white anger for him. He had never been a shouter. "Or are you afraid of me babbling about some Op that would bring the whole country down? You know we don't get that much information. SEALs only get enough information to operate, to perform the necessary tasks or duties. We rarely, as in almost never, get to see the whole picture. That's a privilege for the upper brass."

"Petty Officer, I am simply saying that I cannot approve you to work with a person unless you give me a name and make sure this is a legitimate consultant for our program." The tone of Dr. Johnson's voice was extremely condescending. "Do you understand?"

"I understand that you want the inside track on what's going on in my head. This is real life, Doc. It doesn't unfold in a textbook manner." Jack uncrossed his legs. His eyes automatically checked the clock, and he smiled.

The alarm on the clock buzzed loudly. *Thank God!*

Jack unfolded his body and stood in a single movement. "Good day, Dr. Johnson. See you next week."

He hustled double-time out of the man's presence.

Before he rounded the door, he looked back. The image of the doctor sitting—unmoving behind his desk, with his mouth gaping wide—was reminiscent of a stunned fish on a dock.

Jack was both elated and sad. If this had been a different man, one who was secure in his own abilities and ego, they might have worked together. He would have been willing to give a guy like that a chance to help him.

Instead, being the progressive guy he was, Jack had called the doctor on *his* shit. Another SEAL, or someone secure in his or her sense of self, would have appreciated it and owned up to his or her responsibility. But Dr.

Johnson was the head of the department and the team leader on his case, and nothing short of the man's obvious blunder was going to have him admitting that this PTSD program was flawed in terms of addressing the type of issues Navy SEALs faced. There needed to be a more specialized program that had the doctors working out with them and becoming a part of their world. Then a SEAL might take treatment more seriously.

Jack had heard about and personally knew SEALs who had sustained life-threatening injuries and were told they would never walk again, swim again, or be fully operational again. Ninety-three percent of the time, SEALs overcame their issue and went on to play an important role in another Op. Doctors should never underestimate the human will, or rather, a SEAL's fortitude and desire.

Taking the stairs two at a time, Jack moved quickly through the building and out the front door. When the fresh air hit his face, he breathed deeply, incredibly grateful to be outside. He nodded at a few familiar faces.

Heading around the side of the building, he saw a group of men gathered there. In the center was a medium-build guy in a Hawaiian shirt, with scruffy fuzz on his cheeks and chin, laughing with patients, many of whom looked like they had been injured by IEDs. Stumps were bandaged and taped, and there was dried blood on some of the ends. Jack stopped and listened.

"So, I told the nurse I didn't want to eat. My nurse wouldn't back down. She told me that she would sit right next to me until I did. Honestly, I wasn't going to do it for myself, but the look on her face—for her, I had to eat. I got better too for her, and it took a long time before I was getting better for me. I had to learn that I'm still here, on this earth, because there are things for me to do. People to talk to and pie to eat. Does anyone want some more Julian apple pie?" The man caught Jack's eyes. "Hi, I'm John."

He thrust his hand out and the crowd parted like a wave. Jack caught it and shook hands with a man he knew and could identify as a Medal of Honor recipient, and who was a regular visitor to the soldiers at the hospital. "Jack Roaker. We've met before, at the Wounded Warriors Dinner last year. I've seen you in the halls, too."

"Yeah, had to drag the spiffy rags out for that event. Nice to see you again, Jack." John clasped his hand around both of Jack's holding tight for several seconds. Before he let go, he said, "Stay strong." It was like a punch of energy to his spirit.

"Yes, sir. Thank you, sir." When Jack pulled away, all of his anger was gone, at the doctor and at the situation. Instead, there was a sense of peace. He was somehow part of a larger picture, and though he might not understand it, he would have to keep going forward to see it all.

"I'm John. Just John," said the MOH recipient.

Jack nodded back at him and waved. "See you around, John." The fact that man would say such thing—that he was just an ordinary guy, soldier, man like the rest of them—showed how truly extraordinary he was. His greatness was in his words, his kindness, and the time he took to listen to others, to support them, and to share his own story.

As Jack neared his car, he spied two people whom he had been trying to get hold of for weeks now. Seeley's and Pickens's body language toward each other was aggressive. For the first time in his life, Jack didn't know if he could trust members of his Team.

"What are you deadbeats up to? Nothing good, from the look of it." Jack came upon them from an odd angle and caught them on their blind side. Ah, the looks on their faces, pure shock and a little bit of horror. Not the nicest greeting for a brother who had recently saved their asses.

The men froze for a few seconds, obviously caught in the act of talking about something that Jack wasn't supposed to hear. "So, what the fuck is going on? Are you bastards hanging around the hospital parking lot to pick up chicks?" Jack was prepared to lay it all on the line to find out the truth. The only trick was that he needed to be stealthy.

"It's Croaker! Nice to see you, old man. Looks like you're healing up just fine," said Seeley, pasting a grin on his face. "How's the noggin doing? Seen any more mermaids?"

Pickens said nothing. His face was blank and he looked past Jack as if he weren't even there. This, from a guy who claimed to be a Teammate and friend. Obviously there was an issue here.

Jack stared at them, waiting for them to make accusations to his face or to let something slip. It was like talking to statues.

"Aren't you in a speaking mood, Pickens?" asked Jack as he stepped closer to the silent man. "I've heard that you have a lot to say about me... lately. Anything you want to say to my face?"

"Hey, now, Jack, it isn't what you think. We only gave our reports. You know how it is, we have to be up-front."

Seeley stepped in between the two men. "Don't give us any trouble here, we're brothers."

Jack glared at them. "Team guys don't set each other up. Why do I get the feeling that the two of you are hiding something?"

"We've been ordered not to discuss the Op with you, Jack. And, we won't." Pickens's voice was low and hard. Under his breath, he muttered, "Fucking West Coast do-gooder."

"What?" Jack took a step toward Pickens. Seeley blocked him. There were other ways to skin a goat, and he wasn't going to let someone ruin his good reputation or peddle some other nonsense without a face-to-face discussion. "Would you like to repeat that?"

"Why don't you just let it blow over?" spoke Pickens through gritted teeth. "The report will go through, because you can't remember, and the whole thing will go away. Just ride it out, Jack."

"Because whatever this is about, you're doing it at my expense, Pickens, and the rest of the Team. We don't work that way. Courage, honor, duty… or have you stashed your values in your duffel?" Jack knew he was taunting him. He was prepared to go a lot further, too.

"Shut the fuck up, Croaker. Red Jack, the fucking Boy Scout!" Pickens stepped toward Jack and Seeley was mashed between the two of them. As he spoke, his spit hit Seeley's shoulder and sprayed Jack's face. "Everything's landed on you. Fucking own the situation and move on with it."

"Yo! Take it easy guys. There was so much gunfire— all that ammo we laid down, and there was smoke and dust. Combat can affect your memory, Jack." Seeley was rattling on, trying to smooth things over. There was not enough camouflage makeup in the world to cover this up. "Besides, with the light from the boxes…"

"What light? There was dust everywhere in that factory." A puzzle piece was falling into place. If there was light near the boxes, either a Team member had walked over there or someone else was in that building. This clue could help him, or maybe it was a red herring.

"Shut up!" said Pickens, stepping closer and getting in Seeley's face. He glared at Seeley and murmured, "Stop helping. Just get the fuck out of this."

Jack turned his head to the side like a dog examining something from a new angle, and he saw one. Seeley was the weak link and Pickens was the linchpin.

The new information made him feel more in control; Seeley would continue to spill the beans. He just needed to get the man alone and ask the right questions. "What gunfire are you referring to? The place was a ghost town. Just precisely who were you guys shooting?"

Pickens's eyes were angry, and his jaw clenched. He opened and then closed his mouth. "Fuck off, Jack, there's nothing here. Got it? Just get lost, before you—"

"Before I what? Get hurt? Wait, I did." Jack rubbed his chin. "I get it. You think I have something else to lose besides my swim buddy. Nope, that was it. Everything that was important to me stood next to me during that Op." It was clear to him that two of his brethren had sold him out for something and Don had died at the expense of whatever those two guys had valued more. Problem was, he couldn't prove a damn thing. Yet.

He stared each one in the eye and then he left. As he

made his way to his Jeep, Jack could feel the heat of their eyes on his back. He wished he knew every detail of what they said. If there was a hearing and he was brought up on formal charges, he'd hear every detail— that was certain. Until then, everyone was keeping a tight lip.

Nearing his vehicle, he could see them reflected in the driver's side mirror. They were arguing and Seeley looked like he was getting slammed.

"The truth always rises, in the same way the sun always sets," Gich was known to say. Come hell or high water, Jack was going to make sure everything came out.

Getting in his Jeep, he fastened his seat belt, turned the key, and pulled noisily out of the lot. He powered up the Bluetooth and called Laurie. Her voice mail picked up. She must have been in session.

He decided to leave a message. "Hi, Laurie. It's me. Call when you can. I have some rather interesting information to share with you." Another call was coming in, so he ended his message and picked up the incoming call.

"Roaker," said his XO. "Get your ass to my office ASAP."

Chapter 11

Kill one, terrify a thousand.

—Sun Tzu

JACK PULLED INTO AN EMPTY PARKING SPACE IN FRONT of the SEAL Team ONE Quarterdeck. He jumped out of the Jeep and double-timed his step until he was at the XO's door. He knocked and waited.

The hallway was bustling with activity and his nerves rattled a little.

"Enter," barked XO James "Chick" Stockton through the closed door. He had gone through BUD/S training being called Chicken Stock, and the "Chick" part stuck. He was in the process of growing a beard for an upcoming deployment and looked like a plucked bird with feathers sticking out in places.

Jack took a deep breath, let it out, and then turned the knob. Hot air pummeled his face. The XO hated air conditioners and kept the place as warm as a stove. "Jack, take a seat."

The XO was using his first name. That made him nervous, but it set the stage for things to be a bit less formal—not that SEALs stood on formality. "Listen, I didn't call you in to bust your chops. I want to know what you remember now from the Op."

"Quite a bit, Chick." Jack related the whole story as

far as he knew it, with every bit of sensory detail he could remember and highlighted the areas where the holes still remained. "I know I'm close to finding out the rest of it, too. I just need a little more time."

The XO nodded his head. "Good job, Jack. You're on track, that's good. It's a luxury—medical leave—that needs to be short-lived. Understood?" He cleared his throat. "Not that you're hearing this from me."

"Yeah, Chick, I get it."

"Good. Um, there's one other thing. An issue about how you're going about finding your answers…"

That pussy Doc Johnson must have contacted the XO. "Chick, did you get a call?"

"Yes, from a, uh…" The XO looked at his desk, and said, "Dr. Derek Johnson."

That fucking, pompous paper pusher! "Chick…"

Holding up his hand, the XO said, "Hear me out, Jack. The regulations are straightforward. A civilian cannot treat military personnel when national security matters are at stake. Since a formal complaint has been registered by Dr. Johnson, I have to ask you not to see this therapist again in that manner."

"Permission to speak freely, Chick." Jack's words were clipped. He was fighting a wellspring of emotion at the thought of not being able to see or speak to Laurie again. He was so close to the truth.

Waving his hand, the XO replied, "Dammit Jack! We're alone. When have SEALs ever stood on ceremony? You're the damned formalist jackass around here. Speak!"

"Thanks. This isn't some Army doctor. Laurie, she's a physical therapist, a woman who has accomplished more in just a couple of sessions than the whole damn team at Balboa has done since I got back here. Top that off with the fact that she's the daughter of a SEAL and grew up in this community. It's not like I'm talking to some fucking *stranger*, Chick." The words flew out of his mouth at rapid-fire speed. "I can't disengage, not see her again. This is my best opportunity to learn what really happened."

The XO shook his head. He lifted up a document and held it so Jack could see it. "Stop. I didn't hear it. This is a copy of the formal complaint added to your file, about your visits with a civilian. I printed it out, because I knew you'd have to see it to get it through your thick skull. I *have* to order you not see her. I have no choice, Jack." The XO studied him. "Johnson, he's an insecure asshole, I get it. There will be repercussions for you and for her if there is any contact. So, say you understand, and get the hell out of here."

Picking up his pen, he looked at the paperwork on his desk. "Jack, a SEAL psychoanalyst will be back from deployment in nine weeks. You could take it up with him then, if you'd rather wait."

"That's a long fucking time." The wind had gone out of his sails. Jack didn't know what to say.

"Yes, it is. The issue will have to be dealt with before then. By my estimation you have about seven and half weeks left to get to the truth." The XO dropped the sheet of paper and it landed without ceremony on his desk. "You've heard me. I see your head nodding. Good. Now, get out and go do what you have to do to heal."

Damn headshrinker. "Chick!" said Jack, his eyes

held the XO's gaze as he tried to convene the pain this would cause him… losing Laurie.

"Please…" Inside, Jack was panicking. He needed her. She was healing him—his mind and his heart. His chest tightened.

The XO sighed as he put the page back with the rest and shut the folder that obviously documented Jack's military career.

They stared at each other.

Finally, Jack turned away from the XO's desk. He hadn't been dismissed, so he turned back around. Unlike Don, who had disobeyed practically every command, Jack had never disobeyed an order in his life. But the thought of never seeing Laurie again was like being gutted.

The XO studied him and then said, "Dismissed."

Jack turned and left. Salutes were not big in the Teams, and unless it was a formal occasion or a sign of respect to someone important, they just didn't happen often. The Teams were a giant equalizer where everybody got dirty, including the officers. That's why SEAL Teams worked so well: everyone trained together and operated together as one unit, one arm, and one force.

Today, though, Jack felt like a man on the outside of everything. He wanted back into the action—to be put in play—but nothing was going to change until he could fill in the blanks. Without Laurie, he didn't stand a chance.

He walked straight to his car. He opened the door and reached underneath.

Unlocking a combination box secreted under his front seat, he withdrew his gun case. More than anything, he needed to think. As he headed to the shooting range, he knew that he'd have to come up with some way to find the answers. Without Laurie's body alongside his or her guiding hand, he didn't know where to begin.

His phone beeped. A text message scrolled through: Group therapy on Tuesday.

A phone call came fast on the heels of the text. It was Laurie. He needed to tell her that he couldn't see her professionally or personally for a while. There was no boundary between the two roles right now, and he didn't trust himself to keep his shit on one side or the other. The cell phone in his hand was his work line and it would register that he had taken her call.

His throat tightened. Christ, he wanted to hear her voice. But if he never spoke the hated words, then maybe there would be some chance in the near future. Better to leave it alone for now.

He closed his eyes, unwilling to think of a life without her. Silently, he prayed for the first time since he was a little boy. He didn't know if it would help, but he couldn't imagine it would hurt.

Another text shot into his phone. A picture of Laurie's face all squished up as if she were kissing him. He couldn't stop himself from saving the photo to his phone and sending a copy to his computer. "Fuck! What am I doing?"

Pushing a button, he deleted the photo from his phone. Inside, he knew the image was seared on his brain.

Large dark clouds sped across the sky, blocking out the sunlight. Birds landed on the ground, tucking themselves next to large buildings. Planes zoomed overhead aiming for North Island, and they appeared to be going faster than usual. A storm was coming in and it would be here quickly.

Drops of rain landed on his hands and face—first a few, and then the skies opened up, sending down a deluge. Had to love this time of year.

Jack yanked up the soft top and secured it to the frame. The rain had already poured inside, soaking the seats. It would dry, and yet it seemed so unimportant compared to what was happening to him. His main concern was… Laurie.

What would she do when he followed orders and just disappeared? Would she miss him? Would she hate him? Would she ever be able to forgive him? Thinking about her reaction made his emotions spike.

If only I could tell you… what you mean to me. I fucked up big time, and I don't know how to fix it.

Instead, he would be the Navy SEAL jerk who *never* called her back, and he didn't even have an Op as an excuse for the lack of contact.

Chapter 12

I don't mind being called tough, since I find in this racket it's the tough guys who lead the survivors.
—Colonel Curtis LeMay

THE MORNING HAD BEEN EXTRAORDINARILY DULL. Sunbeams streaked in her window one moment and then were gone the next.

Wednesday—the hump day of the week—usually progressed at a snail's pace, but today seemed even slower and more fraught with frustration. With only two appointments on the log, Laurie knew she should have done something to fill her time: taken a spin class, gone grocery shopping, anything but sit around, staring at the computer.

Lately, she felt miserable. There were very few things that could make her smile.

Scrolling through her cybercalendar, Laurie checked today's date for the twentieth time. Over six weeks had passed without any word from Jack. Having run the gamut from rage to worry and then back again had been tough on her psyche.

She'd left ten voice mails and had sent him more text messages than was actually attractive, but she knew she had good reason. The last time she saw Jack, they had planned on speaking within hours of his meeting with the therapist. He had been so gung ho on having another session that he made her promise to keep time in her schedule for him.

Now, here she was, still waiting for any word from him and worried as hell! "The man is on medical leave. There is no reason for him not to get back to me ASAP." Her words sounded flat in the empty therapy room. She wished she had giant windows to throw open and let the sunshine in. The subdued lighting and lack of something to concentrate on was eating away at her tiny amount of forced harmony.

With over three hours until her next two appointments, the only tasks at hand—that she could do in here—were pacing the confines of this space and worrying about what was happening to Jack. Anything else she could think of—organizing receipts for taxes, organizing her notes, updating all the files, getting a manicure and pedicure—had already been attended to.

Images of her dad kept invading her mind. They wove into the questions she had about Jack until her brain felt like it would explode. Was this why she'd never wanted to date anyone from the military? Being shut out was hard to take.

She asked herself the scariest question aloud. "Is he a player, like Dad?" She didn't believe it. Couldn't face it, even as a possibility. Yet the idea of having committed so much of herself to him made her stomach do flips. Falling for him had been almost unavoidable. One minute she had decided to keep her distance, and then Jack was there—making love to her in the shower, toweling her dry, and cooking for her, even bringing her breakfast in bed.

How could she deny this man who rained attention on her?

Jack couldn't be… a man like her father…

Running for the bathroom, she threw open the door, flipped on the light, and made it just in time as the bile rose up her throat and exploded out of her mouth.

As quickly as the feeling came, it left.

Leaning her forehead against the cool porcelain, she was relieved that the pressure in her stomach was gone. Expelling made her feel slightly better physically, but confirmed something she could not deny any longer.

Priorities first. Unable to stand the taste in her mouth, she pushed herself to her feet, went to the sink, and splashed cold water on her face. Then she swished with mouthwash and brushed her teeth.

Staring in the mirror, she thought she looked pale. There were dark circles under her eyes and her neck was splotchy. The necklace she used to wear all the time sat on the edge of her sink. Twisting it at least a hundred times—like worry beads—had given her small bumps on her neck. She didn't know whether to laugh or cry that they looked like the hickeys Jack was notorious for leaving on her body.

"You've looked better, doll." Patting her cheeks, she raised a little color and then added a few layers of lip gloss. The pampering helped her self-esteem, so she pulled out her makeup bag and went to work: mascara, eye shadow, bronzer, a dash of blush, and a double dollop of under-eye cover-up.

Pleased with her appearance, she reseated herself in front of the computer and logged in to the calendar program again. She selected the two-month display and counted the days again.

"I'm pregnant!" *Holy moley! No fucking way! No, no, no.* "It can't be. This is just nerves. I've made myself sick from emotional fantasizing. The lack of closure on this situation is making me loopy." She took a deep breath.

Cradling her head in her hands, she closed her eyes and wept, trying to force all of the pent-up stress out of her system in one tear-filled session.

Maybe she should go out—kayak, swim, bike, or hike, anything to keep her mind from wandering. When the sobbing finally ran its course, she looked up, staring blankly at the computer screen in front of her as she backtracked through her memory files. "When did we have unprotected sex? We didn't. We couldn't have. Did a condom break and we didn't know it?" she murmured to herself.

Her chin bumped her knuckles, sending a shimmer of pain up her jaw and focusing her mind. The only time she could think of was… after the incident in the parking lot between Gich and Jack, where she had been inadvertently struck in the jaw. She and Jack had gone back to his place. She'd been consumed by the pain in her jaw—okay, and by her libido, too, as well as seeing his space for the first time. She groaned. The Vicodin.

Crap, crap, crap! If it were true, then they were both at fault here and there could be no finger-pointing.

"Please don't let it be true. I'm not ready." The words hung in the air as if it were something she could swat away.

She picked up her phone and scheduled an

appointment with her gynecologist. "We're not living in the Dark Ages. Rather than buy a hundred tests and freak myself out as they register either a plus or minus, I can be a smart soul and know for sure."

Having made a grown-up decision to deal with the issue, she felt moderately better—more in control. Logging off her calendar program, she shut down her computer, grabbed her purse and keys, and headed out of the office. Nothing could keep her in this room for three hours if she didn't need to be there.

Opening the door to her waiting room, she poked her head out. "Frannie, I'll be back in time for the three p.m. I'm going to run a few errands. I'll just sneak out through the back door."

"Oh, Laurie. Right. Before you go, uh, Mr. Foster and Miss Hennessey canceled for this afternoon. Your schedule is completely clear. They both booked double sessions for next week." Frannie smiled at her. "You can go now, dear. Since we don't have anything scheduled, I'm going to take the rest of the afternoon off."

"You're leaving early?" Laurie was baffled. She stepped into the room.

"Yes, dear. Unless you have additional work." Frannie batted her eyes and waited for Laurie's response.

"Uh, no. You can go. Uh, Frannie." Laurie needed more details. She hated to cross-examine the woman but the cancellations sounded suspicious. "Did they cancel or did you call and reschedule them?"

Her assistant sniffed and then turned around and began straightening her desk. She didn't speak right away, paying enormous attention to her tasks. After she turned off her computer and retrieved her purse from the bottom drawer, Frannie stood and faced her. "I rescheduled them. These walls are thinner than you think, and sometimes a physical therapist needs some time off, too. I may not be a healthcare provider, but I work for one. I've learned a lot from you."

"I... I don't know what to say," replied Laurie after she'd figuratively pulled her chin off the floor.

"Well, you can fire me if you'd like. You know that I am very discreet, but I'm partial to you—been with you since you opened, and I plan on coming to work every day until they lay me in the ground. Unless you feel I need to be fired for my actions." Frannie stood her ground, willing to take the consequences either way. It was hard not to admire a woman with such guts.

"Do you hear the clients when they are on the table or in the chair as they discuss their personal issues?" asked Laurie. "I'd really need to do something about the sound."

"Of course not! When you have them sitting, I can barely hear a murmur, though occasionally I hear a scream or groan. Your desk is just on the other side of the door and, well, you're like a daughter to me, or a younger sister." Pointing her index finger in Laurie's direction, Frannie said, "When my boss is pacing up and down the room, slamming books, bolting for the bathroom, and worrying aloud about being pregnant, I can certainly be enough of a friend and assistant to make sure she gets what she needs. Understood?"

Shock riveted Laurie to the spot. Nodding her head in a bit of a stupor, unaware that anyone else knew of her dilemma, she finally found her voice and replied,

"Thank you, Frannie. Next time, though, please let me make the choice, okay?"

"Sure thing," said Frannie with a wink and a big smile. Approaching Laurie with wide-open arms, she hugged tightly, holding on too long. The air felt like it had been squeezed out of Laurie's body, but that sweet, tender Frannie smile was on the woman's face when they pulled apart. "If you're inclined, I'd like to know the outcome. You got me! I'm here either way, and I love little ones. I can bottle-feed and burp with the best of them, as well as answer phones." With that said, Frannie trundled out of the office, locking the front door behind her.

The knot in Laurie's throat was too big to swallow. She wanted to sit down on the couch and cry, but she had spent too much time doing that recently. Now was a time for action, and Laurie Smith was on the move.

Determined, with car keys and purse clenched in her hand, she headed back through her office and into her apartment and exited through the rear of her office/ home. Getting in her car, she headed for the ultimate joy, one she knew would bring her comfort.

She sped along Rosecrans Street and onto the I-5 freeway. The best spot in the whole world was Gator Beach, with one pit stop along the way for an ice cream from MooTime Creamery.

—⁓—

A triple-decker ice cream in a waffle cone, loaded with all the candy fixings, was exactly what she needed on a hot November day. While the rest of the world was plunging into winter, Coronado residents were still en-joying a relaxing autumn heat.

Deciding to stroll along Orange Avenue, it occurred to her that leaving her wallet in the car might stop her from impulse buying. Whenever she was in a heightened emotional state, there was a temptation to buy everything she could get her hands on to comfort herself. The best control technique was leaving the plastic—her credit cards—where she couldn't reach them. Stopping at her car, she stashed her purse in the trunk and pocketed her keys with a smile.

Ready for her relaxing walk with her luscious treat, Laurie strolled. Pausing at the bookstore, she noticed the display of new romance novels and mysteries. If the store had allowed ice cream, she would have been in there instantly, making a stack for her TBR—to be read—pile. But the sugar was providing so much comfort right now, she thought, she'd swing by the car and grab her purse and then stop in there on the way back. So much for willpower and good shopping techniques…

Hey, books are food! she told herself. *I can spend money on them.* Grinning, she knew novels would always be the only exception to her purchasing rules.

Her eyes caught a rather extraordinary display in the far window. The sign read Baby's First Books. Many of the stories had been ones her mother had picked out for her, before she was born. Several of them had helped her learn to read. Precious memories teased her mind, bringing her overwhelming feelings of security and joy.

A hand went to her belly, and for the first time she consciously considered what it would be like to have a baby. Could she be a mom? She waited for the panic of uncertainty to set in, but none of it came. Instead, there was a calm that permeated her system—a sense of well-being and capability. Her whole life, she'd been around kids and babies and was always comfortable with them. Next was the realization and understanding that she could really do this—be a mom.

Seeing the reflection of herself in the window—one hand on her belly and the other holding an ice cream cone—she contemplated how she would look pregnant. She smiled. "I'll be beautiful."

"You already are! Very sexy, too," said the coffee guy as he strode by her and into his little booth, positioned less than five feet away. "How about a date? Or would you like something to drink?"

Heat rose in her cheeks. She knew she was blushing. "No. Thanks. I'm good."

She knew he had just been flirting, but it was kind of sweet. Nice to know she was still desirable. Continuing her stroll down Orange Avenue, she passed the Mexican restaurant with wonderful garlic and onion smells coming from inside. Next to that was a tourist shop selling Coronado and Life Is Good T-shirts.

Women dressed in workout clothes, pushing babies in strollers, passed by her, and she realized she was suddenly seeing children everywhere.

As she crossed the street, she heard laughter coming from McP's. *Maybe I'll visit Greg. I haven't seen him in months. Oh, they have delicious potato skins, too.*

"It was too fucking funny!" That voice! Was that Jack?

Her steps quickened, drawing her closer. Scanning the faces, her eyes found him before she fully believed it was actually he. *Yes! It's Jack! He's alive!* And he was sitting at a table in the McP's courtyard, surrounded by women. The bastard was perfectly and absolutely fine.

That motherfucking jackass! I'm going to kill him!

Without realizing exactly what she was going to do, she parted the bevy of cackling women and walked right up to him. Jack Roaker stared at her as if a demon had just materialized.

Everyone was dead still as they stared at her. "Excuse us," she said to the women.

Without uttering a single syllable to the accused, she dumped her favorite ice cream treat on his head—cone and all—and then turned and walked away. That was it! She had nothing more to say to him. That rat bastard!

"Laurie! Wait! Laurie, I can explain everything." Jack caught her arm, stopping her retreat. "You owe me that much."

"I owe, you? Fuck you, Jack. I owe you nothing!" She held a hand on her belly. A noise was buzzing in her head, and she desperately wanted to throw up. *I am the daughter of a SEAL. I will not cry, and I will not throw up!*

"Wait. Please let me talk to you—face-to-face." As he turned her to look him in the eye, she felt her gut convulse as she threw up all over Petty Officer First Class Jack Roaker. "These ladies are from…"

Chunks of chocolate and strawberry streamed out of her mouth, landing all over his navy-blue running shorts and white T-shirt with the words *Doing It Dirty* written in gold. It seemed oddly appropriate to her, because Jack was all about mucking around in the dirt and with the ladies…

The chunks and liquid slid down his shirt and shorts and onto his golden skin. His grip was firm. He kept holding her arm, not moving. She had to give him a tiny amount of credit for not thrusting her away. She wasn't sure she could have been still while someone threw up on her.

"Shit! Laurie, are you okay?" Rather than wait for an answer, he scooped her up—carrying her at arm's length—and placed her in a chair. After she was seated, he brought her a glass of ice water from the waitress bar located only a few feet away from the table, at the back gate.

Grabbing a wet bar rag, he wiped himself off, and then seated himself across from her. He propped his elbows on his thighs, those heavily muscled legs that begged for a woman's touch. "Laurie. Listen to me. There's a lot, so much, I have to tell you…"

At this point, she was so numb, she didn't know what to say. She could see his mouth moving, but his words didn't penetrate. Wavering between anger and attraction, her brain was just too confused. What could he possible say that would resolve this intensely crazy situation?

Literally, she had caught the man red-handed…and blond-handed, and brunette-handed, too.

Heaven help her! The worst nightmare she could ever imagine had just come true: being knocked up by a military guy who screwed around and was completely dishonest with her. What could be worse?

The bevy of ladies drifted by them as tears filled her eyes. The brunette frowned at her and stuck out her tongue.

Laurie did not care one whit as the ladies left the bar. She just stared at Jack as he babbled on. Shaking her head, she decided she just didn't want to hear one more syllable come from his mouth. It was a jumble of discordant noises, and she couldn't take it one second longer.

"Don't worry! I'm not asking you for a damned thing. I want nothing from you!" Gulping in air, she attempted to steady her nerves, but she had so much more to say. "Stop! Just stop, Jack. Please. I don't want to hear it! I might be pregnant, and this is my choice, my decision."

Jack was trying to say something even as his eyes looked like they were popping out of his head. He looked shocked beyond words.

Taking several deep breaths, she said, "Listen. Don't talk to me. Don't come find me. Not at home. Not at work. Just let me be." Standing up, she wavered for a minute and then steadied herself. "I'm a strong woman, Jack. I'm just disappointed, and very sorry; you're not the man I thought you were. I don't need a person like you in my life. One SEAL that dicked around was quite enough in this lifetime. Good-bye, Jack."

Keep walking. Don't look back. This is for the best! She repeated the phrases as her feet took her forward and walked her out of McP's.

The pub had always been a safe place. As a child she had played on the patio; when she was a teenager, dates had taken her there for a meal; in the summertime, Gich and her father had brought her to enjoy the music on Sundays; and now, she'd just told the man she loved she might be pregnant and never wanted to see him again.

Had she come full circle? Or was life very much like the past—doomed to repeat patterns?

In the car, she started the engine and pulled into the rush of traffic. Cars sped by, beeping their horns at her.

The speedometer read twenty miles per hour, and she pushed the accelerator to make the car go faster.

Everything felt out of sync as she squeezed the steering wheel. Her fingers ached at the pressure and she had to loosen her grip. Fishing in her purse for her cell phone, she contemplated calling Gich and ratting on Jack. Rarely had she allowed herself to push that particular panic button, but was she justified here? What if she changed her mind and wanted to get together with him? "It'll never happen. I'm too angry."

Images ran through her head of the men brawling. "He'd kick Jack's ass if I asked him to." Staring at the ten digits, she just couldn't bring herself to call. Gich would be so disappointed in her, and Jack would be toast. Years ago, he had told her he wanted love, marriage, and a happily-ever-after for her. Now, she realized she wanted that, too, but fate seemed to have a different plan.

Dropping the phone on the passenger seat, she abandoned the call. In her heart of hearts, she just could not believe that Jack was a player. Something else must be wrong! Without the answer, though, her heart was breaking one tiny piece at a time, and pretty soon there would be nothing left.

A car cut her off, almost causing an accident. Her body shook.

Tears streamed down her face, making it too hard to see, so she put on her blinker and pulled over. Turning off the car engine, she put her head on the steering wheel and wept.

Thoughts whirled in her head. What had she done? She'd just kicked the man whom she loved out of her life! What was she, a complete idiot?

Confusion made the tears come faster. Her hands slammed against the steering wheel.

A loud rap on the window startled her. Laurie looked up to see a police officer. She turned the key halfway and lowered her window. "Y-y-yes."

"Ma'am, are you okay?" The police officer looked concerned. She needed that right now.

"No," she sobbed. "I'm not. I might be pregnant and I just told the father to take a flying leap." Groping in the center console, she found a small packet of tissues. She blew her nose. Speaking very fast, she asked, "Did I make the right decision? I mean, I did, right? I caught him with other women, and that says he's a jerk! Right?" She was now weeping with an open mouth, so she could breathe.

"Christ," he muttered under his breath. "Ma'am, is there someone you can call? I'll wait with you."

"P-p-papa G-g-gich," she stammered. Grabbing the cell phone from the empty passenger seat, she shoved it into the cop's hand. "I want Papa! Waaaaaahhhhh!"

A part of her brain knew she was opening not just a can of worms, but a box of vipers by inviting Gich into the situation, but the stress of the moment had gone well beyond her ability to cope. If ever a girl needed her daddy, it was now, and Gich was the closest thing she'd ever had to a parent who cared.

"Sir, this is Officer DeGines. Is this Papa Gich? Your daughter is sitting in her car on Orange Avenue in Coronado. I think she's going to need a ride home." The cop paused. "No, sir, she was not in an accident, but the, uh, hormones of her pregnancy might be adding to the, uh, situation, sir."

"What? Pregnant!" Gich's voice shouted over the phone, and she could hear him clearly. "Well, that fucking asshole! I didn't see that one coming. I'll be right there."

It seemed as if only a few minutes passed before Gich's truck pulled up in front of her car. The cigar stump usually clenched between his teeth was missing, and he was wearing a clean button-down Hawaiian shirt. He'd probably done that for her, made himself respectable so the cop would let him take her home.

Gich shook hands with the police officer. They traded comments and then Gich helped her out of the car. He didn't utter a single negative word as he placed her safely inside the cab of his truck and then fetched her purse and locked her vehicle behind him. "I'm here, sweet Laurie. You can relax."

She blew her nose on the wad of crumpled tissues in her hand. Suddenly, familiar scents tickled her nostrils: Gich's musky aftershave, the faint scent of his robust cigar, and sea air.

Help me! Would Gich take her to his home? Living in a small house on the edge of the ocean in Imperial Beach made everything smell like salt water. As a child, she'd adored it. Life was easier then.

Lying down on the seat, she placed her head on his lap. His hand stroked her hair for a few seconds and then settled on her shoulder for balance while he snapped the seat belt around her, and then he started the truck. Of course, he never put one on. He detested being restrained by convention or the law. The rebel instinct was alive and well in him. But he always made sure she was safe.

Slowly he pulled away from the curb and headed toward home. "Thank you, Papa Gich."

"I'm here, Laurie girl. I'll always be here." His words drew a few more tears to drip from her swollen eyes. She loved him more than she could say and was grateful for his presence in her life.

The tears dried, and unfortunately, hiccups surfaced from deep in her diaphragm to accompany them on their journey across the bridge.

"I love you, Laurie," he said, his voice heavy with emotion. "I will always stand by you." She knew he was telling the truth. Gich was always true to his word—the one man she could count on.

"Papa Gich will make it better," he said as she closed her eyes. Gich would take care of everything—just as a daddy should always do for a child.

Chapter 13

Keep your eyes up and your ass down.
        —Favorite saying of Moki Martin, retired SEAL

"ROAKER! YOU SELFISH SON OF A BITCH! WHAT THE hell were you thinking?" Gich appeared in front of him on the street, almost as if he had materialized there. The man flew under everyone's radar, and it didn't surprise Jack that his mentor would seek him out.

"Took you long enough," said Jack, annoyed. "For the record, those ladies had just toured the base and Spasick—Team ONE's Intel Officer—asked me to drop them off here. He had back-to-back commitments."

"Do you think I give a flying fuck about tourists? I'm talking about Laurie." Gich pointed a finger into Jack's chest and it felt like a spear skewering his heart.

He had nothing to say. No words. Whatever was coming his way, he'd own it like a man, but fuck, he wished he didn't have to do this.

"Oh, so that's how you're going to play it. No words. No defense. You just going to take it." Gich's face was red and his fists were like two large hams. "I'd like nothing better than to beat you senseless. Pretty fucking futile if you didn't fight back."

"Aw, you called me, pretty!" Unable to keep the sarcasm out of his voice, Jack shook his head. Emotions pounded his heart and brain, making his head feel like it was about to explode. When he looked up, Jack sought Gich's eyes with his own.

Tears slid quietly from his eyes. He didn't bother to wipe them away. "Gich, what the hell am I going to do? My whole life is screwed up and I'm hurting the people who are most important to me."

His gaze held tight and then slowly the fury slid off Gich's face. The man scratched his chin, hemming and muttering to himself. Finally, he took Jack's arm and led him to a table tucked next to a local café. They sat down on opposite sides of the table.

Jack couldn't stop the waterworks. Silently he wept as Gich watched him.

After a time, Gich punched Jack's arm and said, "C'mon Jack, crying lets the pain out, and now it's time to stop and address the problem. Give me the Sit Rep." This was one of the reasons Gich was a top BUD/S Instructor. He was always teaching the newbies life lessons.

Shrugging off the mantle of frustration and upset, Jack wiped his face on his shirt and looked Gich in the eyes again. "She told me not to contact her. I'm not letting her go through this alone. I want to marry her. I will provide for her and the child. And I need her to get that."

Leaning back in his seat, Gich stroked his mustache. "My boy, the fact you started this discussion focusing on her, with all the crap you have going on, shows me that you have honor. But I knew that about you—you stepped up in the past and continue to do it in the present. So then, why didn't you call her for six weeks?"

"The XO forbade it, ordered me to withdraw completely, and I follow orders. What happens if I don't? The repercussion for *not* doing as we are told is—I would be thrown in the brig, and Laurie could be in trouble for eliciting information that threatens national security." His emotions rode so high, Jack spoke as if he were running a race. "I know, it sounds like a load of shit! The killer hook was the fact that Laurie helped me. The fucking doctor who put all of this in motion couldn't and he hated that fact!"

Slamming his fist on the table, which made the steel and wood frame vibrate, Jack shook his head, wishing it were a big mistake. "I shouldn't have told that doctor anything. Not a goddamned thing! I was so fucking thrilled to have some of my memory back that I babbled like a two-year-old. Why didn't I think first… think about the fact that the XO would be reviewing any important notes with the doc?"

Gich's eyebrows lifted. "Well, well, well, that is interesting. All of your 'sessions' are confidential and the XO didn't have a right to know those exact details unless your doc's a dick and you pissed him off. Though the Navy does have a few peculiar regulations when it comes to National Security and civilians." He stretched his legs in front of him and said, "Let's face facts, Jack, you're a SEAL. You could have found a way around 'not talking' to her. Texting. A letter. Or calling your old mentor for a drink and asking him to pass a message on to the lady I didn't want you to date."

"Fuck! Why didn't I think of—?"

"You didn't use your noggin, Jack! Half of me wants to believe this cock-and-bull story of yours, and the other half feels like you're blowing smoke." Signaling the waitress, who had been lingering just inside the door, he ordered. "I'd like a black coffee with a shot of whiskey, and he'll have the same, but unleaded. Don't tell me that you don't have whiskey, because I saw your cook, Charlie, less than twenty minutes ago buying a bottle for some fancy damn recipe."

The waitress laughed and went off to fill the order.

"Jack, you're up Shit Creek and I don't know how to give you a paddle." Gich studied his fingers. "Laurie is my daughter. I adopted her, way back when her dad died, and I have to put her first. She isn't like you or me. We can make do. We can make something out of nothing and be fine. Our lives are hard and filled with pain and torment, but we chose it. She was born into it, yet that doesn't mean she wants to be tough all the time."

The waitress placed the coffees and some napkins in front of them and left. Gich sipped his drink that looked more whiskey than coffee. The cook knocked on the window and Gich toasted him with the mug.

Gich pressed Jack further. "What else did the XO say? I can't believe he didn't give you any other out."

"Fuck! Fuck! I can't believe I didn't catch that!" Jack sat up straight in his chair and looked Gich square in the eyes. "He told me to do what I needed to do—to heal. Fucking asshole, this was my out. Why didn't I see it before?"

"Because you got stuck on emotion—missing her— and not on how to maneuver around the equation." Gich snorted derisively. "Okay, now let's see if I can wrap my brain around this, Jack. This was a miscommunication of sorts, and you like Laurie, is that right?" Putting his arm on the table, Gich leaned forward, staring at Jack, almost daring him to be a lothario.

"Of course, I like her!" Jack was incredulous. "I more than like her. And… and I know I owe you an apology, too. I should have come to you. I'd like to do that now, ask you if I can be with her."

"That boat might have sailed, my brother. Laurie's not like other people. She's strong and can handle the truth, but deceit really pisses her off and her memory is eternal." Gich stroked his mustache in contemplation. "What are you going to do about that?"

"Everything I can possibly do… with your help and blessing, of course," said Jack. "I'll marry her if she wants a ring; otherwise I'll support her and be there when I can."

Gich finished his coffee and then said, "I'd refine that speech. You're not going to win agreement from her with that crap. Either love her and be with her or don't bother." Gich shrugged. "I went through something similar once. There was a lady I liked. I couldn't own it, and she married my best friend, my swim buddy. The life I should have had went to someone else, and I've spent the rest of my life picking up the pieces of one of my biggest mistakes."

Leaning back in his chair, Gich continued. "I'll be honest with you, Jack, you're not good enough for Laurie. No one is. But if it has to be a Team guy, then you're one of the best I know. Don't do this—go any further with Laurie—if you're planning to ring out. She doesn't need the heartache and neither do I."

Jack's gaze was steely. "I don't quit, sir. That word is not in my vocabulary."

Gich nodded. "We've got a long road ahead of us. I'll do what I can to bridge the gap, and the rest of it will be up to you."

"Thank you, Commander." Jack grinned and then added, "Dad."

A shiver went through Gich. "Shit! I guess that means I'm going to be a grandpa. I never thought I'd see that day so soon. And don't you be spreading the gratitude so swiftly. You're not secure, Jack. Not yet." Gich wiped his nose on the back of his hand. "Come on, let's go to McP's for a real drink. This is going to require a serious strategy and thorough planning."

Bringing another shot of tequila to his lips, Jack slammed it back and placed the empty glass on the table. The liquid burned a fiery trail to his gut. His head was already swimming and he knew it probably wasn't the wisest move, but whatever challenge Gich put in front of him, he took. In many ways, it did numb the pain.

Fuck me!

His stomach rolled, preparing to toss the contents of three hours of drinking steadily. Jack stood, nodded to Gich, and actually made it to the men's room before he hurled seven shots and six beers into the toilet.

When his stomach was empty, he leaned his head against the wall. *Why am I doing this?* Within ten minutes of arriving at McP's they'd achieved a plan. Gich was going to talk to Laurie and convince her to hear her former lover and, he hoped, soon-to-be husband out.

Hell! A husband! I'm not ready for marriage. Yet Laurie was different. The woman was capable of pushing his head and heart ten different ways. Feeling his cock slide into her was a slice of heaven he'd be happy reliving for the bulk of his days.

God only knew if it would change things in their relationship, being married. Some of his brethren said it did and others really liked the security of being married. No more going from woman to woman or having to play "Guess your insecurities" or "Are you more fucked-up than me?"

The throbbing in his head lessened and he made his way to the sink. He washed his hands and splashed water on his face. Using his shirttail as a towel, he mopped his eyes and mouth and then straightened his clothing. Knowing this was as presentable as it was going to get, he left the washroom and headed back to the table.

Two more shots were waiting for him. Gich eyed him and then nodded. "You should have plenty of room for more, now."

Jack wasn't exactly sure what made him shake his head. Nonetheless, he sat down at the table and said, "I'm done, Gich. I've never been a drinker and I'm not going to start now."

"Good on you, son," replied Gich as he reached over and downed the drinks. "I knew you had a steady hand on the helm, Roaker. Now, keep thinking and living that way. Between us, I had to know that you would say your limit." Placing the glasses on the table, he signaled to the waitress for a check. "Laurie's biological daddy drank until everything disappeared. You and I have spent enough time together that I have a pulse on your personality, but I had to know if you had a line."

Digging bills out of his wallet, Gich dumped them

on the table next to the check. Then he leaned forward. "Toe the line, Jack."

"Yes, sir." That was a promise. "Out of curiosity, if I had kept drinking, what would you have done?"

Gich shrugged his shoulders. "Probably sobered you up and made you drink again, until you showed me a line." He scratched his chin. "Though I could see the part of you that wanted to take the punishment I was dishing out. There's a wiser part inside that wouldn't let you put yourself in jeopardy and was quite done with the game."

"Yeah," said Jack was a slow grin. "My gut said it was time and I listened. Guess that's good."

"Always," said Gich. "Now help an old man over to that Mexican restaurant on the next block for some food. I'm not going to waste excellent tequila by being a sissy bear and throwing it up. Instead let's get some tamales and really give the alcohol something useful to do."

"Sure thing. I need coffee," said Jack as he accompanied the only man alive who could bring him to his knees and build him back up with a single look. Today, though, all alone he'd turned a corner. A piece of him had grown—away from Gich and patriarchs and "must dos"—to be independent of the past and to know how clearly he was taking deliberate steps to shape his own future.

He was sure some men missed the signal to take a life-changing turn. The tools to make his life what he wanted it to be were right here, inside of him. It was about desire. In his mind anything was possible, if strategized properly.

Chapter 14

Pain is inevitable. Suffering is optional.

—Anonymous

THE SCREEN DOOR SQUEAKED AS LAURIE OPENED IT wide to reveal Gich standing on her welcome mat. Somehow, she just didn't feel particularly welcoming at that moment. "Hi, Papa Gich."

"That has to be the most unenthusiastic, forlorn greeting I've ever heard." He lifted his eyebrows. "Are you going to invite me in or am I going to have to stand outside?"

"Sorry. Come on in." As she walked into her living room and over to her favorite stuffed leather chair, she said, "Since when do you need to be invited?"

Gich sat down in the twin of her chair. They had been a gift from him when she had moved in here, and the supple brown chairs had always been a comfort. Today, the weather was a little warm and her skin stuck to the sides as she moved. When Gich stared at her with a certain deadeye gaze, she knew that either she was in trouble or a sensitive topic was about to be broached. She wasn't in the mood for any of it, but what choice did she have? He was the closest thing she had to family, and if he had taken the time to come here and speak to her, she would listen.

"Hey, baby girl. How are you?" he asked.

"Fine," she said nodding her head. "The ob-gyn is going to call me back in a few hours."

"You look better, Laurie." He nodded at her. Gich didn't look very comfortable in his chair either. "Did you get the tears out?"

"Yeah. You know, there are always more," she replied. She couldn't take the tension and finally said, "What did Jack say?"

Gich sighed. "Christ! Laurie, you're too intuitive for your own good." He scratched his mustache, smoothing the corners into place, and then spoke slowly and thoughtfully. "Jack got slammed for seeing a physical therapist outside of the military medical system. He was ordered not to talk to you again. Of course, that dumbass wasn't using his brain. He could have found another method for getting a message to you. All that's beside the point now. Of course, I talked to him." He paused to watch her. When she didn't say anything, he continued. "He cares about you. Laurie. He's not perfect, but he's a good guy."

She'd been chewing the edge of her lip as Gich spoke. She looked at her clasped hands. The fingers were white-knuckled from being squeezed so hard and she unknotted them. Flexing her hands to get some blood back into them, she stared out the window.

Hundreds of thoughts swirled in her head. Her greatest hope had just been fulfilled. She was important to Jack and another factor had kept them apart. Yet she felt disconnected, empty. Had so much emotion passed that she could not rally even a little bit of excitement?

Straightening her shoulders and adding some steel

to her backbone, she looked at Gich. "Are you here with an olive branch to start a peace treaty between Jack and me?"

His eyes traveled up and down her and then focused on her gaze. "Fuck, no!"

"Then, what are you doing here, Gich?"

"I'm a parent, caring for his child, and I'm sharing a message that should have been conveyed six weeks ago." He watched her. He had this way of doing it that made her feel like a monkey in a zoo.

"What do you want me to say?" She needed more information. She was a little perturbed that Gich seemed to be on Jack's side right now. Her foot began tapping, a surefire sign that her temper was coming into play.

"That you'll judge the situation with a logical mind and not with a full head of steam." Gich stood. Closing the distance between them, he touched her cheek. His eyes were gentle as he spoke. "Laurie, go find out the truth. Whatever you do from there, I support you."

He drew her slowly into his arms as if he were deliberately gathering a wild beast, to soothe and calm it. "Getting hurt is one of the ways human beings learn. For example, if this is a learning lesson, what do you want to get out of it?"

Her words were somewhat muffled against his chest. "Don't date military men."

He lightly smacked her backside. "You can do better. Come on."

"Okay, you're right." She rubbed her face against his shirt. The scent of Gich wrapped her in the familiarity of cigars and coffee and home. "Why isn't this easier? Aren't the right relationships supposed to just fall into place?"

"Hell, no! Physically, they are easy. That's basic chemistry. But you have to be willing to face the tough stuff. Someone who can call you on your shit is more precious than gold, especially if it is mutual." His explanation hit a home run for her. As much as she hated to admit it, Gich was right. The annoying part was, nine times out of ten, he was correct. *Dammit!*

"Got it?" As Gich pushed her back to arm's length, his large strong hands held firmly to her shoulders.

"Yeah." She sniffed.

"Don't take too long. Time can build a wall, if you allow it." He chucked her gently under the chin.

Her whole life, Gich had encouraged her to see beyond a problem's emotional impact. He'd asked her to look at the root and to examine life from an instinctual gut sensibility. Teaching her to go toe-to-toe not just with bullies, peers, and men… but also with life itself. How could she do less than he requested?

"Okay, Papa Gich," she replied, feeling appeased even if still a wee bit confused, contrite, and still frustrated with Jack. Some of her thinking was clear and had revealed itself in this discussion, though none of it had included an apology from Jack or solutions to what her future path was going to have in it. Her world had gotten significantly more complicated in a short space of time and she needed help.

Would he marry her? Did she want that? Could she raise a child alone? Yes. But she wanted a father figure in her child's life. A whole family, so her child would not have to grow up the way she had. And the only father she desired for her child was Jack.

"I gotta go." Gich spoke with that signature kindness

that had melted her heart for an entire lifetime. He drew her closer one last time, smelling of sweet cigars and his undeniable warmth, and kissed her forehead before releasing her.

Turning away thoughtfully, he walked slowly to the door. Before he opened it, he said, "Just remember, I'm here if you need me. I'm only a phone call away. Your dad is always here."

The emotion was thick in his voice.

Her throat choked up, too. Without him, her world would have been hell, and she loved him dearly. "I know. Thanks." Laurie knew she had lucked out by having him in her life. "I'll call you later."

"Great, baby girl." As the door squeaked open, he paused. "I'm proud of you. I don't tell you often enough, but I love you, Laurie." Then he was through the door and walking away.

The screen door protested as she pushed it wide. "I love you, too, Gich. I'll always be your Laurie, your baby girl."

Cars passed by and the street was empty of pedestrians. In the blink of an eye, Gich had disappeared. Always the stealthy SEAL, and forever the heroic dad, she would appreciate him and love him for all of her life.

The sound of her cell phone ringing drew her back inside. She allowed the screen door to bang shut, and then scooping up the phone, she answered on the next ring. "Hello. Hello, this is Laurie."

"Hi, Laurie. This is Dr. Gainer. We have the results from your blood tests. You're not pregnant. I believe..." His words droned on as she tried to understand what she was hearing. The rush of blood in her ears and head was so loud, she had to swallow several times to try to calm herself.

"Dr. Gainer. Can you please repeat that?" Her voice shook and she had to wrap both hands around the phone to keep it positioned to her ear.

"The blood test was negative. You're not pregnant. Your hormones are out of sync due to your previous use of the pill. Oftentimes, women who have been on the pill for many years have a rather dramatic reaction once they go off it. If you had let me know ahead of time that you were planning to go off the pill, then I would have suggested you switch to another brand and taper down. Is that what you'd like to do?" He paused.

She searched her brain, trying to find the right words. "I'll get back to you."

"Fine. In the meantime, I suggest you start back up on the dosage you currently have. This should get your hormone levels back into the proper cycle. If you have any difficulty, let Mary know, and we'll get you into the office immediately. I see by your records that you should still have a two-month supply."

"Yes. Thank you." Her answer felt far away, breathy, and very unsteady. Could he hear that she was freaking out?

"Good. You're all set then. Good-bye, Laurie." Then he hung up.

Slowly she disconnected the phone and laid it gently on the table next to her. Her legs seemed to lose all of their strength and she sank to the floor. Her body felt boneless.

Seeing clearly the mess she had made of her personal

life, and the stress she had caused herself and her loved ones, filled her with regret.

Mainly, though, it was the loss of a child that had never been that felt like a dagger in her heart. She knew now she really wanted a child, and to experience the joys of being a mom. This fact was clear for the first time in her life. This was what she truly and desperately wanted for herself and her future.

Chapter 15

I only regret that I have but one life to give for my country.
—Nathan Hale

A NIGHT AND DAY HAD PASSED SINCE HIS TALK WITH
Gich. Somewhere in there, the hangover had finally dissipated to a manageable dull throb. Jack liked beer, but he didn't have a taste for hard liquor. He had no interest in developing one, either.

He locked his apartment door and headed for his Jeep. Sliding into the driver's seat, he switched on the ignition, turned over the engine, and pulled into traffic. About twenty minutes ago, he'd received a call from Chalmers. Both he and Billings had been moved out of ICU and into a patient ward. They wanted to talk to him.

Traffic moved slowly. It figured that this would be one of those times that he wanted to zip over the bridge and arrive at his destination quickly, and it wasn't possible. Patience was his friend. He'd spent days stuck in a hole in a jungle before waiting for the "go" on an attack. Urine and waste had run down his pant leg, and yet he held his position. He'd been lucky that the place he was waiting in stank, because it had covered his own stench.

Practicing isometrics in the tiny cramped spot and moving slower than an inchworm to drink water or eat a power bar had made him capable of anything. The enemy had been only four yards away and they had not discovered him until the call came and he rose with knife at the ready.

Sitting in traffic was a piece of cake compared to that experience. His eyes tracked a seagull as it flapped its wings, soaring high. The winged surfer caught a current and sailed for at least half a mile.

Some of life's best moments had that "sailing" aspect, an easiness that sat right in the heart and gut. He could list a handful of people who really sat well with him. Chalmers and Billings were on that list. He hoped his buddies were in decent shape. Man, he was really looking forward to seeing those guys.

The traffic finally let up and his Jeep roared over the bridge and onto the Five. Taking the exit for Balboa Naval Hospital, he drove up the hill and found a parking spot. It felt good to be coming here for a purpose other than group therapy.

Stepping through the front door of the building, the smell hit him, some kind of heavy-duty institutional cleaner mixed with rubbing alcohol and fear. God, he hated this place! Nonetheless, he hotfooted it past the welcome desk and loads of people asking questions, and took the stairs up to the correct floor. Winding his way through the building, he located the ward. His Teammates were there, and he was going in no matter what! Fuck, he wanted them to be okay!

Jack took a deep breath and walked inside the room. He spotted Chalmers immediately. Team banter popped out of his mouth like a reflex. "What the hell are you slackers doing sitting on your asses?"

Chalmers looked up. He was sitting in a chair next to Billings's bed, and the growing grin on his face was an excellent indication that he was pleased to see Jack. Chalmers's retort was swift. "It was my turn for ass patrol, want to take over? Hey, Roaker, how're you doing?"

"Hell, yes! My ass could stand to grow a little. There's only muscle back there for the ladies to hold on to," said Jack, going over to Chalmers and hugging him. The man wrapped his right arm and the stump of his left around Jack and held tight for a long time.

When they released, Jack nodded at Billings, who was out cold. "How's he doing?"

Chalmers shook his head. "I don't know. Hey, let's go over to the window, okay? I want to feel the sun, but I don't want to leave the room in case he wakes up." There were some bandages around Chalmers's legs and back, and his ass was hanging out of the back of his gown. The man was moving about with ease, though, which was a good sign.

They walked less than ten feet to the other side of the room, where the window was opened as wide as it could get. They both stood there, staring out. The silence was comfortable, and the people moving about below looked calm, reassuringly ordinary as they went about their business.

Jack waited. He knew Chalmers would speak when he was ready, and Jack was not in any rush. His apology to Laurie would have to wait a little longer. Being there for his buddies was enormously important to him. When he was in the hospital, he hadn't been able to speak to anyone and that had been tough on him, like being cut off from his family, who were also his best friends. It was hard on the psyche.

Finally Chalmers spoke. "Listen, Peter's not doing so well. Every time he wakes up, he starts screaming. For now, he's sedated; they gave him a shot about a half hour ago. Bullets tore up one leg, and he lost a chunk of his calf off the other. He'll be able to walk with a prosthetic limb and eventually even be able to run again after a lot of therapy. You know, he's a marathoner? He'll adapt, because that is our way. The tough part is that his whole world was action and SEAL Team." The SEAL's face was grim. "None of us do well when we're benched."

Chalmers didn't look like he'd slept in a long time, or if he'd had sleep… none of it was peaceful. Most likely Peter was getting him up. His own nightmares were certainly beginning to haunt him. God knew Jack understood that! Maybe he could figure out a way to give him a break.

"What about you? Is there anything you need?" Jack asked. It was doubtful that Chalmers would ever be deployed again, either. It was the Navy's loss, too, because these guys were incredible in the field. They had the right attitude, killer reflexes, and were as dependable as the sunrise.

"All I want is to change the outcome of that Op," said Chalmers. The makings of a beard had begun on his face, and he scratched it thoughtfully. "Though I could be scoring a lot of pussy this way." He waved his mangled arm at Jack, and then he sat down in the chair next to his bed. "Listen Jack, I want to thank you for saving my life."

"Shit, Chalmers, you don't need to... Fuck, you would have done the same." Jack didn't seek anyone's gratitude. He just wanted his buddies safe and alive, and he wanted out of this current memory mess.

"Hell, yeah, I would! Still, let me say it, okay? 'Cause when Billings comes out of this, he's going to go from screaming to angry before he gets anywhere near acceptance, and I don't want you to take anything he says to heart or have it kick you in the gut. Eventually, he'll be glad he's alive. Maybe doing that marathon crap with him will help. He'll have an advantage over the guys who have already been doing it in chairs, because his arms are like forty times stronger." Chalmers took a long deep breath and slowly exhaled. He looked seriously spent. "Fuck, I'll make it work."

"You guys have always been tight," Jack added, leaning against the edge of the window frame. The air from outside blew gently across his skin, bringing him ease. If he had a choice, he'd spend more of his day outdoors.

"As you know, Billings kept me from going over the edge when Betty and I divorced, and then when we remarried again. She's back East with the kids right now, at her parents' house in Virginia. I told her to stay there until I'm discharged. I want Billings to be in a good place. Hell, I'll take him back East with me if I have to." The comment was solemn and sober. Chalmers's eyes went to Billings's bed briefly. They were swim buddies and had operated together for many, many years.

Slowly his eyes tracked back to Jack, and he allowed him to see the acute sorrow, and then it was gone. He'd hide it and so much emotion from the rest of the world, but a Team guy was inner circle.

Yes, we tell it like it is.

Chalmers cleared his throat and asked, "How are you doing, without Don?"

The question hit Jack in the gut. Everyone wanted to know the answer to that horrifically nightmarish question, and yet Chalmers had been the first person to ask it boldly and straight to his face. The rest of the world danced a jig and used leading questions, just expecting him to spill his guts. That would never happen! But one of his brothers asking… well, God bless him. For Chalmers he'd deal with his feelings and slog through it!

Jack's throat was clogged with sentiment, but he managed to say, "How do I feel? It fucking sucks! There aren't enough swear words in existence…" Shaking his head, Jack couldn't push the horrible feelings away. "I feel like I'm missing a piece of myself." Jack realized what he said, and then laughed. Would his buddy take offense? "Shit, Chalmers! I'm sorry…"

Waving his stump at Jack, Chalmers gave a short burst of laughter. "No worries. If I can't joke about it, I'm screwed! As to Don… yeah, I get it. Fucking crazy." Keeping this light, he grabbed his cock through the thin hospital gown. "At least I can still make love to my wife. At the end of the hall are the guys who have to use bags to crap. Man, I'm not ready for that stuff."

Chalmers punched Jack lightly in the leg. "Lighten up, Roaker." Humor and seriousness danced together in his eyes. "I want your oath, if it ever gets that bad, just take Billings and me out to the desert and leave us alone with some C-4. Got it?"

All three of them were Explosive Ordinance Disposal. It was pretty rare to be both EOD and a SEAL, and there were only a handful of those guys in the Teams. Each of them even had their own stashes, not that they'd share that info with anyone else.

"I promise, Bill." Jack didn't give his word lightly. He'd give his life to keep it. The men shook hands. Then Jack said, "For me, I'd rather my chute didn't open on a free fall." Jack leaned in. "It'd be a death with a great view."

"Are you fucking nuts? What if you just break some bones and really bang your shit up without doing yourself in? Hell no." Chalmers's eyes were point-blank earnest behind the joking. Jack knew what he was asking. He would want someone to do the same, if he couldn't do it himself. All of them were a long way off from that destination. There was a lot of life still surging through each one of them. The Teams made sure guys who had been injured understood that they continued to be an important part of the Navy. Unfortunately, it would take some time for those two to get back to work.

"Ah, man, I just realized, they're going to make you do group therapy. I feel for you," said Jack, kicking Chalmer's foot.

"Motherfucker, I hate that shit! You got any e-x-p-l-o-s-i-v-e-s in your Jeep?" Chalmers winked at him.

"Sorry, man. Fresh out." Jack grinned. In truth, he had a few guns and a bunch of ammo in locked boxes as well as some knives under his seats. Made him feel better, to be armed or at the very least prepared for an emergency. "Hey, uh, have Seeley and Pickens been here?"

The emotion slid out of Chalmers's eyes as he leaned toward Jack, and his voice was instantly defensive and very cold. "Why do you ask, Jack?"

"I've heard that they're soiling my name." Jack had

to know the truth, and he had been waiting ages to speak to Chalmers and Billings. This could be a golden chance to find out what was really going on.

"Not to me. They wouldn't dare. Knotts, Billings, and I were in the same class, and of course you, Don, and Duncan were two below us." Settling back in his chair, Chalmers's eyes moved up and down, studying him. "Those guys! They always hit me wrong, like they're walking out of sync with the rest of the Team. When they were patients here, Seeley came and found me in the ICU and told me some cock-and-bull story about you setting off a bomb, and that's why everyone got hurt. I told him he was an idiot and that I saw you dive onto Don when those shots were making his body dance. Then you were lifting him and running.

"I was firing everything I had. It didn't seem to make a bit of a difference." Chalmers sighed and then he squeezed the bridge of his nose as if this were the source of his pain. When he dropped his hand, he laid it thoughtfully on the armrest. "There was an explosion in the factory. I don't remember much after that, except waking up twice, once while you were carrying me and the other time in the hospital." His hand banged the fabric of the chair, punctuating each sentence. "I'm glad we could come here rather than heading to Walter Reed. Yeah, it would have been closer to Betty and the kids... but I needed to deal with all of this by myself first, before they see me. Good thing they love Peter."

Jack knelt in front of his buddy. Their eyes were level now. "Bill, I wish things were different. I'm sorry."

"Me, too." He looked away for a few minutes, studying the floor, and then his gaze snapped back. "Jack, don't apologize, though. You saved the whole Team. Dead or alive, we never leave a man behind, and you got top marks." Chalmers shut his eyes and pushed on his eyeballs with his thumbs. "Fuck this! Let's change the topic before you have me crying like a little girl." When he opened his eyes again, Chalmers's character- istic spark was back. "Do you want to know what I'm dying for?"

"A beer," replied Jack easily. A knot loosened in his gut. Bill Chalmers had always been honest and plainspoken. The man's story fit with Gerry's version, and now, he just needed his own puzzle pieces to be revealed so he could view the entire picture and under- stand what happened.

"Damn straight. Got any?" Chalmers wagged his eyebrows.

Jack admitted, "I've got a cooler in the back of the Jeep. They aren't cold, though." The happiness on Chalmers's face was priceless. He'd fill the room with kegs to see that look again.

"Bring them on. It'd do my spirit a world of good to taste that barley tang on my tongue." Chalmers stared at him as he blasted the order. "Well, hop to it, son. The minutes are passing and I am thirsty!" Grabbing the bedpan off his nightstand, he held it up for his friend to see. Offering a grin, he said, "Ice will cool 'em, and I can't think of a more appropriate vessel."

Having spent time with Chalmers bolstered Jack's spirit. Peter Billings didn't wake while he was there. Jack would go back in a few days. Knowing that his

Teammate was struggling meant he was going to help out more. It's what they did for each other. Next time, though, he'd bring a cooler filled with Beck's and Bud Select, and a bag of burgers.

His mouth was dry and he was thirsty. After having only one beer, because he was driving and had a major event to go deal with, he considered grabbing a bottle of water. Time wasn't in his favor.

Glancing in the rearview mirror, he caught sight of himself and quickly smoothed his hair. He had shaved twice since this morning, making sure his chin and cheeks were baby-bottom smooth. When he and Laurie made up—and he was determined that they would—he didn't want his rough stubble to scratch her delicate skin.

A red Porsche behind him sounded its horn. *Beep. Beep!*

He checked the speedometer. Sixty! Hell, he was driving his Jeep on the Five like a little old lady and he had a death grip on the steering wheel, too! His foot hit the accelerator and the Jeep shot forward, giving the Porsche room to maneuver and, of course, pass him.

Taking the exit toward Rosecrans, he squealed around the corners, moving at lightning speed. Traffic was bunching up ahead of him, and he took his foot off the accelerator.

"Give me a break," he murmured to himself. "I'm overthinking this thing. I'll go. I'll speak to her and then we'll make up." God, he hoped there would be sex in that equation!

He caught a string of green lights and sailed down the street. Spotting an empty parking spot close to her office, he pulled in and set the emergency brake. He turned off the ignition, banged his hands on the steering wheel to let go of all the energy, pocketed his keys, and then grabbed his stuff and headed in the direction of her office door.

"Crap!" His palms were sweating again. He balanced the load in his arm as he wiped first one hand and then the other on his jeans for what seemed like the tenth time, before he reached the front door of her office.

The last time he'd been this nervous, it was an hour before Hell Week was over and the instructors had been busting their chops hard about how only one or two men would be making it through. The rest of them would be kicked out to sea, which in layman's terms meant being stuck back in the Fleet, or whatever branch the soldier originally hailed from. For him, if he hadn't made the Teams, he would probably have been a sailor stuck on a carrier, swabbing decks for the next twenty to thirty years.

He'd nearly crapped his pants with relief when the instructors had told him that he was secure. Instead, he'd asked for permission to use the head, ran to the bathroom, and sat. Shit! That had been a memorable moment.

Mental experiences punctuated by physical outcomes stuck with him. He knew that about himself. If he had to learn a piece of knowledge, he could tie it to something tangible. For example, his grandfather had taught him multiplication tables as they played catch. Another trick was to process his emotions through exercise, which had always served him well. Also, it had made him into a tough-as-nails SEAL, and those skills would get him through this latest challenge. He was sure of it! Even if he had to climb the jagged mountain of Laurie's wrath, he was going to scale it deliberately and with a full pack of ammo.

In his arms, which were overladen, were a teddy bear, chocolates, red roses, and a bottle of sparkling apple juice. Jack used his foot to open the front door of the business and went inside. The air-conditioning was blasting full force and it felt good. His polo shirt was almost completely soaked and he needed to air-dry.

"F-F-Frannie isn't in today and L-L-Laurie l-l-left a note saying she was r-r-running l-l-late." The voice came from the teenager sitting in the corner of the room. The darkness hid her, and he had to squint to make her image out. "You're Jack, aren't you?"

"Yes. Who are you?" Jack sat down two chairs away from the teenage girl. The young woman was most certainly in high school, pretty in a girl-next-door way, and shy.

She spoke slowly and very precisely, pronouncing each syllable succinctly. "I am Clarissa."

"Nice to meet you, Clarissa. You're a patient of Laurie's, right?" Jack almost smacked his head when he saw a look of embarrassment on her face. "I mean, I'm one, also."

"Yes, it's okay. I am overcoming a jaw injury." She hung her head. Then her fingers found a clump of hair near her face and she pulled it with harsh-looking tugs. "It's fucking frustrating!"

"Well, your swearing is pretty good." Jack grinned at the teenager, giving her his gentlest smile. So young, and so much yet to go through. Were the kids at school

kind or cruel? His guess was that they were jerks. High
school had been rough for him and he'd never want to
go through it again.

The nice smile must have worked, because Clarissa
smiled back.

Then they both laughed. The awkwardness was broken and they sat comfortably in silence for a few beats.

Jack was worried about what he should and shouldn't
say to Laurie. Finally, he couldn't take it anymore and
decided to do some recon with the kid. "Hey Clarissa,
you're a girl and you know Laurie, right? Could you
give me some advice? You know, some pointers."

"Sure." The teen nodded her head in agreement.
Perking up, she straightened herself in her chair and
even turned toward him. "Shoot."

"Great! Here's the thing. I screwed up. Majorly,
too. Enormously. What could I do to get her to forgive
me?" Jack hoped the teen had some good idea to add to
acting like a lovesick horse's ass or asking for mercy,
which he hated to do. There had to be an easier way to
talk to women.

Clarissa considered his question for a few heartbeats
and then she replied, "Well, it's always good to apologize. And you could remind her of the h-h-happy times,
relive the h-h-happiness. FYI, g-g-girls do not like to be
kept in the d-d-dark."

"Good to know," said Jack. He was elated. This kid
was a fucking genius! Not just for the advice, either,
but for being candid. "Thanks, Clarissa, you're terrific."

She'd given him an idea on how to patch his own
memory, and how to attack his own problem of how he
could re-create the Op. Man, he prayed Laurie would

forgive him, because he would definitely need her help to carry out the plan.

"Pumping the kid for information, are you?" asked a rather terse and angry-looking physical therapist answering to the name Laurie Smith. The beautiful woman stood in the doorway—framed by sunlight—looking like some kind of an avenging angel or Boudicca, Briton Queen. Hey, he loved PBS, but not like this!

Strangely enough, before Laurie, he couldn't remember ever saying he was sorry to anyone. Now, here he was for a second time, bowing his ego to woo her—the woman and the professional. Personally, he'd rather not fuck up that much! "Laurie…"

Laurie held up a hand, halting his words. "Clarissa, may we switch our session to tomorrow?"

"Yes," said Clarissa with a bright smile. A clever spark in her eyes spoke volumes of her understanding of the situation. The boy that captured that young lady's heart would definitely be walking a straight line. "I'll c-c-close the d-d-door be-h-h-hind me."

The teen gathered her books and bag and headed out. She gave Jack a little wave as she left.

He liked her. "She's a great kid."

"Clarissa is a fifty-year-old in a teen's body." Laurie made sure the door was shut and then she locked it. Marching past him, she went straight through the waiting room and into her office. "Are you coming?"

"I wish I were," he murmured, and then he was following in her footsteps, treading the path into the sanctuary of her office. The air-conditioning was set to subzero temperatures and he couldn't imagine that clients didn't complain when they started to suffer from hypothermia.

On the other hand, he supposed that Laurie's clients would probably stay awake—teeth chattering, knees knocking, and just plain cold!

"Look at this!" Laurie held a piece of paper in front of her as if it were an award certificate. She waved it in front of him like a flag. Her gesture was starting to piss him off a little bit. "I need you to focus, Jack."

He needed to get this apology out of the way before she launched into something new, so he started talking over her. "Laurie! Can't you at least hear me out, before you give me a restraining order? Dammit! You're making it really fucking hard for me to apologize."

Jack pushed the paper aside and started pacing in short lengths in front of her desk. "I'm sorry. I made a huge mistake and I want to make it up to you. There were circumstances surrounding my inability to call you, but I should have found a way to communicate with you. I realize that now."

He stopped pacing and looked at her. "I want to be with you. I think of you day and night, and it's making me nuts—not being able to talk to you, touch you, and make love to you. If I have to spend the rest of my days, I'd like to—"

"Jack!" Laurie screamed at him, effectively cutting him off. She looked annoyed and happy at the same time. Now, he was confused.

"What? Laurie, what?" Jack sighed. Didn't all women want men to grovel at their feet? Shouldn't she let him continue, because his tolerance for humbling himself was about five minutes long? "Laurie, help me out here."

"Yeah, Jack, I got the apology. Not only from the

run-on sentences but also by the look of the greeting-store-style make-up gifts. Thank you. I get it! I accept it, and I need you to see this." She thrust the paper into his overfilled hands. The gifts shifted into his other arm as he managed to grab the single page she gave him... except for the bear, which landed on the floor.

Picking up the teddy bear, she held it as a woman would a baby. When she looked up, he was smiling at her, and he touched her hand. The sweetness filled him.

Methodically, he put the other gifts on the table and grabbed the sheet with both hands.

Slowly, she smiled back and then laid the bear on her desk next to them. "Jack, the page."

He studied the piece of paper with a fax number, date, and page information at the top. Was this an important document? What the hell was it? The abbreviations and list of numbers meant nothing to him, and he had no idea what he was supposed to be excited about. He shrugged. "I don't get it. What is this?"

"I'm not pregnant." She said the words slowly. Then repeated them. "Jack, I am not pregnant. Did you hear me?"

There was a long pause as they stared at each other.

When he opened his mouth, the question that he couldn't keep out of his brain came out. "I heard you. I just... How does that change things for us? I want to be with you, Laurie. No matter what, do you forgive me?"

She seemed not to hear him as she fingered the foot of the bear, because Laurie launched words out of her mouth like missiles. "I mean, I could be one day, but not right now. I had a hormone imbalance. Isn't that amazing? Right before we got together, I had gone off the pill and my body flipped out." She squared her shoulders and stepped toward him. "It's my turn to say I'm sorry, and I hope you can forgive my outburst to Gich! I'm a pretty private person, and I usually keep my personal life—our life together—under wraps." When she let go of the bear's foot, she looked at him. Her sorrow was crystal clear, as were her feelings. She cared about him.

"Of course. Sure I will," said Jack, sitting down. Relief swept through his body. "We all have our moments, Laurie." His feelings were definitely mixed now. On one hand, he wanted to be a dad someday, and on the other, he was glad the time wasn't now. He wanted the news of the birth of his child to be greeted only by joy. Could he tell her that he was both happy and sad?

As if she were reading his mind, she said, "You really can't hide emotion from me. I can read it in your eyes. I have mixed feelings, too. We do have a lot in common, don't we?"

"Sure. Did you hear me say that I want to be with you?" he asked.

The plainspoken words touched her. His honesty released the pain, and the wall that had been crafted by childhood fears crumbled. This man, despite all odds, wanted her just as she was, and he was willing to be real about his own feelings and life. "Oh, Jack, I want to be with you, too." She lightly stroked the top of his hand and then smiled.

She turned it over so that she could tease her fingers over the center of his palm. "We're both nuts, aren't we?"

"Probably." He nodded his head. There was a good probability they could survive this… this experience.

Was she ready for the good stuff now? "Is it time for make-up sex?"

"Almost." Her eyes sparkled and Jack decided she had never looked so beautiful. "But first, I owe you something."

Laurie didn't give him time to expect it as she turned to the side and elbowed him in the gut. The air whooshed out of him. When he could speak, he asked, "What did you do that for?"

"Who were those women at McP's?" She raised her eyebrows.

"They had just had a tour of the base. I'd taken them to McP's for our Intel Officer. Besides which, they were waiting for Jackson and Kirby, who were running late and asked me to meet them. The brunette is Kirby's kid sister and those were her sorority sisters. They just did an auction for our Morale, Welfare, and Recreation Fund." Jack sat in the chair, making his body a less open target. This lady was definitely full of surprises, and she certainly had a jealous streak. He'd have to remember that.

"Oh!" she said as heat bloomed up her cheeks. Her eyes were wide open. "Jack, I…"

He waved her words off. He didn't need any explanation. The truth was obvious. "I know what you were thinking. Just remember, appearances are rarely what they seem. In the future, don't give me your doubt, just give your faith. Okay?"

"Yes. Can we… get past this?" Laurie looked nervous as she sat down on her desk chair. She scooted closer to him. "I've majorly screwed up here."

"So have I." He took her hands into his. "We just need to communicate better. Any suggestions?"

The edges of her lips quirked and then she smiled. "Why don't we set up our own Rules of Engagement— the 'Rules of Relationship'—you know, the ways we do and don't interact?"

"I like that." He nodded his head. "You first."

"Okay, first, when in doubt, call, text, visit, or communicate in some way, and the other person must answer back." Laurie squeezed his hands.

Jack nodded his head in agreement. "My turn. There will be no public displays of emotion or affection unless it's an emergency or agreed upon."

"Yeah, those people who dry hump each other in public are really unattractive." Laurie tilted her head to the side. "Third, whether we're physically in the same location or apart, we are faithful. Also, if there are any health or mental issues—or something life changing—we always keep the other person in the loop."

"Fourth, we will not dictate how the other person lives or makes their money. I'm a career SEAL. I'm putting in twenty and maybe even thirty years. Got it?" He laced his fingers through hers.

She pursed her lips, obviously considering her words before she spoke. Given their misunderstandings of late, he was glad she was taking the extra steps. "I may hate the idea of you being in danger, but I do know the score. I can handle the pressure and the lack of knowing what's happening to you, if you keep talking about us—you and me—kissing me, and the rest of the good stuff."

"Such as doing the funky monkey?" he said, wiggling his eyebrows up and down and giving her his best cheesy grin.

"Oh, that is the least romantic label I have ever heard

for making love!" she exclaimed, pulling her hands away from him. "Get away from me."

Jack refused to let go and instead pulled her onto his lap. "I'm Navy, ma'am. There are about a hundred ways I can describe sex, but none of them come close to describing what it is like to make love to you."

Her face lit up as if he'd just given her the best gift ever. All he had been doing was speaking from the heart, too. His instincts usually led him onto the right path, and they kept shouting that Laurie was a very special someone. It had been worth raking himself over the coals to hold her again.

She laughed softly as she squeezed his hand tightly, and then she released it and stood up. "Jack."

"Laurie." He followed suit, his eyes taking in her beautiful body. She challenged him, and he liked her more for the experience of it.

They opened their arms and walked forward, meeting each other halfway. On equal ground, they embraced, and though there would undoubtedly be more to discuss, the life preserver had been grasped by both of them. Neither one of them was drowning anymore.

Needing to taste her, feel her closer to him, he brought his lips to hers and kissed her. It was like drinking ice-cold water from a bubbling, fresh spring on a hot day. Before he realized he was doing it, he'd walked her back to the table and was undressing her. When his pants hit the floor, he stopped and looked at her. "Shit. I'm sorry. Can… can we do this?"

"I'm able if you are." She gave him a wink. "I went back on the pill, and everything will be back in sync soon enough. In the meantime, using a condom would definitely be wise. Double our protection until we're, you know, ready."

Slowly, he leaned forward, giving her every opportunity to pull away. Instead she leaned in, and their lips touched.

Her lips against his were downy soft. He kept his hands still, holding her balanced on his lap as her arms wound around his neck, drawing her body flat against his. Hard nipples teased through her clothing. The swell of her breasts made him long to touch them, cup them, and worship them with his particular brand of attention. The slow languorous kiss took over his senses. All he wanted at that moment was to strip Laurie naked and really get their forgiveness on track.

Pulling back from their embrace, she said, "We have more to talk about." Those words had to be the fastest cause of death to a hard-on known to man.

"Could we do it in your bed, after..." He kissed her lips once, twice, three times, hoping she would let their lovemaking continue. Being skin on skin was an important connection.

"Yes," she sighed. "I guess we've put each other through enough. Let's go get 'oinking from the boinking'!" With that, she pushed off of his lap and sprinted for her apartment.

"That's 'smoking from the stroking,' baby!" he yelled as he ran after her in pursuit.

On her trail, he followed her through the bathroom and into her apartment. Two feet from her bed, he knew he had her. Making a flying leap, he grabbed her, wrapping his arms tight, and took her down to the bed with him.

As they fell, he'd spun her so she landed on top of him. She was laughing so hard that her body vibrated in his arms. "Those are some mean reflexes you have there, Red Jack. Can you show me the meaning of that Red nickname again?"

He liked the teasing and needed the laughter in his life. Ask any man what is important to him and after he mentions sex, being laid-back, easygoing, and having a sense of humor will be on top of the list. Laurie had all three and more. "Aha! I knew you liked my particular brand of adoration. But I'll make sure it isn't too hurried for you."

"Oh, great!" Her laughter turned into breathy silence as his hand cupped her breast. Through her bra he could feel the heat of her body and the beat of her heart. It felt good to know he could make her pulse race that fast.

Gazing into her eyes, he knew he could spend a life-time loving her.

He kissed her, and for the first time, he could have spent an hour just exploring her mouth and tasting her lips. Somehow this kiss had taken on a life of its own, and his hand slid from her breast up to cup her head and get lost in the silky strands of her hair.

When they came up for air, she blushed and looked down. "I have never been kissed like that before."

"I've never kissed anyone like that before."

She kissed him sweetly, shyly, and then slowly Laurie removed his clothes. When he was to her liking, and sheathed in a condom, it was his turn. He reached for her, removing her bra and panties and just as patiently adding tiny caresses with hands and his lips.

At last, together on the bed, their hands explored each

other as if this were the first time. Their relationship had hit a new level of intimacy and a place he had never been before. Each touch brought heat racing through him and excitement speeding up his pulse. He had never felt this close to a woman before.

"I need you now." When she pushed him down and crawled on top of him, he held his breath as Laurie firmly guided him inside of her. When his cock reached the top of its hilt, his breath eased out in one whoosh. She was already leaning down—to kiss him, to tease him, and to drive him wild with need.

"Laurie, you feel so good." His hands clasped her hips, urging her to move.

She waved a finger at him, not in a mood to be ordered about. This was a woman who could deal with his shit, and he was figuring out how to handle hers. He'd always craved a woman this independent, hoped she existed, and in Laurie, he had found her.

Then, acting like the alpha male he was, he bucked his hips high, sending Laurie into the air and down on his cock. His body and mind focused every sense toward her.

"Jack!" She laughed breathlessly. "Do it again!" And he did.

They played and caressed until neither of them could stand the tension anymore. Then Laurie set a rhythm that he could feel deep in his gut, and he could have sworn that this little lady was leaving an imprint on his soul, too.

"Jack, you blow my mind," she sighed as she pulsed up and down his cock, her back arched and her arms held high as if he were some kind of wild bucking bronco.

She moved wantonly, inciting him until he began to drive his cock harder.

The climax built. His body tightened, preparing to cum, sending heat scoring through his veins. His fingers clasped tightly to her hips, guiding her to move faster and faster. The tension blazed out of him, his eyes, and the very pores of his skin as he tried to hold on longer. But she moved in circular hip sweeps that drove him to the edge of pleasure and pain as he tried to hold on.

His eyes stayed locked to hers. Feeling more exposed, yet connected, to this one special woman, he watched passion flow from her eyes into his. She threw back her head and then she screamed his name. "Jaaaackkkkk!"

Everything in his body was tightening. He couldn't hold on any longer. He came hard and fast, with his seed pumping into the barrier he had put in place.

"Laurie. My Laurie." She was the purest praise on his lips. The release was exquisite, because it was with her, his Laurie. And as he watched and felt her final climax shiver through her body, she lay down upon him and he wrapped his arms around her tightly.

He rocked her closer until the grooves of their body fit together as if they were pieces of a puzzle. The picture was whole now. She was by his side and here to stay.

Freeing one hand, he held the bottom of the condom and drew his cock out of her. He flipped the used rubber into the small vanity trash can by the side of the bed, and then he resettled her against him.

Their energies had combined. The closeness and the physical connection had cemented something important for him. As his pulse fell into sync with hers, as their heartbeats found a synchronistic rhythm, he knew he could get used to this, and he wanted to. The easiness, the rightness, and the perfection of the moment wove itself tightly around him as they fell asleep wrapped in each other's arms.

— ᴡᴡ —

He tossed and turned on the bed. His body was slicked in sweat.

"Roaker, come on, buddy. You have to get up."

Jack's eyes snapped open, but there was nothing but silence and darkness. A shadow moved near the patio, and Jack pushed back the covers and slipped out of bed. He left Laurie sleeping soundly as he made his way through the small apartment and onto the patio.

At the small stone wall stood Don. The moon showed his face clearly. Displeasure was written on it. "Time is ticking, Jack. You need to fix this or you're going to get desked."

"Don?" Jack couldn't believe his eyes. He moved forward to embrace the man, but there was nothing… only air. Spinning around, he looked for him. "Don, where are you?"

"Where I've always been. Right beside you!" And he was. Just as suddenly as he was gone, he was there again. "I can't stick around for much longer. You only have a short time to save your ass and learn the truth."

"How do I do that?"

"Revisit the Op. There are answers in action." Then, his swim buddy was gone.

Pain squeezed the back of Jack's skull. He laid his fingers against the ache, but it spread throughout his brain, accompanied by a high-pitched sound. Crouching down, he gritted his teeth, determined to get through the pain. As his stomach churned, preparing to expel its contents, he laid his head against the cold stone of the wall.

Within seconds, the pain was gone.

He was sitting up in bed, and his body was shaking. Anxiously, he looked around the room. Nothing was there. *What is real? Did I see Don or was it a dream?*

Looking beside him, he could see her. She was solid. He sought her, pulling Laurie's lusciously soft sleeping form into his arms. Wrapping himself around her, he breathed in her scent and mulled over the facts, trying to decide what he should do next.

Chapter 16

Whatever the mind can conceive and believe, the mind can achieve.

—Napoleon Hill

HER BODY WAS SORE IN ALL THE RIGHT PLACES. WAKING up in Jack's arms had been a very healing and intimate renewal. She was surprised at how different it had been, as if they were lovers and partners even. Spending time together, talking and making love, had cleared the rift between them and set them on a better path.

Forgiveness wasn't an easy concept, but starting with her own mistakes had helped her forgive his. Now, peace surged through her. *What am I going to do with this happiness? I guess, revel in it!*

Wow! She had an odd wish to hum or sing. Would it be too much if she did? Sappy love songs ran through her head.

"Hey, are you with me?" Jack asked, taking a big sip of his coffee. Placing the mug on the table, he ducked his head and tickled his finger under her chin.

Embarrassment heated her cheeks as she waved her hand. "Sure. Please continue."

Guess humming a few bars will have to wait. She had to pull it together. Her man was working a plan! The two of them were sitting companionably at her table, talking like regular people in a relationship. Her fingers traced a scar on his thumb. With more chunks of the puzzle, it was easier to gain some ground on both the way his injuries had occurred and the current situation. Though there were still some unknowns to conquer, and he was eager to pursue them.

"As I was saying, I can't go it alone, Laurie, I need you." Jack eyes held steadily to hers. They drew her in until she felt she was gazing directly into the personification of courageous spirit. She could feel herself becoming excited about aiding him. She was completely head-over-heels, or rather heels-over-head, about him. "I need you to help me for this to work."

His eyes bored into hers. This was the first time she'd sensed his desperation about this plea. "Will you do it?"

"Yes, Jack, of course. I told you I'd help you with anything you need." She closed her eyes for a few minutes to give herself time to think. His plan had her as the control in a rather dicey situation. "But I'd like to go on record and say that this, uh, sounds sort of complicated and could be a little dangerous."

"Headshrinking just isn't my game. Let's try this… and if it doesn't pan out, then I'll go through the Balboa system and do it their way." The comment cost him. He was putting all of his hopes on his plan working.

"Okay."

"Great. Let's war-game the plan," said Jack, point-blank. Neither of them had a problem speaking their mind or respectfully listening to the other's thoughts and concerns.

With that in mind, she began at the top of her list of worries. "Okay. There are no safety elements. I don't want to get hurt, and I don't want to see you harmed either. You have proposed taking a boat to a secure government island where you can set off explosives and walk through the paces of your last mission."

Her comment stopped him in his tracks. "Wait, I don't want to hurt you, Laurie. How could you be harmed? I'm taking the risk, and you're working the camera. There will be a satellite phone in your pack, and I will take all the chances."

"You could bludgeon me. Shoot me. Blow me up. Have a psychotic break... just to name a few thoughts off the top of my head."

"I wouldn't do that." His eyes searched hers with an element of frustration. "This is the best plan I've been able to find that makes sense to me. What other suggestions do you have?"

"I know you wouldn't intentionally do it." She took a deep breath and considered his questions. She'd been racking her brain for alternative options to this scheme that involved fire, ammo, and a trip to a secluded and patrolled island, and still she hadn't found a different viable solution. "Other than doctors, none. I don't have anything else."

"Then, trust me. Guards patrol the island from 0700 to 1600, with two to three flyovers at night unless the weather is foul."

Oh, how I hate those two little words, and yet... I do trust him. With all of my heart and soul, I believe in you, Jack. But a government island in the dark... Even the thought of it makes me nervous.

"Okay, you want me to trust you, let's review your plan."

His posture relaxed. He drained the cup of coffee and then grinned at her. "I'll bet you never thought your boyfriend would be asking you to go on a super-secret Op with him." Jack's teasing was not helping.

He smiled and then leaned over and kissed the tip of her nose. His whiskers tickled and she resisted the urge to rub the itch away. Seeing him this relaxed and at ease was wonderful. Even his hair was growing longer. The buzz cut was gone, and he'd probably need a haircut before long. SEALs weren't required to keep it short like the Marine Corps or Army. If she had to guess Jack's preference, it was probably fairly neat and tidy. He didn't seem the type for a mustache or hair that flopped in his eyes.

"Anything else bothering you?" He rubbed his brow. There were more wrinkles there now, deeper crevices—at least it seemed like it to her. The time apart had most assuredly aged him, and learning more about his situation with his SEAL Team and the amount of stress he was under, she wished he could take a break from it all. Perhaps when this was done and the answers were found, she could talk him into a mini vacation.

"Laurie, you look like you're daydreaming."

"No, just thinking about stuff." It was sort of refreshing that he could identify what was happening in front of him. "How about we set up a code word so you know if this mission becomes too much for me and we can scrub it."

He didn't look convinced. "Such as?"

"Orange," she said as she started peeling one. She'd just picked it from the tree outside and the smell was pungent.

He took it out of her hands and placed it on the table. "Look at me. Tell me now if you don't want to do this. Either we are both in one hundred percent, or we are both out. No halfway marks. Because, as you know, half-assed shit will get someone hurt or killed. Got it?"

She nodded. Entwining her fingers into his, she asked, "How do you keep from being afraid?"

"Fear happens, but you can change fear into a productive emotion with a plan.

"Comfort zones are created by familiarity. So create parameters for yourself to be comfortable operating in, and when you go outside of them, have a set of reactions to fall back on." He let go of her hands and reached for the pen and pad of paper near the phone. Placing them on the table, he opened the pad to a clean page.

"You know the Kenny Rogers song about 'Know when to hold 'em, know when to fold 'em, know when to walk away, know when to run'? Well, here are some examples of how to operate. We continue on the path and do not deviate from the plan. If one of us is hurt—bleeding in a life-threatening manner—or a circumstance prevents us from continuing, such as a broken limb, discovery, or loss of personal safety, then we head for home or call for assistance." Showing her the list, he waited for her reply.

"Okay, that's the first plan. Thanks for agreeing to plan B." Hell, she was a healthcare professional and she'd be an idiot not to encourage him to have something else in place.

He sighed. "I'm not fond of plan B."

"Yeah, I know, but thanks for having it. In some small way, doesn't it take the pressure off?"

"Nope, because sitting in a stuffy room is the worst,

especially when I could be blowing shit up." He smiled at her. "That's my story and I'm sticking to it."

Scratching his chin, he said, "There's another option. I could do it alone or I could get one of my Teammates. Gerry just got home. He might be willing, in a couple of days, to help me out."

She frowned. "I see the merits of having a Teammate help you, but you told me time was running out fast. Plus, you seem to remember more when we work together. You and me."

"Yeah…" He looked away, staring out the door toward the ocean.

Standing up, she walked around the table and tugged his chair toward her to make room in his lap. Then she sat down and kissed him. "I'm a part of this journey. So, let's do it. To think, when I first met you I thought we'd just be bed buddies and nothing more. No one can be prepared for everything, Jack. Just know I believe in you, and we're burning daylight."

"Thanks, Laurie. Means a lot to me." He wrapped his arms tightly around her and squeezed. Then he ran his hand up her leg until he reached her thigh. "By the way, this is a night Op. We have a lot of light to burn."

He stood up with her firmly in his arms. "Want to help me count your freckles?"

"Jack!" she squealed as he walked with her to the bed. "Again?"

"And again, and again…" Gently, he laid her down on the bed. His hands caressed her. "Thanks, Laurie."

She nodded. Then slowly, she reached up a hand, cupped his head, and brought his lips to hers. "Love me, Jack. Love me like it's our last day on earth."

—✺—

"Time is not my friend." His words rattled around her brain like a bad song. Wearing a black sweatshirt, matte-black spandex leggings, and black ankle boots with a black silk scarf made her feel more like she was a heroine in some kind of low-budget spy movie than a girlfriend helping out her lover. "Why can't I add a dash of color, again? Don't answer that, it was a rhetorical question." But the look on his face had been priceless as if she had asked why they couldn't send out engraved invitations to everyone in the community about their supersecret event.

"Laurie…" That word said it all.

Even joking around hadn't taken the seriousness out of it, yet she couldn't stop trying. Humor was her mask; when she wore it, she was usually scared shitless!

Laughing, she replied, "Jack, I'm on board. One hundred percent. You know that. I trust you and the Op you have brewing in that SEAL brain of yours."

An intense feeling flooded her body. The truth always did that, and she couldn't remember ever trusting a man so fully, except perhaps Gich. "So, MacGyver, what do you have in mind?"

"Yeah, yeah, MacGyver. I like that. Just don't call me that in bed. I prefer Red Jack." He winked at her before he leaned over and kissed her. His lips were warm and soft, and she allowed herself to become lost in the kiss.

As they pulled apart, Jack took a deep breath, obviously regretful at ending the contact. Reaching behind her, he snagged a black band with a box-looking thing on it and fitted it around Laurie's neck. Next he handed her a receiver. "Here, put this in your ear. This is a throat mike and receiver. It will allow us to communicate when we're apart. Use it like this. Press here to send; release when you're done, so you can receive."

Jack reviewed the motions several times. She was grateful he was checking her out on the device so thoroughly. There was nothing worse than being in the field and not being able to handle equipment you were depending on. "You good?"

"Yes," she replied before she carefully removed the receiver and mike and returned them to him for inclusion in their gear packs.

"Okay, babe, this is where I am putting the first-aid kit on your left hip. The satellite phone is located here—this flap will be easier for you to reach—so this is why it's on your chest. An extra flashlight will be on your right hip. When you connect the straps across your waist, the access points will make sense. When I finish loading and strap you in, we'll go through it again."

"If I'm carrying all of this, what will be in your pack?"

He grabbed his pack and flipped open the top. Looking in, she was speechless. The man had brought cakes of explosive into her house. "Don't look so shocked. There are no detonators."

"Dude, I'm a woman. I can detonate my anger in about two seconds flat!" She teased.

———

Laurie clutched the edge of the black canvas, lighter-weight pack that Jack had assigned to her and tried to be excited about their upcoming trip. He had nixed the use of her favorite army-green backpack with its iron-on

Brownie decal and sewn-on Girl Scout patches on the outside. *Killjoy*. She followed close behind as he hefted the abundant operating gear and headed for the water. As she walked onto the rocking dock toward the rubber inflatable boat (RIB for short, she knew), she couldn't shake the nervous feeling. The night air nipped at her nose, making it drip. Without a tissue, she wiped her nose on her sleeve.

Jack steadied her.

"Slowly… and quietly," he whispered as he helped her sit and become settled in the boat. Gripping the side of the control panel, she made herself as small and steady as possible and then felt Jack push the boat into the ocean with a lurch.

Her stomach moved with it and it surprised her how uncomfortable she felt. Maybe it was the fact that they were "sneaking" out to sea in a Navy boat.

Implementation is a bitch!

Jack paddled adeptly away from the dock. It seemed prudent to ask if they'd get in trouble for borrowing the craft. She'd lived with SEALs most of her life, and they had several unspoken mottoes they adhered to. "Apologize later… if necessary" was a common one, but "Don't get caught" was rule number one.

Her father had been big on "Don't ask permission, just do it now." Of course, his alcoholism had always taken it too far. There were too many times that he'd borrowed things from the neighbors and had never returned them or returned them broken or damaged, including one time, crashing the neighbor's car. She'd had to call Gich on that one.

Jack was different. More responsible than her father,

Jack didn't love a vice more than the people in his life. She was certain of it.

Laurie bit her lip, unable to turn her brain off. At least he wasn't a psychopath who had a complete mental break with reality. Crazy snippets of television shows shuffled through her brain, followed by questions she could never imagine relating to Jack. Wasn't this a perfect way to get rid of a lover? Take them to sea and dump them into the middle of the ocean. Did Jaws really live out here? Sharks twenty feet long had been sighted off the San Diego coast. Could one of them topple the boat? What other sins could the darkness hide besides drowning, death, and dismemberment?

The water looked black. If the RIB turned over in the water, it would be up to Jack to save her. She wouldn't know which way to swim to reach the shore. An empty water bottle bounced around the RIB, threatening to fly over the side into the water. She watched it for a few seconds and then secured it under a strap.

The look on Jack's face was pure excitement. He loved this. *Get it together, Laurie. Enough drama. Just do your damned job!*

Taking a deep breath, she stowed her uncertainty and gave him her best "I'm on board!" smile. He nodded at her and then went back to his compass and instruments.

The boat curved smoothly to the right, then the left, and back to the right again. Water splashed in her face, jarring her out of her musings. *Thank you, God! I needed that!*

She was grateful for the wet wake-up call as she wiped the salt water from her eyes and cheeks just in time to get another wet smack. Shifting her weight toward the center of the boat, she tried to avoid the next jolt of the RIB on the waves. She came to the conclusion that she was just destined to be wet and gave up as the next splashes of water soaked her shirt.

Jack didn't take his eyes off the ocean as he maneuvered them through the waves. He was in his element, the captain of the sea, and the RIB was moving so swiftly that it didn't look like he would slow down for King Neptune himself. This SEAL was driven.

She stared at him, bathed in darkness and looking like some avenging angel. Her feelings were overwhelming. He was one very intense, seriously hot turn-on.

"Nice night." She smiled at him.

"Oh, yeah." His answering grin was pure sea wolf.

The inky darkness of the night sky seemed to swallow everything around them. The nighttime fog had already descended on the top of the water, and the clouds kept the moonlight and stars at bay. According to *Papa Gich's Bedtime Stories for Small Children*, this was the perfect time for an Op.

A strange feeling came over her. Exhilaration. Excitement. Anticipation. She was living an experience that thousands could only dream of. It was amazing!

She leaned into the next wave as Jack sailed the RIB over it. The splash made her laugh out loud. He looked back at her and winked.

Yeah, this is great!

"Go faster," she yelled.

He heard her and cranked up the speed. If anyone had seen them, they would have witnessed twin grins of pleasure.

Suddenly, he slowed. "We're almost there. Hang on!" Jack spoke without taking his eyes off the upcoming landmass. The boat came to a crawl. She'd stopped holding on and tumbled forward, landing spread-eagled on the bottom of the boat.

Water had gathered on the bottom of the RIB, instantly soaking her clothes all the way down to her panties. She wasn't a sissy girl by any means, though when her underwear got wet, that was a childhood signal that it was time to go home. Tough PJs! She was wearing big-girl panties, and they would dry.

The engine stopped. Carried forward on the momentum and by the motion of the waves, the RIB lifted up and down again and again until it connected with a lurch to the sandbar.

"Oh, good, you're sitting. I was going to suggest you do that while I haul the RIB into shore." One minute he was speaking softly against her ear and the next he had slipped over the side and was tugging the boat quietly up onto the sand.

Marveling at his expertise as he pulled the RIB in rhythm with the waves, she was mesmerized by the man. His efforts were pure genius—by using the tides coming into shore, he conserved his strength and minimized the noise. He was Hercules, bringing his maiden ashore.

Laurie grinned and stood up in the boat. As she started to step over the side onto the beach, Jack materialized by her side, molding his arms around her. His wet body soaked hers more thoroughly and she began to squirm. "Stop," he whispered and then he kissed her.

Wrapping her arms around his neck, she kissed him back, rubbing her body against his. The kiss turned hot and wild, and she felt her body aching for his.

A light shone down on the boat from a helicopter

overhead, and then just as quickly, it moved away and disappeared.

He broke the kiss. "I was hoping for that. The timing was right on the dot."

"What?" She was puzzled. "I don't understand."

"We took a Team boat, so if we were caught, any guards would think we're here for some slap and tickle." Jack grabbed her bag and gently took her elbow, guiding her toward the trees. He secured a rope to a tree, assuring the boat would not be pulled out to sea by the current, she supposed, and then he was assisting her up a makeshift path.

"Have you done this before?" asked Laurie, feeling a little suspicious.

"No. But I have inside Intel. Don did it all the time with Sheila. He shared a few secrets about this place." Jack released her elbow, transferring his support by taking her hand. "Come on."

Laurie was silent as they walked through the trees. Moonlight illuminated the path in patches. The eeriness made her heart race. Was this what it was like for Jack on a mission?

Her foot crushed a dead branch, making a loud snapping noise.

He whirled around and looked at her.

So much for being sneaky! I suck at this.

Jack, God bless him, didn't seem fazed. Instead, he calmly guided her around the other noisemakers, showing her how to pick out the better path.

"Thanks," she whispered after they were past the obstacles.

He smiled and then he grabbed her hand and pulled her gently and yet firmly up the path of soft dirt. The thicket of trees was suddenly past and they were out in the open as they climbed a hill.

Fat gray clouds obstructed the moonlight, leaving only an inky blackness. Clutching the strap of the backpack, she allowed him to pull her up the hill. When they reached the top, she was panting from the climb. Looming in the distance was a large shell of a building.

As they drew closer, she could see that it didn't have any windows, and only a few doors. Nothing was around for miles except for a few trees. Her feet trampled spent brass—bullet casings—as they neared the building, and the smell of gunpowder and something else, crushed leaves and damp earth, made her nose wrinkle.

He dropped his own bag of gear on the ground and took out two dry T-shirts. He handed one to her and kept the other for himself. Stripping his wet one off, he put the dry one on. Pulling out a gun, he put it aside and put their wet shirts in a waterproof gear bag and then stuffed it into his pack.

Laurie stared at the gun. "Uh, Jack. I didn't know you would be bringing a firearm."

"My 9mm doesn't have any bullets," he said. "I need something familiar in my hand to ground me in realism."

Nerves smacked her hard. "Show me that there are no bullets."

He released the magazine and showed it to her, and then he drew back the slide and let her see into the empty chamber. When she seemed satisfied, he reinserted the magazine into the gun and released the slide back. For good measure, he clicked on the safety, though there was nothing in it. "I wouldn't put you in that kind of position, Laurie. Trust me a little, okay?"

His comment rubbed her wrong. "Listen to me, Jack Roaker, if I didn't trust you, you never would have gotten back into my bed or my life. Also, I would not be here right now. Got it?"

"Yes, ma'am," he said. "Your turn. Show me what you have in there."

Oh, crap. She didn't want him to know what was in there, to see the stuff she'd added. As he lifted his flashlight over her tie-down straps, she knew she'd have to come clean. Her fingers worked the knots until they opened. As she lifted the flap, she said, "Please don't judge me."

Jack peered inside and then started to laugh. He lifted out a roll of zebra-striped duct tape. "What's this for?"

She grabbed it and stuffed it back into the bag. "In case I need to restrain you. There's zip ties in there, too."

He shook his head. "I think I get your drift, but those things won't work on a SEAL." Digging into his pack, he withdrew a small gun. "Laurie, do you know how to use one of these? It's loaded with sedatives."

"Yes." Her father had collected revolvers, and as a child she had learned about gun safety. Every now and then she went to the shooting range, too, but she'd never been to a place where she might have to actually shoot at a real person instead of a paper target. Nervous energy crawled up her spine.

"I'd rather you didn't use your pink Taurus .38 on me. That has real bullets, doesn't it?" He quirked an eyebrow.

"Yeah, but it's for wild animals. I didn't know what to expect." She shrugged.

"Well, don't wave it around. This is Navy property, and I don't want to see you get in trouble. Got it?" He pushed a sweater over her pink gun, and then tucked the gun loaded with sedatives into a small hidden pocket under her left arm. "All you have to do is reach, pull, and shoot."

"I promise not to shoot you unless you're out of your mind," she said, nodding her head. But the teasing didn't alleviate the seriousness of the moment.

"Where is the satellite phone?" he asked.

She pointed to her chest.

"Extra flashlight."

She pointed to her right hip.

"First-aid kit."

She looked at him cross-eyed and pointed to her left hip.

"Great." He adjusted the camera that was secured to the front of her chest strap and then he tightened the waist strap. "Too tight? Too heavy?"

"I'm good to go."

His kissed her. One brief soft touch and then he moved away, setting up a small hunting blind to shelter her and store their equipment. When he returned, she knew in her gut it was time to begin the mission.

The sky opened up in a cacophony of lightning and rain. It was mesmerizing and for a few minutes all she could do was stare at the sky-savaging flashes. Thunderous waves of energy echoed around her and the wind picked up, blowing trees and bushes around and swirling dust, dirt, and small debris into the air. She was glad to be tucked away, safe in a small hidey-hole far from the area where Jack was working.

Laurie filmed him as he laid out the C-4 and prepared the site, following his every action as he glided through the ground cover. He looked like the Shadow—or some kind of comic-book superhero—as he slid in and out of the darkness. As long as she faced him, the camera mounted on the front of her pack would capture everything he did.

Jack wired up the last of the explosives, made another obsessive safety check and, having confirmed that they were indeed alone, headed toward her. This had been one of the conditions of their plan, as they didn't want any cannon fodder.

As he neared her—his Teammate—she could see he was wet. *So much for having changed clothes*. She sighed.

"Okay. We're set. I picked this place because it's a similar terrain to where the incident went down. Also, we practiced for the Sundial Op here." He looked at her. "Any advice?"

Laurie considered it for a moment. "Let your senses lead you."

"They always do. Ready?"

She took a deep breath, swallowed the last of her misgivings, looked Jack square in the eye, and nodded.

Boom! Boom! KA-BOOM!

On cue the thunderstorm played into the scene, adding nature's light and symphonic displays to Jack's man-made pyrotechnics. The concussive force of the explosions reached them, pressing on their faces and skin. It was followed by the smell of ether, earth, and the distinct odor of the canvas it had been stored in—all of this sensory data carried to them on the storm's wind. Even the scent of ozone smacked her nostrils.

Jack hefted his sidearm in one hand, dropped into a crouch. He grabbed Laurie's arm with the other and pulled her forward with him into the darkness.

Chapter 17

Nothing makes a man more aware of his capabilities and of his limitations than those moments when he must push aside all the familiar defenses of ego and vanity, and accept reality by staring, with the fear that is normal to a man in combat, into the face of Death.

—Major Robert S. Johnson

SEVERAL HOURS OF WALKING AROUND THE AREA HAD gained him very little until he accidentally scratched his arm on a rock. It was a superficial wound, but the coppery smell, combined with the dirt and mud and the flashing lights, penetrated the shell. As if a switch had been flipped, he started seeing it in his head and acting it out from the beginning.

The pieces fell into place. He could see himself fast-roping into a clearing in the trees. Felt his feet hitting the ground and at the same time he lifted his gun.

He moved quickly out of the way as Don came down right after him, swiftly and silently taking the spot next to a bush. Lowering himself to one knee, Jack scanned the area. It was standard operating procedure.

Jack's voice was barely audible as he began to vocalize what he was seeing on the viewing screen of his mind. "From the corner of my eye, I could see Don landing on his feet, like a cat, and lifting his gun. The Team was accounted for; the helicopter took off as we moved into the jungle. Very few animals stirred as we went into stealth mode." There was a slight grin on Jack's lips, and then it slowly drifted away. "Except for Seeley, who got friendly with a snake and jumped about a mile out of his boots.

"Other than that one occurrence, no one spoke. There was nothing to say." Jack crouched down low.

Laurie followed closely behind him. It was odd and yet his comments made her feel like she was right there, on the Op with him. She needed to keep him on track, though. "Unless there's something important here, speed ahead. Stop when you're at your goal."

Jack complied and moved closer to the building. "We're at the hill overlooking the factory. There is no one around and the place looks deserted. I'm uncomfortable, but I've already voiced my doubts about the mission and the Intel. Knotts says over the comm, 'We don't change horses in midstream unless something makes us.'" Jack paused, blinking as if he was trying to see or hear more of the scene playing out before his mind's eye. "But already we spot a few IEDs half-buried in places along the hill."

"Okay. Then what's next, Jack?" asked Laurie.

"We noted the path in case we had to return this way and then we made our way single file down to the factory. The rest of the Team goes forward and into the building. Don and I were designated rear security. He was carrying the big gun, tagged the Peacemaker, and I was humping additional ammo as well as my own gear." Jack took several steps and then stopped. Tilting his head, he looked like he was listening. "We stopped behind an outcropping of rocks. Don and I had a good visual, though there was nothing in sight. Then Pickens and Seeley called us inside.

"Don said, 'I'm getting spooked by this place. What the hell could be of interest to the brass? No one has been here in months, maybe years.' Then Don whispered, 'Jack, you were right to be uncomfortable. Your instincts are dead-on, man. I'm sorry I didn't give you more support during planning.'"

Jack motioned for her to move ahead and together they entered the building. "I said 'Thanks, Don. I'll take that to mean you're buying the beer when we get home.' I checked the door. There were no trip wires around it, so I opened it and went in. Don followed me.

"There were layers of dust on the stacks of boxes. I could see six sets of footsteps on the ground in front of me. No one except my Team had been in here for a long time.

"Don tapped me on the shoulder and pointed. About five steps in, something was in the corner—thick shadows. I was using my night-vision goggles, but couldn't get anything useful. I just knew something was wrong. So, I pulled them off and grabbed my blue light, and that's when I spotted them… at least a dozen bodies in various states of decay… staked out on poles.

"Some had their skin peeled off. Others had missing teeth or fingers… How had the rest of the Team missed this? The victims had most likely been tortured. There was stuff scattered around: knives, needles, barbed wire, steel bars. Christ, some items were still sticking out of them! God, what a horrific way to go!

"The suits were CIA. I've worked with spooks

before. They're pretty identifiable." Jack took a slow long breath.

"Don's radio wasn't working so I used mine to communicate with the rest of the Team." Jack's voice was barely audible.

"Jack, what were you afraid of?" asked Laurie.

Jack shook his head as if he didn't want to answer; her question was throwing him off. The pieces... the pieces were coming together in his head, and he frowned as if he didn't like the picture that was forming.

His tone changed, going back to reciting the incident. "My Teammates had retraced their steps. Sure enough, they had confirmed seeing more explosive devices, trip wires, et cetera, and had thus far avoided setting them off. Down below were cases of guns and ammunition as well as several million dollars worth of cocaine. It could be a plant, or this could really be someone's stash.

"There was no way we were going to investigate a booby-trapped building without knowing the area was completely secure. We don't like surprises."

He looked at Laurie. "I asked the team, 'Did you guys see those bodies?' Nobody answered until Knotts finally said, 'I'm getting that bad-mojo feeling. We're scrubbing the rest of the mission. Let's move.'"

Jack paused and then turned back to the door. His head tilted. "I saw Don turn toward the door, retracing his steps very carefully. He checked the door again. No wires or anything were there, and then he slowly opened it. Don walked about three feet and then the bullets hit him."

The memories rained down on him then, thick, hot,

and fast, knifing him in the gut and knocking him to his knees. "Don's body danced in the gunfire. I dove onto him, bringing him to the ground. The firefight was going on over his head. The helos were trying to get to the landing zone to extract them, and only one made it as flames consumed the other. The victim of a rocket-propelled grenade. The explosions. The bodies. Everything. Every sight. Sound. Smell. Emotion. And the frustration." It was all there. His memories. Down to the last grain of sand and sour taste of fear and grief in the back of his throat. *Oh God! Oh holy, fucking glory.* He knew. He had everything back and the pain was the worst he'd ever felt.

He was panting; his entire body shook with the stress and grief of the memory.

"Jack?"

Strong fingers grabbed Laurie's forearms, wrapping tight like steely bands. They bruised her but she didn't care. He drew her close to him. His face was only inches from hers and his eyes searched hers wildly. "I remember. I remember it all, Laurie." Then he hugged her and she wrapped her arms around him like a vise.

They held each other for a long time. When he broke contact, his face was solemn. "Can you… can you give me… some time?"

She nodded.

He escorted her back to the relative dryness of the blind and made sure she was safely ensconced, and then he walked away. She couldn't help admiring him for wanting to know the truth and for confronting the pain. A cry cut through the wind and she was instantly on her feet. It took all her will to stop herself from going to him. But she said she would give him time, and she meant to honor that.

Silently, she sat on the ground and pulled her knees up to her chin, hugging them. She thought of the sorrow he must feel for his best friend, and the trauma he'd had to slog through to find the truth. Her tears fell for him and for the ones who didn't make it back.

She must have fallen asleep, waiting for him to return, because sometime later she felt Jack move her onto a blanket. Then, he curled up beside her. His heat warmed her. Laurie closed her eyes and sent her love into him, willing him to heal, or at least feel comfort from her presence beside him.

His arms squeezed tight, his breath soft and shallow on her neck as she slipped away into a dream, held safe in his arms.

—◆◆◆—

Later on, the rain woke them, forcing them out of the no-longer-waterproof duck blind and into the semidestroyed building. The fine mist of rain had turned into a barrage of wetness as they ran the short distance and settled themselves inside. When lightning fired up the sky again, he turned her toward him and cradled the back of her head. He murmured her name and then kissed her.

Lightning crashed around them, and yet she felt perfectly safe here with him, especially with his arms wrapped tightly around her body.

"I need to get our packs," he whispered against her mouth.

"So romantic," she quipped as she watched him run outside. She'd have bet a trip to Hawaii that their shelter would be completely dismantled, too, and nary a trace of it would be identifiable.

"I'm home." When he came back in, the lightning illuminated him in the door, and he looked like the mythical Thor, God of Thunder and son of Odin.

Stripping his clothes off, he stuffed them into the wet sack, and then he came to her and removed her wet clothing. His tenderness touched her deeply, especially after everything he'd been through. Then he was touching her, smelling her hair, rubbing his cheeks and lips against her throat and breasts until she moved into him, silently asking him to take her.

Pulling a condom from his pack, he sheathed himself. Lifting her up, he turned her away from him, putting her hands on the walls. Gently pushing her feet apart, he played his fingers between her legs, making her juicy and wet until she sighed with want. "Jack."

Then he turned her around, dropped to his knees, and buried his mouth between her legs, licking and lapping a path to her clit and making her move wildly against him. His tongue tormented the tiny nub over and over as a climax crashed over her senses.

"Yes!" she screamed.

Wetness bathed his face and her thighs as he spread her wider, and he stood and slowly teased his cock at the entrance of her. With one push, he thrust himself into her.

She came again, and as the climax wound down, he began to move in earnest, thrusting in and out, harder and harder, pounding his body into her with an edge that was almost violent and yet reverent. And when the climax hit, they both shouted their release.

The night was not over, though, as Jack laid her on the blanket. He explored her—her breasts, her neck, her hair, and the curve of her rear. They cuddled, touched, kissed, and renewed themselves with each other's energy.

They didn't talk about Jack's experience again that night. Laurie knew he had the answers he'd sought, and she wasn't going to interrupt the time he needed to process it all. The best thing both of them could do... was live.

──₩₩──

Morning came too soon for Laurie. Birds chirped and the sun pushed through the window, lighting the barrenness of the old building they had slept in. She loved the outdoors; camping was definitely her thing.

Wrapped around Jack, who was like her own personal heater, she never imagined she could be this warm and see her breath at the same time. The only thing she lacked now was a steamy shower and hot cup of coffee, which weren't the only two things that woke her up.

"Look at this!" said an unfamiliar voice. "Who's that hot dame?"

"Jack," she whispered hurriedly. Laurie's eyes had sprung wide open. She was awake now and very alarmed. Pulling every piece of clothing within reach on top of her, she rolled away from Jack. *Shit! Shit! Shit! Don't look!*

"What?" asked Jack sleepily, throwing an arm over his eyes. "I know those voices. Don't worry. They're fine. Go back to sleep."

Shoving her feet against his body, she pushed him with all her strength. "Get up, Jack. I'm naked!"

Jack rallied. He sat up and said, "Laribee. Hanks. Good to see you, guys. When did you get back, and who did you piss off to get stuck with morning patrols on the island?" Then he got to his feet and just stood there, shaking hands with the two guys who had discovered them.

Laurie was incredulous. Why didn't Jack care if his cock was hanging out for the entire world to see? What? Did they just like the fact they had one that much?

"Two weeks ago. Don't ask about the extra duty. I could live without going through that particular hell again," said Hanks. "What brings you to Bomb Island?"

"Sorry to interrupt," said the stockier one with a shit-eating grin. He leaned down and presented a hand to her. "I'm Laribee, ma'am. If you ever get sick of this loser, give me a call. I've got more in the, uh, manhood department than this FNG."

The fact they were teasing each other about being fucking new guys meant they were friends. Only buds teased each other with such callous pleasure.

Despite the lighter mood, Laurie could feel a blush rising from her toes and going up to the top of her head. God, she was a prude when it came to public nudity! Wrapping one arm tightly around the clothes that were pinned in place, she freed a hand and shook his. "Gee, thanks." Unfortunately, his enthusiastic shake sent her clothes askew and she had to scramble to make sure her, uh, assets were hidden.

"My BUD/S class was two before you. Who is the new guy?" corrected Jack as he stretched. She couldn't believe he was still just standing there, naked. Why did men look like Highland warriors—all sexy and godlike—and she just wanted another layer to cover up?

"Put me on the list, too, ma'am," said the taller one. "I'm Hanks. Jeffrey Handel Hanks. No relation to the composer, unless that helps my case."

"Would you guys get the hell out of here so my lady can get dressed? And for your records, she is *mine*. Got it?" Jack pushed them toward the door, laughing. "Head toward the landing. She's got a gun, and she'll use it if you stand there and stare in the window."

"Crap! I was hoping he wouldn't think about that," said Laribee.

"She had nice tits. A really sweet ass, too," added Hanks.

"Is that anyway to talk about a fellow Team member's lady?" asked Laribee.

"Hell, yes! It's better than asking what he was drinking when he landed a total dog. Arf! Arf!" Hanks joked.

Their voices were drifting away. Laribee said, "Shut up, Hanks!"

"Woof! Woof!" barked Hanks.

Laurie shook her head. "So, that was a compliment?"

"Yes," he said, pulling a dry change of clothes out of his bag. "Either you can put on your damp clothes or you can give mine a try."

"I'll take yours. I'm not proud, and there's probably a very cold ride back to shore ahead of us. I'd rather be warm than freeze." Laurie pushed the damp garments off her and stood. "Maybe we should go away somewhere warm. I'd enjoy romping in the wild with you."

"We're on the same wavelength. I'd like to add, you do have a spectacular body, Miss Smith," said Jack with a wicked gleam in his eye. "How about a little sookie-sookie before we go?"

"No!" squeaked Laurie as she grabbed the proffered

garments and danced out of reach. "Jack, I don't want those guys to see us, you know. I want our lovemaking to be between us."

"Understood," he agreed, rather disheartened. "Though if you change your mind..." His cock was still ready to do battle, but seeing her frown of disagreement, he covered himself rather speedily with his clothes from last night. Those guys must not have bothered him at all, because he gathered the gear together and was ready to go almost instantly. "Do you need any help?"

"No, thank you." She had just finished buttoning the last button when he asked. The clothes hung on her body. One good stiff wind and they would be falling off. Her hand held firmly to the top of the pants and the edge of the shirt to anchor them in place. If there were going to be more guys to encounter on the way down, these clothes were most certainly going to stay put.

He put his pack on and took hers. They left the building, making their way down the hill, through the trees, and down to the small alcove. A light marine layer floated on top of the water as Jack helped her climb on board and secured their gear. This man had a way of making physical feats look effortless. She really admired his abilities and was determined to improve her own. Maybe she'd start jogging every day again.

When she was in high school, Gich had had her doing five miles a day. They'd talk every morning... about the weather, boys, or whatever took their fancy. It was a very nonjudgmental space and had been a nice way to start the day.

Sunlight teased the water, glistening on top like millions of tiny diamonds. Pelicans flew overhead in formation. And the ocean seemed vast from here… as if it went on forever.

The wind whipped her hair about as the RIB flew over the water. Errant squirts of water splashed her now and then, and this time she laughed.

Dolphins swam alongside them for a time and then dropped behind, diving in and out of the wake of the boat. Nature's glory truly awed her.

Soon enough, the dock came into view, and the RIB was drawing alongside. Jack secured the ropes and retrieved the gear. He tossed it up on the deck and then turned to help Laurie topside.

They stood there together for a few minutes, watching the sunbeams peek through the foggy wet layer on the water. Suddenly, a rainbow appeared, making them smile as they gazed at the glorious spread of colors.

"All set?" With the fog lifted—in more than one way—it was now time for them to get on with their lives. "I have to go," said Jack as he turned Laurie toward him.

She nodded her head and handed him the pack with the camera in it.

Jack hugged her tight. "Thank you, Laurie. God, there aren't words enough to show how grateful I am." Kissing her on the ear, he released her and started walking down the gangplank. "I'll call you in a couple of hours, okay?"

Chapter 18

Individuals play the game, but Teams beat the odds.
—U.S. Navy SEAL saying

JACK POUNDED ON THE DOOR WITH HIS FIST. HIS CHEST was heaving from running, and he was completely incapable of keeping the grin off of his face. The answers were in his hand, captured by videotape, and this time he was looking forward to a meeting with the XO.

"What the hell?" asked the XO in a gruff voice as Jack yanked open the door. His eyes traveled up and down the panting SEAL, and then he nodded and said, "Roaker, come in. Would you like to take a seat?"

"Chick, I, uh…" Within two steps, Jack was in the office and headed for the XO's computer. "Sir, I'd like to stand. But could you please, uh, hook up this vid to your computer? Before it starts, I would like to explain, to tell you how I gained this footage. The Balboa therapy system has long been ineffective for SEALs, and it was imperative that I use the most efficient method to regain my memory. That's precisely what I did. I reenacted the Op and remembered everything, sir."

The XO nodded his head. "Proceed." He gestured to his computer, and Jack plugged the device in. Immediately, the segment uploaded and opened. Jack forwarded through it until he found the point where the action began. As the video played, the XO's face changed from his usual affable good-ole-boy Texas demeanor to a deep-lined frown.

Halfway through, the door opened. They both looked up.

"Jim, could you…" The CO stared at the two of them huddled behind the computer. "You're not looking at unauthorized materials, gentlemen. Are you?"

Both of them stood at attention.

The XO responded, and then he looked at Jack. "Depends what you mean by unauthorized. Jack, I'd like the CO to see this."

Jack nodded his head. "Yes, sir."

"Henry, Roaker has been very creative in finding a way to access his memories. He's been successful, and I believe you might be interested in seeing what he has learned."

The CO crossed the room and took over Jack's spot in front of the computer. Checking his watch, he told them, "I have twenty minutes until a conference call. Go!"

The XO restarted the segment. Jack stood across from them, listening to the audio and watching their faces. When they reached the part where Don died, he felt the lump in his throat. But the truth was there. He could look Don's family in the eye and say, "I know what happened." As difficult as that would be, the closure was important to Sheila, Kona, and him.

As the video completed, the XO closed the computer. "Roaker, thank you for working diligently to fill the holes in your memory. It clarifies quite a bit. This action is in sync with the majority of the Team's account. All of this footage was gained with the help of your friend, the civilian therapist, is that correct?"

"Yes, sir," replied Jack, studying their faces.

Picking up the phone, the CO dialed a number. He talked into the receiver. "George, this is Henry. Between us, I'd like to ask you a question about Operation Sundial." The CO pushed the speaker button.

"Now, Henry, I'm not at liberty to speak of that mission. You know how the CIA feels about that," squawked the voice on the other end of the line.

"Yes, of course, I just wanted to get clarification. When did you commandeer the factory?" asked the CO.

There was a long pause at the other end of the speakerphone. A choking sound, and then a throat was cleared.

"About a year ago. We stationed a few people there six months after that," confirmed the voice. "I really can't say any more. I have to go." The call disconnected.

The CO pushed a button, shutting the speakerphone off. "He's already confirmed information that wasn't in the Intel. I'm inclined to believe we weren't given the entire picture. I'll take that piece of this incident upstairs." Moving around Chick's desk, the CO sat on the edge. "Roaker, this recording isn't evidence, but it fits the phases, the progression of events, of the Op. Well, with the exception of Pickens and Seeley and their report." His eyes gazed forthrightly into Jack's. "I'll only ask you once, is this your Official After Action Report, SEAL?"

"Yes, sir." Jack stared into the CO's eyes without wavering. He put everything he had into that scrutiny—his integrity, his courage, and his willingness to act with honor. They would either believe him or not. His fate was in their hands. Of course, he had never in all of his eight years of service done anything to violate that trust, and he was depending on that now.

"That's good enough for me," the CO said with a nod and then he stood. He walked to the door and then he said to the XO, "You'll be speaking with Seeley and Pickens…"

"Aye, aye, sir. I'll take care of it," said the XO.

"Jack, there will be a Quarterdeck rededication on the Grinder in two weeks. I look forward to seeing you there." The CO waited for Jack's nod and then he left.

Jack and the XO were suddenly alone. The pause was dramatic, and for Jack, filled with relief. "Sir, about Doc Johnson and group therapy…"

"I'll take care of it," said the XO, waving a hand. "You'll probably have to go through at least one more evaluation, but I'll get the process moving so you're not stuck there for weeks on end. And I'll make some recommendations to the psych department brass. With any luck, maybe they will relocate Johnson to one of the hotter outposts. Who knows, perhaps we can get your civilian consultant on the payroll, too. Though I don't want any details about what type of physical therapy you're receiving, Roaker."

"Yes, sir. Thank you, sir." Jack was elated. "Permission to speak freely."

"Christ, why do you always ask that? We're alone, Jack. What else do you want to say?" The XO teased him and the annoyance was obviously welcome.

"Chick, I just wanted to say… thanks. You know, for believing in me." Shaking his head, Jack didn't have words to share his gratitude. In one fell swoop, between recovering his memory and this moment, he'd gotten his life back. The odds were in his favor that he would deploy again, soon, and his reputation was whole and unblemished. Both of those things meant a lot to him, more than most people would realize.

"Yeah, yeah…" Grinning, the XO picked up the phone and dialed two phone numbers that Jack knew by heart: Pickens and Seeley. He said the same thing to each. "I want you in my office ASAP! Together."

Laying the phone on his desk, he said, "Why don't you wait outside of the door, Roaker?"

"Yes, sir." Jack gave the XO a salute and a very happy smile. A golden opportunity was coming his way—for Jack to hear two guys get reamed out. He could never remember being happy at someone else's pain. This time these assholes had it coming. They were going to sacrifice him for their own reasons, and that shit didn't rock this boat!

Stepping outside of the office, he closed the door behind him. Then he leaned against the wall, watching the clock. Seeley arrived first. It only took him eight minutes. He must have been somewhere in Coronado. Pickens took thirty-five minutes to arrive. By that point, Seeley was sweating and chewing his thumbnail down to the quick as he waited to be called in.

Pickens gave Jack a dirty look as he took his place next to Seeley. "What's going on?"

"I don't know," said Seeley in a high-pitched and obviously nervous voice.

The XO must have been be able to hear a pin drop, because his door shot open and he walked out like Patton taking the front line.

Lieutenant Commander Stockton looked all of the men up and down, and then in a low voice he growled, "Seeley. Pickens. Inside." Both men passed by Jack; then the XO swung the door behind them, leaving it open almost an inch. Sounds could carry like a loudspeaker through that kind of opening. "Men, many comments are running through my mind. The first one of which is why you had the audacity to accuse a fellow Team member without taking the primary responsibility of discussing the question with him. We humble ourselves before each other that we might be stronger. Arrogance and pride will only show you the exit door faster. As a SEAL, it is your responsibility to protect your Teammates. Now, I get that things might appear to be different in Team ONE—we're tough on discipline. But we are a Team—first, second, third, and fourth—and together, we win. That's why we're successful! So, let's begin with the reason you put Roaker in the line of fire, and let me share this, this is your *only* chance to set the story straight."

The XO's chair protested as he sat down in it. His hand slammed down on the desk. "Prepare for a long discussion, because whether or not you stay in SEAL Team or see that door comes down to you…"

—∿∿—

Jack's Jeep screeched to a stop in front of Laurie's place. Driving like a kamikaze pilot brought him a tremendous measure of pleasure. He knew it made her give him the disapproving frown, but he kind of liked it and he knew she would get used to it, eventually.

He looked at her office and home. The building sat

on the edge of the water. Kayaks were perched on the wall with a line coming off them tied to a peg in the stone. Laurie lived and worked in the same spot, and this woman was comfortable with who she was. He liked that! And he respected her. He was completely confident in the fact he would have a great time getting used to being with her.

He saw her standing in the window. Her hands fluffed her gorgeous hair as she walked to the ancient screen door and opened it wide. She waved at him.

Hopping out of the Jeep, he grabbed the case of Karl Strauss beer and his overnight bag and headed for her. At the door she ambushed him, kissing him—leaving lipstick all over his face. *Ah, well, that's my Laurie. Mine!* He was pleased that she primped for him and was excited that he was there. He could enjoy that kind of attention forever.

Walking through the apartment, he deposited the case on the kitchen table and tossed his bag onto the bed. "I'm home, honey."

She laughed and then she stumbled as she was walking toward him.

"Did you start the celebration without me?"

"No, of course not!" she said, laughing. "You just bowl me over sometimes."

"Gee, thanks," he said with a grin, and then he scooped her up in his arms and tossed her in the air. With her light frame, his gorgeous lady flew.

"Jack," she squealed. "Jack!"

He did it again, and then he caught her to him and squeezed her tight. "Don't worry, I won't drop you, not ever." She wrapped her arms around his neck and the delight in her eyes hit him full force. Damn, he could stare into those beauties forever.

"Before we disappear between the sheets, please sit and tell me what happened." The look on her face was one of serious curiosity, and given everything she had done, he owed it to her.

Taking her to the couch, he sat with her still in his arms. He helped her get comfortable and then he shared the story. "I arrived at the Quarterdeck shortly after I left you. The XO was already in, and we hooked up to his computer and watched the video. Great idea, by the way—it added a lot to the explanation, and my story connected almost exactly with Knotts and Chalmers." He sat there, quietly reflecting on the notion. He wanted Laurie to meet them. Was she doing anything this weekend? They'd give him a lot of grief when they first met her, but it would be worth it.

"Come on, Jack. Don't stop now. That can't be it." Laurie wiggled in his lap, making him think about something other than the Op explanation. "Give me a break. I need more."

"Yeah, I thought you might." He lifted her up and gently placed her alongside him on the couch. Releasing her hand, he went to the refrigerator and took out two bottles of beer, popped the tops off with the magnetic opener on the front of the freezer, and came back. He sat down on the couch next to her and handed her one of the cold brews.

Jack stared at the bottle for a long time, thinking of how to share what had been hard for him. God love his lady, Laurie was generously silent, allowing him to gather his impressions. When he finally spoke, she smiled at him. "The device worked exactly as you said it would. I wasn't prepared to see myself, to hear the words coming out my mouth, and to go through everything again with my XO and the CO sitting right there. But I handled it. The truth was heard."

He continued. "Afterward, we spoke about the implications of the Op and what the situation told us. I gave him my permission to send it to the brass, and to basically use it to nail the CIA for *not* disclosing information that got a Navy SEAL killed and several others seriously wounded, in addition to the horrific deaths of the helicopter crews. I hope they fry those CIA bastards! They used us to try to get their assets back, and it cost us dearly. They need to be held accountable.

"Then there's Seeley and Pickens who thought I was dirty. All I was doing was following my gut. My instincts shouted that the Op had problems. We all learned Swepston's Rule of Three. But those guys would rather think the worst of me instead. So much for Team loyalty! The XO read them the riot act for implying without knowing the truth." He rolled his shoulders and then his neck. "If there is a question next time, the XO told them to honor their Teammate and go fucking ask him."

As he settled back in the chair, his voice became softer, and lower. "Hardest part was… letting it sink in… that Don died in my arms. Before I rigged up the gear to hold pressure on his wounds in the copter, my… my swim buddy was already dead. No part of me wanted to accept it. Still don't… But I'm not sure that reality gives me much of a choice." Lifting the bottle to his mouth, he took a long sip. Coolness bathed this throat. "To you,

Don. I miss ya." He took another pull. "Best elixir in the whole damn world is beer. Well, in moderation."

"Jack, I'm sorry about Don."

"Me, too."

"What's next... for you? For work?" asked Laurie as she trailed her fingers on his arm, comforting him.

"I'm good to go," he said, nodding his head. "The brass is already getting to the root of the issues, and the XO, CO, and the rest of Team are cool with me." He gave her a very toothy grin. "Also, I'm going in for a physical and X-ray tomorrow. If I pass it, then I'm off medical leave. Probably will be a while before I deploy, but I can get back to work. No more sitting on my ass and no more threats of doctors and group! Except for you." Grinning intentionally like a jack-o'-lantern, he tickled her side. "Want to take my pulse, Miss Therapist? I bet it's racing."

Looking at the clock, she smiled back at him and then winked. "I'd love to, Jack, but I'll have to take a rain check. Gich will be here any minute."

"Fuck, what did I do now?" Jack shook his head and did his best hungry hound-dog impression. "I thought we talked about *not* having Gich in bed with us."

"Ew! Jack, bite your tongue! That's gross!" She pointed her finger at him. "You said, 'It's time for a family celebration.' Those were your words, big man, and he's family. So, live with it.

"Besides, I've always wanted a normal life." Shrugging her shoulders, she said, "You and Gich are everything to me, and we are going to grill some steaks, roast some potatoes, have some salad, and drink some beer. We're going to talk and laugh and eat until the fireflies' butts start glowing. That's probably as sane as our life will get. Are you good with that?"

"Aye, aye, ma'am!" he said with a salute. "Where's my duty station?"

"To the grill with you," she ordered, and her smile could have lit the Pacific seaboard.

Hearing a set of brakes squeal, he knew Gich had arrived. The man drove the same way he did, like a bat out of hell.

Jack watched Laurie make her disapproving face as she marched to the screen door and pushed it wide. "Could you drive any slower? You're like an old lady! You better not get back in that car and try to drive away. I see you, Gich! Get your ass in here!" Laurie shouted at the top of her lungs at the man who was her mentor, her daddy, and her best damned friend. Her voice echoed the screeching sound back to him.

God, he loved her, too! She was his warrior woman.

Chapter 19

If you're in a fair fight, you didn't plan it properly.
—Nick Lappos, chief R&D pilot, Sikorsky Aircraft

TWO DAYS LATER AT TEN HUNDRED HOURS, TWO RIBs pulled away from the dock, loaded with personnel. The boats moved at a slow pace, keeping the participants dryer and lending to the seriousness of the occasion, as they traveled side by side toward the center of the Pacific Ocean. The individuals on board were dressed in formal attire: military uniforms, black dresses, and fancy suits and ties. Their faces were similar in repose, all of them solemn as the wind tousled their hair.

Clear blue skies stretched overhead as far as the eye could see. A pod of dolphins swam alongside the boats, diving in and out of the waves as pelicans dove and flew about, angling for fish. This ordinary nature's play was the flag of "smooth sailing" to the sailors on board even as the RIBs moved steadily over the whitecapped chop to perform this final rite of passage, a burial at sea.

Four jets streaked overhead, racing past them. They performed the missing-man formation. F-18s rolled, twisted, and flew together and then three jets shot forward... as one peeled off, flying away alone and, the rest... went on.

Emotion churned in his guts as Jack watched the display. Then, a signal was given. The RIBs slowed and the engines were cut.

The Chaplain of the Amphibious Base, Commander Deckard, cleared his throat and then spoke aloud. "We are gathered here today to honor Petty Officer Second Class Donald Dennis Kanoa Donnelly, nicknamed Don. He was a SEAL who sacrificed his life for our country, for the principles we all believe in, for the brothers he walked with, and the wife and child he protected. We have our freedom today because of his willingness to defend this nation. We honor your courage, Don. May all here today witness that Don's sacrifice was courageous. He will live eternally in the house of the Lord, and may the Lord watch over his family and guard them as he has always done.

"From the King James Bible, the Twenty-third Psalm, 'The Lord is my shepherd; I shall not want. He maketh me to lie down in green pastures: he leadeth me beside the still waters. He restoreth my soul: he leadeth me in the paths of righteousness for his name's sake. Yea, though I walk through the valley of the shadow of death, I will fear no evil: for thou art with me; thy rod and thy staff they comfort me. Thou preparest a table before me in the presence of mine enemies: thou anointest my head with oil; my cup runneth over. Surely goodness and mercy shall follow me all the days of my life: and I will dwell in the house of the Lord for ever.'" The Chaplain nodded. "We welcome his swim buddy, Petty Officer First Class John Matthew Roaker, to say a few words."

A speech was folded neatly in Jack's pocket. He'd

reread it so many times he knew it by heart. Taking a deep breath, he exhaled slowly and then said the words that made his heart ache.

"Don was a rarity among men. Like many guys in the Teams he gave generously and without a second thought, as he was always working for the betterment or protection of another's life. But there was a unique ability he had to bring humor into the toughest circumstances. No matter where we were or what was happening, the minute a joke flew out of his mouth… we knew we would survive the situation." Jack swallowed around the lump in his throat.

"His lighter side kept his Team members going and it brought his beautiful wife into his life. He teased her from the moment he met her and they fell head over heels for each other. He once told me Sheila was one of the top three best experiences of his life: his wife, his daughter, and the Teams. These were the things he loved most. There will never be another man like Don… It was an honor to serve beside him."

Looking over at Sheila, Jack could clearly see the outline of Don—standing next to his sobbing wife, with an arm around her shoulders. He held Jack's eye for several seconds; then he dropped his arm and saluted.

Jack saluted back… to his memory of his best friend. He knew in his heart that Don was gone from his life for good. Whether the visions he'd had of Don all these months were a part of his head injury, dreams, or as the doctors diagnosed, his mind dealing with the acute suppression, or Don himself, touching base from the other side, Jack didn't care. What mattered most was that he had been able to honor his friend with the truth. In the end, perhaps this was the greatest gift and, more than most individuals got, closure.

A SEAL, wearing traditional Scottish attire in addition to his trident, played "Amazing Grace," one of Don's favorite hymns, on the bagpipes.

Don's daughter, Kona, placed one of her drawings into the water and set it adrift—such a small piece of colored paper, with a picture of a family on it. She watched it go and blew it a kiss. Then her mother took off her lei and placed it into the water. Together, the items floated away.

Next, Sheila was handed the urn. She opened the top and reached inside. Withdrawing a small handful of Don's ashes, she scattered them into the water. Tears streamed down her face, but she never uttered a single sound of misery. She was a true Navy wife, who could stand the test even as it ripped her heart out.

When she nodded to him, Jack stepped up next to her, following her lead, and took a handful of ashes. It seemed strange to him that the big, hulking, and very vibrant man was reduced to this small box of dust. Staring at the ashes, he couldn't believe that this was all that was left of this indomitable SEAL. Somewhere in the hereafter, peace would come, but nothing could squelch Don's undeniable force.

Strangely, Jack's head injury had been a remarkable gift—allowing him to see his best friend and forcing him to seek out help and bring someone new into his world. Don would tell him that God never made accidents, just opportunities to become better. We might not always appreciate the circumstances, but the life lesson was in there.

Jack blew out a long ragged breath. He was next. "Until we meet again, my friend." The wind picked up as he opened his hand, blowing the ashes into his face. Jack opened his mouth and laughed, tasting the gray dust on his tongue. He wiped most of the ash off his face and from around his mouth. "I guess this is a part of him that will always be with me."

Nervous laughter broke out over the boats. It grew into larger guffaws as each member of the Team tossed ash into the wind and water. The heaviness of the burial at sea had turned lighter, as befitted the man's personality. Jack was pleased that the experience held humor. His friend would have hated for everyone to have a heavy heart because of his death. Rather, he'd have preferred to be remembered with laughter and joy.

The moment belonged solely to memorializing this great warrior, and he would do so with a friendly yet stoic face. Tears would wait for a private moment, when he was alone with Laurie. And later at McP's he would raise a toast in Don's honor, holding a beer high, and he would speak again of his friend's greatest attributes and roast him a little, too. Traditionally, this method was the way for most in the Teams…

"Let's conclude with the Lord's Prayer." When the Chaplain led them in the final prayer, the rest of the ashes were given to the Pacific Ocean. Then the box was stowed and the RIBs were turned toward shore. The engines turned over, fluttering to life as the boats surged forward, gaining speed to race each other to the dock.

Jack felt tiny arms wrap around his pant leg. He smiled down at lovely little Kona.

Picking her up, he held her tightly so she could feel

the wind in her face and see the shore growing ever closer. They watched the pod of dolphins join them on the trip back. The creatures dove in and out of the wake, frolicking.

Kona's fingers locked into the edges of his uniform, and he winked at Sheila, whose belly was around six months along. These two individuals were part of his family. He could see it now and was happy to accept the responsibility and duty of this fated gift.

Today they had buried his best friend, a man who had watched his back and been at his side since BUD/S training. There was a bond very few men would ever understand, and no words could sum up the importance of this man's life. Jack knew he was a better man for having been friends with Don, and he'd stay in close contact with Sheila, Kona, and the baby-to-be. It was a boy, who would be named after his father, Sheila had confided earlier that morning.

Life connections were the purpose of this crazy journey. Jack understood it now.

Freedom to pursue his dream of a wife and family surged through his veins. This was a treasure he could have and relish. Being a SEAL meant being part of a Team both at home and in combat. Yes, he could always operate alone, but given the choice, he chose company for this complex experience known as life.

His eyes eagerly scanned the shore, searching for the flash of dark hair being whipped in the wind. His Laurie. She was the unexpected present that came out of this horrific scenario. From knowing nothing to learning about everything, this lady had accompanied him through the entire journey. Other than a couple of small hiccups in communication, she had more than proved her worth to him, and hopefully, he'd proved himself to her.

The RIBs slowly drew closer to shore, leaving a foamy wake behind them. The waves were small but choppy, yet the drivers knew how to keep the boats steady and their passengers dry and safe. It helped that they understood the rhythms of the ocean and had trained on these vehicles and driven them hundreds of times. If only life were that easy, that the unexpected never came to dislodge the calm and predictable ways of existence. But this is the nature of the world… that we never know what will happen next.

For his future, Jack knew he had found a woman who could hold her own, had an independent attitude toward life, and the willingness and forthrightness to live boldly. Laurie had the entire package, and then some. He knew in his heart he would never willingly let her go.

"Look, Kona, there's your Auntie Laurie. You'll like her. She's special," Jack said into the ear of the little girl in her arms. "Come on, let's wave to her." Freeing one of his hands, he waved at Laurie and Kona joined in.

Sheila smiled at him, and then shouted over the wind, "So, this is what has had you so busy. I look forward to meeting her."

"Yes," said Jack, leaning closer to Sheila so she could hear him. "Laurie helped me get my memory back. I want her in my life, Sheila. Permanently." The last word seemed suspended in the air, and he was fine with that pronouncement.

Don's wife nodded at him and said, "Well, she's

already part of the family, then. I look forward to letting her know what kind of nuthouse she's joining."

Ah, the teasing! Sheila had a natural instinct for banter, as did Laurie. If anyone had told him a year ago that he would meet someone like Laurie and fall in love, he never would have believed it. Now his life was coming full circle.

The boats slowed as they approached the dock. A few sailors ran forward to catch the docking ropes. The RIBs were secured, and Jack helped Sheila and Kona off. Then he walked them down the dock and to the spot where Laurie waited for them. If the RIBs had been bigger, she might have come along. But Don was a deeply admired man in the Teams, and they'd had to turn a lot of people away because there wasn't much room on the boats.

Master Chief Kirby pushed a memory card into his hand. Within its small plastic form would be pictures of the burial. These photographs would help Sheila explain to the children as they grew older how their father had been honored. "For Sheila; she can keep this. Knotts is doing a video at McP's."

"Thanks," said Jack, grateful that the community was always there, watching out for each other. He pocketed the precious item and turned his attention to walking down the gangplank.

Laurie stepped into view, dressed in a blue silk dress. He longed to wrap her in his arms and kiss her. Her hair smelled like lilacs, and he wanted to bury his nose in it and just breathe. She had offered to wait on shore. Already, she understood the intricacies of this world— sometimes she would be by his side and often she would wait on shore. She knew this as a former SEAL pup and now she was his SEAL lady.

"Laurie, I'd like to introduce Sheila and Kona." Jack spoke proudly as Laurie embraced her two new family members.

"My condolences for your loss," said Laurie solemnly.

"Thank you," said Sheila politely and then she hugged Laurie. "I've heard good things about you. I'm glad you're here."

"Me, too. Jack has told me so much about you," Laurie gushed with her usual unwavering enthusiasm. Her buoyancy was contagious, and Jack leaned over to kiss her before giving the women some space to chat.

"I'm happy to meet you. I knew Jack must be up to something. When he told me about you and the entire journey to find the truth, I knew you'd be special." Sheila linked arms with Laurie, dragging her ahead. Looking over her shoulder briefly, she winked at Jack. "I can hardly wait to share all of the dirt I have on your guy…"

Jack rolled his eyes at her, and then looked at sweet Kona, who skipped alongside him. Children were remarkably resilient. Perhaps he wouldn't mess one up too badly if he took the plunge. He really did want one, two, or maybe four kids…

Man, that would make Don laugh! Gich, too! Life is not about how one begins his journey or even how it ends. What matters most is reality right now and how lives are entwined with each other. He was done with his hermit-like existence and usual practice of holding everyone at bay. The human-to-human connection is the journey that gives us some of our greatest challenges and most humbling rewards. What better way to honor that concept than by being a living example?

Jack touched the scar at the back of his head. The injury was healed and he had a clean bill of health. He would be reporting back to duty soon, and he was ready to be in the action. He'd be taking his swim buddy and all those life lessons with him.

"Uncle Jack, are you okay?" asked Kona, tugging on his arm. She looked up at him with those wide brown eyes so much like her daddy's.

"Sure am," said Jack as he picked up Kona, spun her in a circle, and settled her on his shoulders. "Are you ready for a hamburger, Kona?"

"Yes," said Kona eagerly. The child was bouncing energetically. Her eyes were lit up and her smile was beaming. Maybe she was a reflection of her mother, who had lightened up also, or perhaps Jack was in a place where he was prepared to be back in the swing of life. Either way, as they headed toward their cars and the Celebration of Life party at McP's, he knew the Don-shaped hole would always be there, and that all of them would reinvent themselves as much as they could and would mostly be fine.

"Let's eat!" proclaimed Kona. "Mommy, we need to bring Mrs. Popcorn. I left her in the backseat of the car."

"Okay, Kona. We'll get her," said Sheila. "We're almost there."

Jack helped settle Sheila and Kona in their car, and then he and Laurie climbed into his Jeep. "See you there," he told them.

"How was it?" Laurie asked when they were alone.

"Good," he said with a nod. "I didn't give the whole speech. Only the first couple of paragraphs." He wasn't about to drink in his uniform, so he hightailed it to his apartment for a quick change. Zipping through the green lights, he knew he'd be at his destination in minutes.

"Those were the best parts," she said, holding on to the side of the Jeep. "Jack, do you have to drive so fast? We're not pursuing an insurgent!"

"Yes, dear," said Jack with a grin that was both placating and teasing.

"Oh, don't give me that crap!" Laurie replied with a smile. "If you're going to be doing this for the rest of our lives together, then—"

Pulling to a halt with a screech, the Jeep jerked to a stop in front of his apartment. "Yes?" he enquired.

She unhooked her seat belt and climbed over to him. Her lips grazed his gently once, twice, and then she kissed him. Full lip on lip—with its bombardment of emotions—waylaid his intentions.

One minute he was thinking about a retort, and the next he was contemplating carrying her into his apartment and stripping her naked and taking her as they leaned against the wall.

His fingers sought the release for his seat belt and then he was pulling his keys out of the ignition and lifting her into his arms. Having traveled these steps a hundred times, he could do it sleepwalking, and before he knew it, they were at his door.

Fitting the key in the lock, he opened the door, pulled the keys out, and slammed the door shut with his foot. Her hands worked over him, releasing buttons and pulling the clothes from his body.

He did the same until they both stood naked. Then he was laying her down on the floor, reacquainting himself with the woman he loved. Her body was soft and curvy, sexy and familiar, and yet completely new as another layer of emotions played into their lovemaking.

Lifting his head, he stared into her eyes. "Did you really think we would only be bed buddies?"

She laughed, her eyes sparkling with mischief. "Yes, I did. I know how you guys operate. I didn't expect anything, so I didn't get hurt. But I knew I wanted to have fun."

"And now?" He had to ask the question to completely understand the way she felt about him.

"What do you think, Jack?" Laurie's hands tried to drag him back down for a kiss.

"No, wait. I have to say this…" He held himself poised above her, the woman he had gone to for help and begun to fall for. "I have feelings for you."

"I know that," she said, running the tips of her fingers over his ears, trying to distract him.

He captured her hands and squeezed them tightly. "I love you, Laurie. Just for the record, beauty is courage, kindness, joy, and pleasure. Even when you're unsure, I see more of that in you than in any woman I've ever known."

Her eyes widened in surprise. Tears gathered at the corners. "Bravery is honesty even when it's uncomfortable, happiness at simple things, and knowing that every day matters. You have that and so much more. I love you, Jack."

They kissed, and it was one of the sweetest moments of their life together so far. If they have been in a luxurious suite it could not have been any better. He reached for his wallet, breaking the kiss; he found a condom and rolled it onto his cock.

With a sure stroke, he buried himself deep inside of Laurie. His body shook as he balanced himself on his elbows, not because the technique was taxing on his body, which it wasn't, but because this was the woman he loved and his emotional investment was one hundred percent. Every moment with her mattered, and he wasn't going to take anything for granted.

Her hands brought his face closer to hers. She kissed him tenderly on his lips. "I enjoy being with you, Jack. As much as I've wanted to deny it or even be cool about it, I can't. I fell for you the moment we spoke at Dick's Last Resort, and every interaction and hurdle has only brought us closer. You're my ideal, Jack, even when I didn't really know exactly what I wanted."

For the second time today, words clogged his throat. He cleared it and said, "See. You wanted a SEAL. You didn't know that before, because you hadn't met me."

"You're right. You're always right," she teased. "I have everything I want right here."

"Can I get that phrase in writing? No wait. Let's have it bronzed!" He tickled her until she laughed. Then he captured her wicked little tongue until their kiss drove them both into a more primal dance. "Did you mention I was perfect?"

"Jack!" She moved against him, asking for more.

He refused to deny her.

With swift strokes, he brought her to climax twice before he allowed himself to cum. Then he rolled to his side, gathering her close. He could have stayed there forever, but today was about honoring a friend, as well as life and love.

"Is it time to go?" she asked, reading his mind.

"Yeah," he said, kissing the top of her head and then untangling his limbs from hers. "Let me grab some jeans, and I'll be right out."

Laurie jumped up and dashed for the shower. "Okay! I'll be really quick."

"No fair," he shouted back. "It's no fun unless we both smell like sex." Nonetheless, he found the clothes he wanted and headed for the bathroom. She was already toweling dry, and he snapped a towel in her direction, praising her lush curves and laughing at her small squeal of annoyance. His cock started to harden again, so he put the shower on cold and jumped in.

~~~

The courtyard of McP's was packed with people. Jack parked his Jeep around the corner, and then he and Laurie walked to the gathering. From the kitchen of the pub, the smell of frying beef and chicken wafted his way, even from fifty feet away. His stomach growled. He'd worked up one hell of an appetite with this lovely lady and he was seriously hungry.

"Was that your stomach?" she asked, teasing him and then fake-punching him in the stomach. Laurie was definitely feisty tonight. "I'm starved, too!"

He nodded his head, and then ignored his hunger. Banging on the far side of his leg was a fancy paper bag. Laurie hadn't asked what it was, and he was glad. He hoped she'd like the surprise.

The parking lot was stuffed full of cars, motorcycles,

and bikes. To move anything would require a coordinated attack. Most likely everyone would be walking home anyway, and the owner wouldn't mind. He was one of their own. Once a SEAL, always a SEAL.

A sign was taped to the gate saying Private Gathering, and they waded willingly into the chaos. To his left, a keg of Stella was propped on the table. Next to it were several trays of chicken wings and potato skins—Don's favorite bar snacks—as well as several plates of mozzarella sticks with veggies.

Someone had set up a barbecue in the back and the turkey burgers and ribs sizzled loudly on the fire. The smell of a sweet spicy sauce filled the courtyard, in addition to a little smoke.

Their old CO, Jiffy, had once said, "Courage is not in walking blindly into battle, but fighting the battle where you know how high the odds are stacked against you."

Jack's eyes searched the faces. Community—Team guys and their wives—surrounded Sheila and Kona. This group never left anyone behind. Loyalty was forever, and no matter what circumstances faced a family whose warrior father had been killed in battle or training, the community would help.

He nodded at several of his brethren as he steered Laurie toward a couple of empty seats.

The party was getting loud and rowdy. Gich was holding court in the back corner, near a second keg, with a bunch of the Old Frogs and SEALs. Jack gave a small wave to them all and then helped himself to two beers. As he sat down next to Laurie, he asked, "How many of these have you been to?"

"Too many to count," she said grimly. "My dad's was

the hardest death. I was so young, and everyone around me was the size of giants. Kona must be feeling that way. Let Sheila know, okay? I could help, talk to Kona about this, if she wants. It could be now or later… just putting it out there."

"I'm sure she'd like that." He nodded. "Are you going to be able… to do this?"

The implication was there… the larger question of whether or not Laurie would stick through it. Being with a SEAL took guts and a backbone of steel; none of it was easy.

Her eyes held his. "Yes."

He cleared his throat. "You know these are part roast and part what we loved about the guy, right?"

Her eyes studied his, thoughtfully. The fact she didn't answer right away meant she was probably really giving tremendous weight to the inquiry, just as he wanted. "Don't look so worried. I'll be fine. I'm familiar with how it goes. Back then, when my dad died, I had Gich. Now, I have you. I'm a strong woman and I can deal with it all. Just promise me that when we're together, you'll be really here with me and not thinking or wishing you were somewhere else."

"I promise. You are my beautiful, bright, and talented lady, and I won't disconnect when I'm home. If I do, you have my permission to call me on it." Jack was not sweet-talking her, either. "Just don't whack me on the back of the head for a few more weeks."

"Ha ha!"

He reached for her, pulling her into his arms and kissing her in front of the entire bar.

"Get a room!" shouted Knotts.

"Now that's living!" agreed Chalmers. He raised a glass in their direction. Billings hadn't been able to attend—still on heavy meds—but it was good to see that someone had sprung Chalmers from the hospital for a few hours. Good to have most of the family together. Well, except for Seeley and Pickens, the black sheep who had been reassigned to ships rumored to be somewhere in the Arctic.

A few people clapped and yelled more comments at their next public display of affection.

After another long, luscious kiss, Jack released Laurie and stood. Picking up a glass of beer from the many placed on the table for just this purpose, he raised it high. "Hey! I've got a toast! I'd like to raise a glass to a man who knew what love was. From day one, when he met his bride, Sheila, he told me—his swim buddy who gets to see it all—that he knew what the future held for him. Sheila was the only woman he wanted to spend the rest of his life with. Don said someday I'd be bitten, too. Well, he was right! This toast is to Don. Thanks for sharing the fact that love is real, and for allowing me the joy of being part of your world with Sheila and Kona. To Don! Hooyah!"

"Hooyah!" resounded the men and women in unison. "To Don!"

Waitresses brought in pitchers of Stella to be passed around, and trays of ribs, hamburgers, and cheeseburgers, making sure everyone had sustenance and drink.

Jules placed plates of food in front of Jack and Laurie. "I've never seen him so happy. Congratulations!" she said to Laurie. "You make an adorable couple. Now, where did my husband get to?"

"Don't know. Thanks, Jules," said Jack with a grin.

"Thanks," replied Laurie as she reached for a burger. Jack's hand stopped her from having a bite. She frowned at him. Obviously, the woman wanted to eat.

Another waitress placed chips and salsa on the table along with glasses of ice tea. It was quite a banquet.

A few more guys arrived, including Franks and McCullum from Team THREE. Jack greeted them with a nod before returning his attention back to the group.

"One more thing!" Jack yelled, forcing everyone to quiet down again. He hauled Laurie to her feet. "I was once accused of having an empty life, which matched my very empty walls. I'd like everyone to meet the lady I've fallen in love with. This is Laurie Smith, and this is a gift for my lady."

Wolf calls, sexy whistles, and loud shouts, along with clapping, ensued as Jack helped Laurie to stand and face his military family. He handed her the fancy paper bag and said, "Here…"

"What is it?" she asked, puzzled and unusually shy.

"Open it," he said, softly raising his eyebrows. His instincts had led him down this path, and in his mind, this was a super gift.

She gave up her uncertainty and armor, plunging her hands into the bag. Withdrawing an item wrapped in blue tissue paper, she ripped off the top and gazed at it.

"Come on, what is it?" shouted Knotts. "If it's a nude picture, let us know so we can cover the children's eyes."

"Maybe it's a lock of his hair," shouted Gertz, a Petty Officer from Team ONE who had operated with Jack and Don on occasion. He had saved their asses. Of course, Don and he had been able to return the favor. Gertz was a good guy to have come to Don's Celebration of Life. "Or he framed his last pair of 'tightie whities' from way back when… you know, BUD/S! I think my balls are still torqued."

"I knew you'd be the heckler, Gertz. Stow it or I'll show you pain!" remarked Jack jokingly and shooting a derisive gesture at his friends.

Gich raised a glass of scotch in his direction. With a nod, he took a deep drink and lowered his glass.

Jack smiled. He was filled with warmth at the gesture. The relationship between him and Laurie was definitely growing on the old guy. He lifted his cup of beer and toasted back, and then he drained the brew in one long gulp.

Laurie peeled off the rest of the blue tissue wrapping. Gripping the gift in both hands, she stared at it blankly for a few minutes.

A strange smile was frozen on her lips and then slowly it warmed into a wide grin. Laurie turned it around and held the picture up like a prizefighter showing off a championship belt, proud for the entire world to see. Her words were loud. "It's a picture of us."

It was a snapshot he'd taken over a simple morning cup of coffee at the small table in her apartment. Leaning forward, she kissed him. "It's wonderful. Thank you."

"The first of many. I want to fill our walls with memories of us and our life together," he said softly, knowing he was right about her. If he had never risked, made love to her, apologized, asked for help, and so much more, then he never would have had this journey and learned that she was the right woman for him. He had his memory back, too. It was a pretty nifty outcome.

"Yes," she replied with tears spilling out of her eyes. Quickly, she whisked them away with the tips of her fingers and then she waved valiantly to the onlookers. This lady could definitely handle this particular group, and that was a treasured commodity.

"She likes it! Hooyah!" he shouted to the crowd, pumping his fist in the air.

"Hooyah!" his brethren roared back. "Hooyah!"

Around him were the best people he knew. The trek had been tough, and as much as he had questioned if he would ever heal from the experience of this last mission, he had overcome the hurdles and reached his goal. What more could he ask for?

As the SEAL motto goes, "The only easy day is yesterday." Thus, today would unfold exactly as it should and show him its glory. By his side was his lady, and that was one outstanding teammate.

Hooyah!

Acknowledgments and Additional Dedications

With great thanks to:

My wonderful husband—retired Navy SEAL, EOD, and PRU Advisor—LT Carl E. Swepston. Yes, he wrote the Rule of Three and continues to share it and many more stories of his time in combat with BUD/S classes.

Retired Navy SEAL and EOD LT Commander Thomas C. Rancich, an outstanding soul, who answered a ton of questions and gave me a lot of insight on mind-set.

Retired Navy SEAL Phillip "Moki" Martin, a true inspiration; retired Navy SEAL Jerry Todd and his terrific wife, Pete; Greg McPartlin, Navy SEAL Corpsman and the owner of McP's; former Navy SEAL Hal Kuykendall and his lovely wife, Denise; MOH Recipient John Baca, who lets me make corned beef for him and call him friend; MOH Recipient Thomas Norris, who inspires many; MOH Recipient Mike Thornton, a generous and well-spoken man; old goat-roper and good friend John T. Curtis; and to the real Jules, who waitresses at McP's and is a treasure. Also, much gratitude to the Vietnam Era "Old Frogs and SEALs" who contributed comments and stories.

And a MASSIVE shout-out to all of our operational friends—THANK YOU!

To our dearly departed friend, Navy SEAL LT John Lynch—we miss and love you, Jack!

For Chris and Frank Toms (UDT 11/ST1) whose own love story is beautiful. We miss and love you, Chris!

To Suzanne Brockmann, thank you for your incredible support and for being a bright light as well as leading us ALL forward with your wit, charm, brilliance, and friendship!

To Cathy Mann, thank you for being so awesome and for making me laugh as I learn the business!

To my dear friends, D.C. and Charles DeVane, thank you—you are treasures and make more possible than I could put into words!

To my readers—Laurie DeSalvo, aka Lia DeAngelo, and Jan Albertie—YOU ROCK!

Cheers and thanks to good friends: C. H. Admirand; Alisa Kwitney; Kim Adams Lowe; Cathy Maxwell; Christina Skye; Angela Knight; Leslie Wainger; Christine Feehan; Domini Stottsbury; Brian Feehan; Ed and Sheila Clover English; Barbara Vey; Marjorie Liu; Tara Nina; Sara Humphreys; Kate Douglas; Shannon Emmel; Barry Eisler; Amanda McIntyre; Renee Bernard; Lori, Andy, Will and Caite; Sam and Diego; Maria R., Maria M., Gini, Maria N. and Emanuel; Kim and Paul K.; Jill and Carl H.; Brenda S. S.; Anne M.; Stephanie H.; Ing C.; Rose S.; Ginger D.; Laura L.; and the entire BB crew; Frank, Izaline, and Roger D's Clan; and Sara, Lindsey, and Callie, who are always brave and true! To the *RT Book Reviews* magazine and Booklovers Convention—Kathryn, Kenneth, Carol, Jo Carol and Johnnie, Liz, Mala, Nancy, and the whole gang. And, to my terrific agent, Eric Ruben, and his wife, Karen.

Thank you to fabulous editor Leah Hultenschmidt; to the spectacular Sourcebooks crew: Aubrey, Cat, Susie, Beth, Skye, and Danielle; to awe-inspiring Deb Werksman and phenomenal Dominique Raccah.

With infinite love and respect to my parents, always…

Any mistakes are my own. I've taken great pains to make this work of fiction as realistic as possible. Enjoy the journey! HOOYAH!

About the Author

Anne Elizabeth is a romance author, a comic creator, and a monthly columnist for *RT Book Reviews* magazine. With a BS in business and MS in communications, she is a regular presenter at the RT Booklovers Convention as well as a member of the Author's Guild and Romance Writers of America. Her published credits include stories with Atria/Simon & Schuster, Highland Press, Dynamite Entertainment, and Sea Lion Books. She is also a serious Amelia Earhart who is always on the hunt for a new adventure. Anne grew up in Greenwich, Connecticut, and now lives in the mountains above San Diego with her husband, a retired Navy SEAL.